ALFRED KROPP
THE SEAL OF SOLOMON

RICK YANCEY

BLOOMSBURY

Published by Bloomsbury U.S.A. Children's Books
175 Fifth Avenue, New York, New York 10010
Distributed to the trade by Macmillan

The Library of Congress has cataloged the hardcover edition as follows:
Yancey, Richard.
Alfred Kropp : the seal of Solomon / by Rick Yancey. —1st U.S. ed.
p.   cm.
Summary: The last descendant of Sir Lancelot, teenage misfit Alfred Kropp is drawn
back into the OIPEP to battle a group of demons bent on freeing themselves from the
confines of an ancient relic.
ISBN-13: 978-1-59990-045-2 • ISBN-10: 1-59990-045-9 (hardcover)
[1. Adventure and adventurers—Fiction. 2. Demonology—Fiction.
3. Antiquities—Fiction. 4. Conduct of life—Fiction. 5. Orphans—Fiction.
6. Knoxville (Tenn.)—Fiction.] I. Title.
PZ7.Y19197Alf 2007   [Fic]—dc22   2006024989

ISBN-13: 978-1-59990-277-7 • ISBN-10: 1-59990-277-X (mass market)

Typeset by Westchester Book Composition
Printed in the U.S.A. by Quebecor World Buffalo
2 4 6 8 10 9 7 5 3 1

All papers used by Bloomsbury U.S.A. are natural, recyclable products
made from wood grown in well-managed forests. The manufacturing
processes conform to the environmental regulations of the country of origin.

To my sons, for their inspiration
And to Sandy, for her love

From morn
To noon he fell, from noon to dewy eve,
A summer's day; and with the setting sun
Dropt from the zenith, like a falling star.
                              —Paradise Lost

And he asked him, What is thy name? And he
answered, saying, My name is Legion, for we
are many.
                              —Mark 5:9

Integrated Security
Interface System
[ISIS]

<u>User Login:</u>
ChiCubsFan

<u>Password:</u>
●●●●●●●

Welcome ChiCubsFan!

Please choose a task:

Authorized interfaces:

S.E.S
Dossiers
SATCOM System
Current Operations
Archived Operations
Company Directory
Medcon Protocols
Locator Services
Special Weapons & Tactics Division

ISIS
Secure E-mail System
[SES]

<u>User Warning:</u> The Secure E-mail System [SES] utilizes encryption software for delivery, storage, and retrieval of sensitive Company data. Any unauthorized sharing, dissemination, or disclosure of secret, sub-secret, or sub-sub-secret messages or documents is strictly prohibited.

Personnel in violation of SES protocols are subject to immediate termination and forfeiture of all rights and privileges granted to personnel under Section 1.256 of the OIPEP Charter.

All e-mail and attachments of the SES are embedded with self-destructing software. Messages and attachments not saved to individual user interfaces will automatically be deleted seventy-two hours after time of delivery. Users are cautioned to back up any non-time-sensitive data.

<u>Enter SES Password</u>
(CAUTION! This is NOT your ISIS password):
●●●●●●●●

Welcome to SES ChiCubsFan!

You have 1 new message!

Click here to read your message.

To: ChiCubsFan
From: Aquarius
Subject: New Operational Protocol re. Sub-Sub-Sec. Op Utopia

The Operative Nine has issued an Extraction Order for Special Subject Alfred Kropp.

Circumstances now demand suspension of Utopia until S.S. Kropp is neutralized.

Therefore, you are authorized to use all means necessary to neutralize S.S. A.K. before extraction can be executed.

For the purposes of this Order, "all means necessary" includes *extreme* extraction of referenced subject.

Aquarius

PART ONE

Extraction

1

I really thought my life would be different after my death. After all, I had saved the planet from total annihilation, and not a lot of people can say that—well, I can't think of a single living person who can. I'm not saying I thought I deserved a ticker tape parade or a medal from the president or anything like that. I'm just saying I honestly thought my life might be a little different.

I was wrong.

Of course, nobody knew I had saved the world. I wasn't allowed to tell, and who would believe me if I did? There were rumors about what happened when I disappeared from school, mostly based on the news reports that I was involved in a plot to blow up Stonehenge.

One rumor had me as a special operative recruited by the CIA to bust up a terrorist cell. Another said that I was a terrorist the CIA had captured, deprogrammed, and returned to normal life, kind of like mainstreaming someone with a mental condition.

But the most popular rumor was just that I was crazy. "Crazy Kropp," some people called me. Okay, not just some. A lot. Not a terrorist or a mercenary or a spy. Just crazy, off my nut, wacked, loco.

And it wasn't just kids who thought that. Dr. Peddicott, the school psychologist, must have thought it, too, because she referred me to a real shrink, a psychiatrist named Dr. Maury Benderhall, who interviewed me for three hours.

"So, Alfred," he said. "Tell me about school."

"Well, I'm flunking most of my classes. Nobody likes me, and about a month ago somebody invented a new sport called Kropping."

" 'Kropping'?"

I nodded. "Kropping. Basically, it's about humiliating me. Or tormenting. Tormention and humiliation. Only I'm not sure if 'tormention' is a word."

"It isn't."

"Well, it should be. Anyway, Kropping could be anything from tripping me in the hallway to giving me a wedgie. You get more points with something like a wedgie, because it takes a lot of determination and strength to give somebody my size a wedgie."

"I'm sure the school would put a stop to this Kropping if you told someone."

"No, I think it would just get worse."

He flipped a page of his little notebook.

"Let's talk about your fears, Alfred," he said.

"How come?"

"Do you have a problem talking about your fears?"

"It's not something I normally talk about."

"And why is that?" Dr. Benderhall asked.

I thought about it. "It's not something I normally think about."

He sat there, waiting. I took a deep breath and let it out very slowly.

"Well, clowns for one," I began. "But almost everybody is afraid of clowns. Heights. Horses. Thunderstorms. Drowning. Being burned alive. Decapitation. Yard gnomes. Cavities. Gingivitis. Insects. Well, not all insects. Ladybugs are okay, and I'd be pretty weird if I was scared of butterflies. Mostly just biting and stinging insects, though I'm not crazy about cockroaches. Not too many people are, I guess, which is why we have so many sprays and exterminators and things like that. Bats. Well, not the fruit eaters. Vampire bats—or any creature with very sharp teeth. That covers everything, sharks and lapdogs and those kinds of things. Those are the big ones, the top fears. Blemishes. Girls. Well, girls might be one of the top ones. Maybe after thunderstorms, but definitely before the yard gnomes. Boredom. See, ever since I came home from England I've been bored out of my mind. Except for that time at the mall last week, when I saw the little man."

He was staring at me. "Little man?"

"Yeah, this little bald baby-faced guy in a dark suit. I first saw him two tables away at the food court. He was staring at me and when I looked right at him, he looked away real quick. Then I was in Blockbuster and saw him two rows over in the comedy aisle."

"Do you think he was following you?"

"He didn't look like the kind of guy who would rent comedies, but you can't always judge by appearances."

He leaned forward in his chair and said, "Okay, let's talk about what's really on your mind."

I thought about it. "There's nothing really on my mind."

"Alfred," he said. "Anything you say in this room stays in this room. I'm not allowed to tell anyone."

"What if I told you something about a crime?"

"You've committed a crime?"

"Well, I guess technically I did."

"All right."

"So say I tell you about that—wouldn't you have to turn me in?"

"Our doctor-patient relationship is sacrosanct, Alfred."

"What's that—like holy?"

"Something like that." He was smiling. Dr. Benderhall had large yellow teeth, like somebody who smoked or drank too much coffee. "So—what was this technical crime?"

"I beheaded somebody."

"Really?"

"And shot somebody."

"Shot *and* beheaded them?"

"Not the same person. Oh, and I guess I stole a car. Maybe two cars. A cop car and a Jaguar. And the Lamborghini. So I guess that would be three. No, there was the Bentley too. So four cars. You sure you can't repeat any of this?"

He nodded.

"I haven't told anybody since I came home," I said.

He promised me anything I told him would be held in strictest confidence, so strictly confidentially I told him everything.

Then he promptly sent me into the waiting room and I

listened as he picked up the phone and called the social worker assigned to my case. He had left his door open, so I could hear almost every word.

"Clinically depressed," I heard him say. "Borderline psychotic with delusions of grandeur and paranoid fantasies . . . the death of his mother when he was twelve . . . the murder of his only surviving relative six months ago . . . issues with his father abandoning his mother before he was born . . . Alfred believes he is descended from the knight Sir Lancelot. . . . Yes, *that* Lancelot, and that he was involved with an international spy organization in an operation to rescue Excalibur from what he calls 'Agents of Darkness.' He also reports encounters with angels, particularly Michael the archangel, whom he believes took the Sword to heaven following Alfred's own death and resurrection as 'the Master of the Sword.' He also believes the Sword wounded him, endowing his blood with magical healing powers . . ."

Then he said, "Intensive therapy to work out his issues of abandonment, guilt, and betrayal. . . . I'm recommending a CAT scan and an MRI to rule out any physiological abnormality. . . . Yes, such as lesions or tumors. I'd also like to start him on Thorazine, which has been proven effective with paranoid schizophrenia."

I couldn't believe it. He was telling the social worker *everything*, not five minutes after he promised he wouldn't, and he was a doctor. If I couldn't trust somebody like him, who could I trust? I felt lonelier than ever.

When Betty Tuttle, my foster mom, showed up to drive me home, Dr. Benderhall took her into his office, closed the door, and when she came out thirty minutes later, it looked like he had hit her upside the head with a baseball bat.

"I'm not crazy," I told her in the car on the drive to the pharmacy to fill the prescription for the crazy drug.

"Oh, no, no," she said, bobbing her head up and down. "Just a bump in the road, Alfred. Just a bump in the road."

I overheard the Tuttles arguing late that night. Horace wanted to get rid of me.

"He'll lose it completely one day, Betty," he said. "Murder us in our beds!"

"The doctor said—"

"I don't care what the doctor said!"

"Maybe it's something simple," Betty said. "Like a brain tumor."

"Listen to you: 'Something simple like a brain tumor'! I say we send him back to Human Services. I didn't sign up to be a foster parent to a lunatic!"

Every day I palmed the pill and slipped it into my pocket. Then, after dinner, I flushed it down the toilet. I thought about that a lot—if I was crazy. If everyone around you thinks you're crazy, does that make you crazy, even though you might not be?

I thought about proving to Dr. Benderhall I wasn't making it up by putting him on the phone with Abigail Smith, the field operative with OIPEP, who had given me her number and told me to call anytime.

And I *did* call her about six months ago, after I got home from England. She asked how school was going and I told her not very good, and she said working for OIPEP was more like a calling than a job. I wasn't sure exactly what she meant by that.

"Normally we won't consider anyone under twenty," she told me, which made me wonder why she gave me her card in the first place. "And, of course, the training is quite rigorous."

I guessed she meant I was too young and too out of shape.

"So what should I do?" I asked.

"Alfred, I know it's difficult for you now, trying to return to a normal life after what you've experienced. I told you we were interested in your development and we are. Very much so." Then she told me to stay in school, work on my grades, and maybe they'd be in touch after I graduated.

I never called back after that and she didn't contact me. I guessed my jet-setting, world-saving days were over, and in a way I was glad and not glad at the same time.

I was wrong about that too.

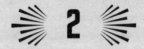

2

On the way home from school, I saw the bald baby-faced man from the video store again, this time through the back window of the school bus. I always sat in the last row, because if I sat anywhere else I inevitably got popped in the back of the head with a paper wad or spitball. One time somebody even threw their dirty gym shorts at me. I bet that Kropping earned them at least four points.

Mr. Baby-Face was driving a silver Lexus ES, so clean and polished, you could see the sky and clouds and trees reflected in the hood.

After I got off the bus, I waited to see what Mr. Baby-Face would do. He just kept driving; he didn't even glance in my direction.

You're losing it, Kropp, I told myself. Maybe Dr. Bender-hall was right. Maybe I was delusional.

I walked two blocks up Broadway to the Tuttles' house. Neither of them had a job: they were professional foster parents. At any given time there were six or seven kids stuffed into their little old house.

My current roomie was a skinny kid named Kenny, with a face that looked like it had been shoved into a vise and squeezed. His eyes were very close together and sort of crossed, so he always looked angry or confused or both. I didn't know his background but, like most of the Tuttles' foster kids, it couldn't have been very pleasant.

Kenny was a mutterer. He made little noises under his breath and repeated the same words over and over. When I was around, the word was "Kropp," and he muttered it as he followed me from room to room: "Kropp, Kropp, Kropp, Alfred Kropp, Kropp, Kropp, Kropp."

It got worse at night. "Kropp, Kropp, Alfred Kropp, it's dark, it's very dark, oh, and I'm thirsty, I'm so thirsty, Kropp, Alfred Kropp, Kropp, Kropp, Kropp." Most nights he was positive someone evil lurked right outside the window, and he badgered me until I got out of bed to check the latch.

But his jabbering never bothered me much. It was soft and steady, like raindrops against a windowpane, and sometimes it helped me go to sleep.

It bothered some of the other kids in the house, though, and they were pretty rough on Kenny until I took them aside and told them if they didn't stop teasing him, I was going to chop off their heads and stuff their headless corpses into the crawlspace. I wasn't exactly a knight, but I was descended from one, and defending the weak is pretty high on the list of knightly virtues.

I hesitated before going inside. I could hear the TV blaring at full volume through the thin walls, probably one of the soap operas Betty Tuttle was hooked on. Horace was usually sprawled in his La-Z-Boy, shouting over the TV at his wife, "Why do you waste your time with these silly soap operas! Bunch of kooks and nuts getting kidnapped or killed or falling in love with their own brother!" While he watched the whole episode, Betty scrambled around making after-school snacks and folding laundry and picking up toys.

But Horace wasn't in the La-Z-Boy when I came in. He was prancing around the living room wearing an apron and wielding a feather duster, his round face shining with sweat, while Betty worked the corners with a broom. She saw me at the door, gave a little cry, and turned off the TV.

"Dear," she whispered to Horace, who had stopped prancing and was standing very still, staring at me. "Alfred is home."

"I know he's home," he hissed back. "These two things over my nose, they're called 'eyes,' Betty."

Then Horace Tuttle came toward me, his short arms flung wide, and I stood there in the entryway, stunned, as he threw those little arms around me. Dust flew from the feathers and I sneezed.

"How ya doin', Al?" he said into my chest. "Good Lord of mercy, you're getting bigger and stronger every day!"

He pulled back, grinning. The smile on his face would give new meaning to the word "creepy."

"What's going on?" I asked.

"Oh, Alfred, the most extraordinary thing—" Betty began, but Horace cut her off.

"Nothing!" he shouted. He gave an embarrassed little laugh and clapped my shoulder hard. He lowered his voice.

"Just a little spring-cleaning, Ally my boy. Is it all right if I call you 'Ally'?"

"No," I said. "And this is October."

"No time like the present!" Horace bellowed.

Just then Kenny walked into the room, muttering, "Oh, Al. Al Kropp. Alfred Kropp."

Horace whirled on him and shouted, "Zip your pie-hole, you pea-brained little halfwit!" and Betty murmured, "Horace, you'll give him a complex." Horace yelled back, "Little late for that!"

"Lay off Kenny," I said, and that shut Horace up.

"Dear," Betty said to Horace. "Maybe we should tell Alfred." She turned to me. "We're having a visitor today."

"Who is it?" I asked.

"No one you know," Horace said. "Here, Al, let me take that backpack for you . . . Dear God, it's heavy—you're as strong as Paul Bunyan's ox! How about that? You learn about Paul Bunyan in school? Kenny, put this away for Al."

Horace slung the backpack in Kenny's direction. It slammed into his stomach, and Kenny went down on his butt.

"That's okay," I said. "I'll take it."

I grabbed the backpack with one hand, Kenny's arm with the other, and pulled him to his feet.

"Thank you," he gasped.

The doorbell rang. All the color drained from Horace's face and he whirled on Betty, one of his stubby fingers jabbing at her nose.

"Great, he's here and I haven't dusted the mantel yet!"

"Who's here?" I asked.

"The visitor," Horace said. He was struggling with the knot in the apron strings.

"What visitor?"

"Didn't we cover this? Betty, go get me a pair of scissors so I can cut off this damn apron . . ."

"I told you to tie it in a bow." She bit her lip and worked at the knot behind Horace's back. The doorbell rang again. Nobody moved. Horace waved the feather duster around in a figure eight. He reminded me of a fat, round majorette, though you don't see many majorettes with his body type. Little dust motes danced and darted in the air. Horace snapped at Betty to never mind and put the broom away. The doorbell rang a third time.

"You want me to get that?" I asked.

"No!" said Horace and Betty at the same time.

Then Horace said, "Al, you take the sofa, but don't sit in the middle. Betty, put the coffee on and do something with your hair. You look like Ozzy Osbourne. Far end of the sofa, Al, you smell sweaty. Kenny, why are you standing there gasping like a guppy? Get outta here."

Horace pulled the backpack from my hand and shoved it back into Kenny's arms. Kenny looked at me and I nodded to him that it was all right, though I really wasn't sure that it was. Kenny left, staggering under the weight. Betty disappeared into the kitchen while Horace tore the apron off.

"*Sit*, Al," Horace hissed. "Act natural! Stick this under the sofa." He handed me the wadded-up apron and I shoved it under the sofa before I sat down.

Horace flung open the door to reveal Mr. Baby-Face, a thin black briefcase in his hand and a puzzled expression on his chubby face.

"Is this the Tuttle residence?" he asked.

"You bet your sweet aunt Matilda it is!" Horace said. "Come on in. Take a load off."

He had remembered the feather duster at the last second, hiding it behind his back as he waved the guy toward the family room.

"I'm Horace," he said. "My wife, Betty, is in the kitchen, brewing."

"Brewing?"

"Coffee. Decaf. Want some?"

"No, thank you, but perhaps a glass of water. It's very warm for October, don't you think?"

"Hot as Africa," Horace said.

The bald guy had come into the family room. Horace trotted after him.

"And here he is," Horace said. "Here is Alfred Kropp."

"I know who Alfred Kropp is," the bald guy said, smiling at me. He had very small teeth with sharp incisors, like a ferret, though I've never really studied a ferret's mouth. He offered his hand and I took it without getting up. His hand was moist and soft.

"My name is Alphonso Needlemier, Alfred," he said. "What a pleasure it is to finally meet you."

Behind him, Horace turned and shouted toward the kitchen, "Betty! Nix the coffee and bring us some ice water!"

"No ice," Alphonso Needlemier said.

"Nix the ice!"

"But chilled, of course."

"Chill it!" Horace yelled over his shoulder. "Take a load off, Mr. Needleman."

"Mier," the bald guy said.

"Mier?"

"Needle*mier*."

Mr. Needlemier sat on the opposite end of the sofa and placed his briefcase on his lap. Horace sank into the lounger and tossed the feather duster behind the chair.

"You've been following me," I said to Mr. Needlemier.

"I have."

"Why?"

"Mostly to satisfy my own curiosity."

"That killed the cat," Horace said. "But who likes cats?" He yelled, "Betty! Water!" He smiled apologetically at Mr. Needlemier.

"The resemblance is not striking, but evident," Mr. Needlemier said.

"The resemblance to what?" I asked.

"To Mr. Samson, of course."

Just then Betty came into the room carrying a tray with three glasses of water. She had pulled her hair back into a bun, but some strands had come loose and hung down on either side of her face. Mr. Needlemier took a glass of water and thanked her. Horace glared.

"Coffee," he said.

"You said nix the coffee."

"Nix his coffee, not mine."

Betty scurried back to the kitchen. Mr. Needlemier sipped his water and then set the glass on the coffee table.

"Alfred," he said, "I am Bernard Samson's personal attorney and executor of his estate."

Alphonso Needlemier pulled a long white envelope from his coat pocket and held it toward me. It read: For Alfred Kropp in the event of my demise [signed] Bernard Samson."

Below the signature were the words, in bold type, Personal and Confidential.

The flap was sealed in the old-fashioned way, with a glob of red wax imprinted with the image of a rider on a horse carrying a banner.

"I would have delivered this sooner, Alfred," Mr. Needlemier said. "But I found it only two weeks ago while going through Mr. Samson's papers. He was a very private man and I promise you I didn't know of this letter's existence."

"Well, what are you waiting for, Al?" Horace said. His voice was shaking. "Open it!"

I slid my finger under the flap and tore the envelope open. Inside were two typewritten sheets of paper. Horace was leaning forward in the lounger. Mr. Needlemier studied me with a sad expression.

"Well?" Horace asked.

It read:

My dear Alfred,

If this letter finds you, then my time on earth has passed. Words cannot express my deep sorrow for not sharing the truth with you while I still drew breath. In time I hope you find it in your heart to forgive me (and your mother) for keeping your true identity a secret. I would have told you of your ancestry, but my journey has been cut short—such is the fate of one born into the line of the noblest of knights.

I pray on this, the eve of my final rendezvous with M. Mogart, that you have found a suitable home. If I have learned anything in my strange and secretive life, it is that Fortune often smiles in the darkest circumstance and it is when we reach that place between desperation and despair that we find hope. I know all too well how you must miss your mother and your uncle . . . I pray only that you understand that I have done everything within my power to see that you are kept safe, far from this dangerous business.

My dear son, I would have taken you in had I not believed doing so would have endangered you and your mother. Forgive me! You are my son, and though I have gone, I remain always your father.

Bernard Samson

I read the letter twice, then I folded it carefully, returned it to the envelope, and set the envelope on the little end table by the sofa.

Nobody said anything for a long time. Mr. Needlemier was looking kindly at me. Horace was glaring.

"Well—what's it say?" he demanded in a loud voice.

"It is a privileged communication, Mr. Tuttle," Mr. Needlemier said.

"And I'm his guardian. Practically family. Nearly a father!"

"Not even close," I told him.

Betty came back into the room carrying a cup of coffee.

"Oh, Alfred!" she said. "I completely forgot about you! What would you like, dear?"

"Maybe just a glass of water."

She left again and Horace gave an exaggerated roll of his eyes. "You married?" he asked Mr. Needlemier. Mr.

Needlemier didn't say anything. He was still looking at me. "Good thing!" Horace said, which covered either possibility.

Mr. Needlemier flipped the gold clasps on his briefcase. Horace gave a little jump at the sharp snapping sound.

"There is one other matter we should discuss, Alfred," Mr. Needlemier said. "As I mentioned, I am executor to Mr. Samson's estate." He pulled a legal-sized folder from the briefcase. He tapped it with his pudgy index finger. "Alfred, his will names you as sole beneficiary."

"What does that mean?" I asked.

"That means you are due to inherit control over Samson Industries and his entire personal fortune valued at . . ." Mr. Needlemier glanced at the papers in the folder. "Yes, four hundred million dollars—give or take a million."

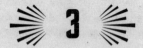

3

A glass shattered and everybody jumped. Betty had come into the room with my water, and when Mr. Needlemier said "four hundred million dollars," the glass slipped from her hand and smashed on the floor. She ran into the kitchen for a towel to clean up the water and broken glass.

All the color had drained from Horace's face. He reminded me of a middle-aged Casper the Friendly Ghost.

"Naturally, as is usually the case in these matters, you are not due to gain control of the money until you reach the age of eighteen," Mr. Needlemier said. "Until then a trustee will manage your inheritance."

"A trustee?" I asked.

"Trustee," Horace whispered.

"Someone to look over your financial concerns. A guardian of your interests, as it were."

"Who's the trustee?" I asked.

"Who? Yeah, who's the who?" Horace whispered.

"Unfortunately, the will does not designate a trustee. That choice falls to me, as executor."

"So who's it gonna be?" Horace asked.

Just then Betty came back with a towel and a whisk broom, saying, "Oh, don't you hate breaking a glass? You never can get all the little pieces and when they get in your foot—"

"So let's stop the pussyfooting around, Mr. Needlehiemer," Horace said. "Who's the trustee?"

Mr. Needlemier stared at Horace for a second. "I haven't decided."

"You haven't decided?"

Mr. Needlemier shook his head. "That is one of the reasons I'm here." He turned back to me. "I want to know Alfred's wishes."

"Alfred's wishes?" Horace asked. "*Alfred's* wishes! You're telling me you're gonna let a kid—and, forgive me here, Al, but a kid with not much wattage in the brains department—decide who manages four hundred million dollars?"

"Actually," Mr. Needlemier said, "the figure is closer to a billion dollars, if you include the assets of Samson Industries."

Horace's mouth came open but no sound came out, as if the word "billion" had sucked all the air out of him.

"I'll have to think about it," I said.

"Of course," Mr. Needlemier said. "It's a great deal to think about."

Horace got some of his breath back and whispered hoarsely, "I'll help him. Alfred. Think about it. Al'll need my help with that. The thinking."

"Alfred means the world to us!" Betty called from the kitchen doorway.

"I was saving the news for a big surprise," Horace told Mr. Needlemier. "But I guess this is a red-letter day for big surprises. See, Betty's right; the kid means the world to us and funny thing is, Mr. Needlemanner, we've talked to our lawyer to get the ball rolling."

"What ball?" I asked.

"We're adopting you, Alfred, you adorable big-headed lug."

Mr. Needlemier gave me his card and said he'd be in touch in a couple of weeks. He told me he was sorry for my loss. I didn't know if he knew about my father being the head of a secret order of knights charged with protecting Excalibur, the Sword of King Arthur, so I decided not to mention it to him. I didn't have the chance, though, even if I wanted to, because Horace was hovering right next to him from the time he stood up till the good-byes at the front door.

After Mr. Needlemier left, Horace barked at Betty to stop sweeping and vacuuming and running a wet cloth over the floor where the glass broke, and get started on dinner.

"We're making your favorite, Al," he told me. "Steak and potatoes!"

"That's not my favorite," I said.

"What do you mean that's not your favorite?" he snapped,

then caught himself and said, "Then you name it, Al, whatever you want!"

"I'm not hungry," I said, and I went to my room and closed the door.

Kenny was lying on the top bunk in semidarkness; the blinds were drawn. He muttered softly above me as I stretched out on the bottom bunk, trying to wrap my Kropp brain around the fact that I was now a billionaire.

Kenny whispered, "What are you doing, Kropp?"

"Trying to figure out how I'm going to avoid becoming Horace Tuttle's son. What are you doing, Kenny?"

"Nothing, Alfred Kropp."

I rolled onto my stomach and glanced under the bed. I flopped back over and said, "All right, Kenny, give it back."

"Give what back?"

"You know what."

After a second I could see the faint light gleaming off the black metal of the blade as he lowered my sword from the top bunk. I knew it was very sharp, so I took it from Kenny carefully.

"I told you not to touch it," I said as I held it against my chest.

"I'm sorry, Alfred Kropp. Please don't be mad at me."

I was running my fingertips along the flat smooth part of the black sword. "Don't bother it anymore, okay?" I said.

"Okay, Alfred Kropp."

I slid the sword beneath the bed. When I first got back from London, I took Bennacio's sword from its hiding place under my bed every day. But as the months went by I took it out less and less. Looking at it created this hollow feeling in my chest. The last time Bennacio wielded this sword it was in defense of the whole world, and now it was just a keepsake. I imagined myself as an old man showing it to the neighborhood kids and croaking, "Look at this, boys! You know what this is? This is the sword of the last knight who ever walked the earth, the bravest man I ever knew." And they would probably laugh and run away from crazy ol' Kropp with his tall tales of magic swords and doomed knights and the singing of angels.

"What are you thinking about, Kropp?" Kenny whispered above me.

"What would you do, Kenny, if you just found out you're going to inherit a billion dollars and Horace Tuttle has plans to adopt you so he can get his hands on it?"

Kenny was silent for a while, thinking about it, I guess.

"I would run away, Alfred Kropp."

"Exactly," I said.

5

I didn't run away that night. Or the next night. Or the night after that. The last time I ran away from Knoxville I left with just the clothes on my back and no planning whatsoever (at least on my part), so this time I was determined not to leave without some clean socks and underwear and a firm destination in mind.

A couple of days after Mr. Needlemier's visit, Horace informed me a court hearing had been scheduled to hear the merits of his petition to make me Horace Tuttle Jr. Then he proceeded to shower me with gifts. He bought me an iPod, clothes, and a cell phone. He started calling me "my boy," as in, "Good morning, Alfred, my boy!" When he wasn't following me around like a puppy desperate for attention, he and Betty were out house hunting, mostly in the fancier neighborhoods in Knoxville. I knew I had to escape from the Tuttles as soon as possible.

Still, I couldn't think of a single place I would run to or what I would do once I got there. England was a possibility: since my father had come from there, I figured there must be relatives around, but I couldn't imagine myself just showing up at their door and announcing, "Hi there! I'm your cousin Kropp!"

On my way to the bus one afternoon, I got seriously Kropped. Four football players jumped me, ripped my backpack from my shoulder, and knocked me upside the head with it a couple times. They took off, leaving me rolling in the grass.

I heard a girl's voice above me.

"Hey, are you all right?"

I peeked at her through my fingers. Blond hair. Blue eyes. Tan.

"You're Alfred Kropp, aren't you?"

I nodded.

"I'm Ashley."

She had a round face and blue eyes—very blue, maybe the bluest eyes I had ever seen, big too, about the size of quarters.

She sat down beside me. We watched as my bus pulled from the curb, belching black smoke.

"Wasn't that your bus?" she asked.

I nodded.

"You need a ride?"

I nodded again. Nodding made my head hurt.

"Come on. I'm parked right over there."

I followed her to the car, a bright yellow Mazda Miada convertible. I dropped my backpack into the tiny backseat and climbed in.

"How do you know my name?" I asked.

"Somebody told me. I just moved here from California. My dad got transferred."

"Are you a senior?" I figured she was, since the car was parked in the senior lot.

She nodded. I thought this was it, a perfect example of the luck-o'-the-Kropp: I get a lift by a gorgeous senior and no-body's around to see it.

"Why were those guys beating you up?"

"Kropping."

"Kropping?"

"You must be new," I said, "if you've never heard of Kropping."

"Why don't you turn them in?"

"It's not the code."

She glanced at me. "What code?"

"I don't know. The code of chivalry, I guess."

"Chivalry? What, you're a knight or something?"

I started to say "No, I'm descended from one," but then she might peg me for a freak, which I kind of was, I guess, but why give that away now?

"There aren't any knights anymore," I said. "Well, except certain guys in England, like Paul McCartney; I think he's a knight. But that's more an honorary title."

Suddenly, the left side of my face felt warm while the right side, the side unlooked at by Ashley, felt cool—cold even. It was weird.

I told her where the Tuttles lived, and she pulled next to the curb to let me out. We sat there a minute, looking at the house slouched there behind the weed-choked lawn and overgrown shrubbery.

"This is where you live?" she asked.

"No," I said. "Just where I exist."

I got out of the car. "Thanks for the ride."

"No problem. See you around."

"Sure. See you."

I watched her little yellow Miada rip down Broadway.

Then I went inside and found some ice for my head.

Over the next couple of weeks, I saw Ashley, the tall, tan, blue-eyed senior, all over campus. One day I looked up and there she was, sitting across from me at lunch. She smiled and I smiled back, but I was a little disturbed, for some reason.

"Hey, Alfred," she said. "How's it goin'?"

I glanced around. "You sure you want to be seen with me?"

"Why not?"

"It could have an adverse effect on your social life."

She laughed and flipped her hair. Maybe I'm wrong, but blond girls seem to flip their hair more than brunettes or redheads.

"I'll risk it."

"I know what it's like," I said, "being the new kid. Only when I came last year I wasn't a senior, I didn't drive a hot car, and obviously, I wasn't much to look at."

"Why do you put yourself down all the time?"

"I don't put myself there. I just recognize that I *am* there."

I noticed she was hardly touching her lunch. When she did take a bite, she balanced the food on the very end of her fork.

"I guess you've heard the rumors by now," I said. "That I'm a terrorist or CIA agent, or the one about me being crazy."

She shook her head. "The only thing I heard was that your uncle was murdered last spring."

"He was."

"I'm so sorry, Alfred," she said, and sounded like she meant it too. Then she changed the subject.

It wasn't until sixth period, right before the final bell rang, that something odd about that whole encounter struck me: the lunch period for seniors was thirty minutes after mine.

That afternoon I saw Ashley on the way to my bus.

"Hey, Alfred," she said.

"Hi, Ashley," I said.

"Where you goin'?"

I pointed at the bus. She said, "You want a ride?"

"Really?" I couldn't have been more surprised if she had asked if I wanted another head.

"Really," she said. So I followed her into the senior parking lot and climbed into the Miata. Ashley tended to drive too fast and tailgate, but the top was down, the afternoon was sunny, and she was tan, so I could live with it.

"We had this neighbor in Ohio where I grew up," I said, raising my voice to overcome the rush of wind. "This old lady who took in every stray dog in the neighborhood."

"Why?"

"She felt sorry for them."

"You think I feel sorry for you?"

I shrugged.

"Don't you think you're a little young to be so cynical, Alfred?"

"Girls like you don't usually notice guys like me," I answered. "Much less eat lunch with them and give them a ride home."

"Maybe I think you're interesting. Hey, I'm starving," she said. "You want to swing through Steak-N-Shake?"

She didn't wait for an answer but pulled into the drive-through lane and ordered two large chocolate shakes, two double burgers, and two large fries.

After our order arrived, she pulled into a parking place beneath the explosion of red leaves of a Bradford pear tree. The milk shake made me shiver and gave me one of those stabbing pains behind the eyeball. Ashley ate that burger and those fries like she hadn't eaten in weeks. She wasn't the first thin girl I'd known who could do that.

"You're really tan," I said. "Aren't you afraid of getting skin cancer?"

"I live for the sun," she said, which I took to mean she didn't give a flip about skin cancer.

"My mom died of skin cancer," I said.

"Your mom is dead too?"

I nodded. "My mom. My dad. My uncle."

"I guess I've lived a sheltered life," Ashley said. "I've never had anything like that happen to me. I mean, your mom and dad and your uncle."

"Oh, it was more than just them. I've lost count now. No, that's a lie; I count 'em up all the time. I've never told anybody this except my therapist, who doesn't count, but I died too."

"You died?"

I nodded. "Yeah, but I came back—only sometimes I feel like a zombie, but I don't have any interest in eating people and I dress better. I guess that's the price I have to pay for sticking around. You know how spiders eat by sucking the juices out of their prey? The body or husk or whatever stays, but all the life's been sucked out. That's how I feel. Husk-o'-Kropp."

She took a long pull from her shake, studying me over the straw.

"Alfred," she said softly, "nothing ever stays the same. It'll get better."

"How do you know?"

"Because you're a knight. One of the good guys."

I wanted to believe her. There were no knights left, but plenty of good guys.

Thinking of knights reminded me of Bennacio, the Last Knight, and his daughter, Natalia, who was the most beautiful girl I had ever seen. She had kissed me the last time I saw her. I thought about Natalia a lot, wondering where she was and if she was okay, because she was an orphan now like me—but mostly because she was the prettiest girl I had ever seen.

We drove back to the Tuttle house. Ashley put her hand on my arm before I stepped out of the car.

"Here," she said, digging into her purse. "I want to give you my phone number."

"Why?"

"So you can call me, silly."

"Why?"

"Because I like you."

"You *like* me like me or just like me?"

"I like you."

My chest tightened and I got out of the car, then turned back and leaned close.

"Listen, I get it. You've taken me on as a project. Poor, big, stupid Alfred Kropp. Well, I don't need your pretty . . . I mean *pity*. Find some other loser to feel sorry for."

I turned away before she could say anything, jogging across the yard to the front door. I missed seeing the gnarled old oak root sticking up in front of the sidewalk, tripped, and sprawled flat on my face in the cool dirt. Could it get any worse? I had been waiting for a sign and, as I pushed my big slobbery bulk from the ground, I realized this was the sign I was waiting for.

It was time to leave.

7

Horace was standing in the entryway holding a gray suit on a hanger.

"What's this?" I asked.

"Your suit, Alfred."

"I don't own a suit."

"You do now. You need to try it on to see if it fits. Tomorrow afternoon is the hearing. And you gotta look nice for the judge, Al," he said.

I brushed past him, went into the bathroom, and proceeded to floss. After a second there was a soft knock and Horace whispered from the other side.

"Hey, Al, I think you forgot the suit. I'll just hang it here on the knob. We're having fried chicken for dinner. Isn't that your favorite?"

I didn't answer and Horace went away.

I went into the bedroom and pulled my old duffel bag

from the closet. It took about five minutes to pack because I didn't have much. The door opened and Kenny came in.

"What are you doing, Alfred Kropp?"

"Packing," I said.

"You're leaving!"

I looked up at him. He started to cry.

"Don't do that, Kenny. I don't want Horace and Betty to know."

"Where are you going?"

"I don't know. I'll figure it out."

"Take me with you."

"I can't."

"Why?"

"I just can't, okay? Look, it's going to be all right. I can't live here, Kenny. Horace is plotting to adopt me and take all my money and I can't let that happen."

He climbed onto the top bunk and refused to come down for dinner, but I ate to keep up appearances, plus I didn't know where my next meal was coming from. I planned to slip out the window as soon as Horace and Betty went to bed.

Around eleven I heard the Tuttles go to their room.

"Alfred Kropp is leaving me to die," Kenny muttered in the top bunk.

I sighed. "Look, when I get to wherever I'm going, I'll call you to make sure everything's okay. And if it's not okay I'll come back and rescue you. How's that?"

"You'll rescue me? You promise?"

"I promise."

I guess that satisfied him, because he quieted down. It was time to go, but I didn't move. What was I waiting for? I had thought Ashley's pity was the sign I needed, but now leaving was the last thing I wanted to do.

Looking back now, I wonder what would have happened if I had gotten off my big butt and left that moment. If I had snuck out ten or even five minutes earlier would the horrors I was about to unleash on the world have been averted?

I'll never know, because I didn't leave that moment. I was waiting for Kenny's breathing to even out. It must have been close to midnight when he yelled, "What's that? I heard something, Alfred Kropp, outside the window."

"I didn't hear anything."

"I heard it. I—" He stopped himself, then hissed: "There's someone outside our window."

"Look, Kenny," I said. "There's nobody outside the window."

But he wouldn't settle down until I checked the window. I pulled up the blinds and squinted through the glass, resting my hands on the sill. I turned my head toward the top bunk.

"See, Kenny? There's nothing—"

Suddenly, the window exploded inward, just like it would in a horror movie, when the teenager turns and says, "See, there's nothing there." Two large, black-gloved hands shot through and grabbed my wrists. I was dragged through the broken window before I could even make a sound.

8

I saw a flash of night sky, a swaying tree branch, and the lawn as it rushed up to meet me. I landed face-first in the grass and something hard pressed into my lower back. I heard someone screaming; I guessed it was Kenny. I had fallen with my mouth open, and now I could taste grass and dirt as a voice whispered hoarsely in my ear.

"Don't fight me."

I twisted to my right, bringing my left elbow up and back, a glancing blow to the guy's head as he leaned over me. He fell away and I pushed myself up, and then he was back on me, throwing his forearm across my neck, pulling back hard, cutting off my oxygen. Black flowers bloomed before my eyes.

He dragged me toward the back corner of the house and whipped me around.

"Settle down!" he hissed. "Settle down!"

He held my arms behind my back and pushed me toward a dark convertible sports car parked by the curb.

He threw me into the passenger seat and brought his face close to mine. I got a heavy dose of spearmint.

"Hey, Al," Mike Arnold said.

I couldn't believe it: Mike Arnold, the OIPEP agent who had betrayed the knights and nearly gotten me killed. Abby Smith had told me they fired Mike for turning double agent. So this wasn't an OIPEP operation. And if this wasn't an OIPEP operation, what was it?

He raced around the front and leaped into the driver's seat of the Porsche Boxster. The car gave a throaty roar and Mike punched the gas. My head snapped back against the headrest. He whipped the car into a U-turn, the back tires locking up and squealing, sending plumes of smoke boiling into the air.

"What's going on?" I yelled. He swerved into the right-hand lane, making for the on-ramp to the interstate.

"This is what's known in the trade as an 'extraction'!"

Mike had cut his hair since I last saw him in Merlin's Cave, wearing it now in a buzz cut, like a marine. He still dressed like a frat boy, though: Lacoste shirt, Dockers, the New Balance running shoes. I could see his 9mm Glock tucked into his belt.

There was hardly any traffic in the westbound lanes of I-40, and Mike pushed the car up to ninety, his eyes darting between the road and the rearview mirror. I glanced behind us. Somebody wearing a black jumpsuit was pacing us on a motorcycle.

"Who's following us?" I shouted over the wind.

"Well, it ain't the Publishers Clearinghouse Prize Patrol!" His lips pulled back and he showed me his big white teeth.

He ran up on the bumper of a lumbering Chevy Suburban, whipped us into the emergency lane with less than an inch to spare, and floored the accelerator.

"Excuse me, Al," he said. He pulled the Glock from his waistband, swinging his right arm in my direction. I ducked, his arm pivoted over my lowered head, and I heard the sharp *pop-pop-pop* of the gun as he fired at the rider behind us.

We jounced over the rough pavement as the speedometer needle hovered around a hundred. I looked behind us again, but the black motorcycle was nowhere in sight.

"You lost them!" I yelled.

He barked out a laugh and cut back into the right lane, right in front of a Best Buy semitruck. Up ahead was the exit for the highway that connected Knoxville and Alcoa.

"Where are we going?" I asked.

"Safe house!"

"A house safe from *what*?"

He faded onto the exit ramp, going way too fast for the curve, and I grabbed on to the door handle to keep from flipping over the door. The highway was deserted, and Mike took the opportunity to push us to 120. My eyelashes felt as if they were being torn from my lids.

"Slow down, Mike!" I yelled.

I heard a rumble that sounded like thunder behind us: two big black attack helicopter gunships came straight at us, screaming out of the night sky, their sleek bodies glistening in the glow of the streetlamps.

"We're not going to make it!" I shouted.

He gave another of those sharp barking laughs. Tall hills

rose on cither side of the highway; we were heading due south, toward the Smoky Mountains. About a mile ahead the hills parted, allowing the Tennessee River to pass between them.

As soon as we reached the bridge, Mike slammed on the brakes. We went into a skid, spinning clockwise until his door smashed against the three-foot-high concrete wall separating the edge of the road from the hundred-foot drop to the water below.

"Here we go!" he shouted as he scooted over the back of the car and ran to my side. Suddenly the night lit up all around us: the gunships were training spotlights on the bridge. They had dropped to only a hundred feet or so above the ground as they bore down.

He flung open my door and yanked me onto the pavement.

"Oh, no," I said. "Mike, I can't swim."

"Good thing I can!"

He forced me over to the concrete barrier.

"It's pretty simple, Al! Jump and live or stay here and get your head blown off!"

I stared at him for a second. "Okay," I said. We climbed onto the barrier. Mike gave me a nudge in the small of my back, and we plunged a hundred feet down, into the murky waters of the Tennessee River.

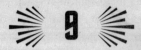

9

I hit the water feetfirst and just kept sinking, my eyes clinched shut, thinking, *This is where Alfred Kropp buys the farm.* I flailed my arms and kicked my feet, but I just kept sinking. My lungs began to ache and my movements slowed down, and then a great sense of peace settled over me like a comfortable blanket. This wasn't so bad. Maybe I'd take a nap. My chin dropped to my chest and I thought of cold winter nights in Ohio where I grew up, snuggling under the warm covers, drifting off to sleep while Mom sat in the kitchen, working her calculator as she balanced some business's books.

A hand grabbed my collar and I slowly started to rise. Whatever was left in me that still wanted to live took over, and I began to kick my feet again. My head broke the surface and I took a huge gulp of air.

"Shhhh," Mike Arnold whispered in my ear. "We're not out of the woods yet."

He gently rolled me onto my back so I was lying on top of him, his arm around my chest as he backstroked toward the south shore. I could hear the *thumpa-thumpas* of the helicopters as they patrolled the river, swinging the searchlights right to left and back again, looking for us. Just our faces were out of the water, though, and Mike pushed us along slowly, causing barely a ripple.

"Nice night for a swim, huh, Al?" Mike murmured into my ear. "Okay, real quiet now; we're almost at the shore. I'm gonna set you down easy. About twenty yards south we've got some cover, but it's gonna be a long twenty yards, Al. Easy now. Almost there."

He took his arm away and I sank about a foot before my butt hit the bottom. I raised my head a little and saw a chopper over the river, so low, the water churned beneath it, the wind of the blades creating little whitecaps in the harsh glare of the searchlights. I didn't see the other one. We were about five feet from the rocky shore. The ground rose sharply toward a densely wooded hillside directly ahead.

"Okay," Mike breathed. "On my mark. Three, two, one . . . *mark*!"

I was a couple of seconds behind Mike. I never was good at races. In PE the whistle would blow and everybody would be six feet in front of me before I took the first step. Mike was already out of the water, running doubled over, his knuckles practically touching the ground, before I even reached the shore. I told myself as I started to run that the roar of the helicopter behind me wasn't getting louder, but of course it was.

Mike had reached the edge of the trees, waving his arms frantically, as if that's all I needed to run faster.

About halfway between the water and the trees I froze.

The second gunship had risen from behind the trees; I was trapped between them. The air began to whip around me as they bore down, and I stood still, pinned like a bug by the blinding searchlights. I could hear Mike screaming my name.

I don't know how long I stood there, river water pooling under my wet tennis shoes, waiting for the bullet to rip through my brain. All I know is after a lifetime or two Mike made a decision and came to get me, grabbing me by the shoulder and hurling me toward the safety of the trees.

I stumbled once, tearing the knee in my jeans on the rocky ground. Mike yanked me up and half dragged, half pushed me into the crowded underbrush of the wooded hillside.

He pushed me face-first into the ground and put his hand on the small of my back as he whispered in my ear, "Don't move!"

The choppers circled slowly overhead. Sometimes they sounded right above us; sometimes the blades' thumping sounded very far away. The searchlights stabbed through the canopy, and they looked like white columns, the kind you see on Southern mansions, as they illuminated the misty air.

The columns of light kept moving farther and farther away, and after a while I couldn't hear the helicopters' engines at all. Finally, I couldn't take it and told Mike I had to pee.

"When you gotta go, you gotta go," Mike said. So I went behind the nearest tree, and when I came back Mike was sitting up. He unwrapped a piece of gum and carefully folded the stick into his mouth. I sat down beside him and examined the tear in my jeans. My knee was bleeding.

"Catch your breath, Al. We got five, maybe ten minutes,"

Mike said around his fresh wad of gum. "They're looking for a place to land."

"And what happens after they land?"

"They'll come for us on foot. They're very determined little suckers."

"Who are determined little suckers?"

He didn't answer at first. He picked up a stick and commenced to jabbing it into the rocky ground.

"The Company," he said.

"OIPEP?"

He nodded. "OIPEP."

"Why is OIPEP trying to kill us, Mike?"

"I don't think they're trying to kill *you*, Al. It's me they want."

That didn't surprise me. Mike had betrayed the knights and OIPEP, but I still didn't understand why he had kidnapped me. Did he think I still had Excalibur?

He stood up and brushed the leaves and dirt from his butt. "Look at this! I just bought these," he said, referring to his Dockers. "Stain-defenders!"

He turned to me. "Sorry for snatching you like that, Al, but I'm in a bad way now and like it or not, you're the only port in this particular storm."

"What storm? What are you talking about, Mike?"

"Well, you could say it's all a big misunderstanding. But it's more a matter of the left hand not knowing what the right's doing. You ready?"

"Ready for what?"

He walked past me, deeper into the woods, without looking back.

"It's your call, kid. Stick with me and you got a fifty-fifty chance of seeing your sixteenth birthday. Hang here and you got a hundred percent chance of having your head snatched straight through your backside."

I followed him up the slope, and to me it sounded like we were making enough noise to wake the dead. We reached the top of the hill and now I could see the lights of the interstate about a mile to our left. To our right was the Knoxville airport. And, directly below us, the parking lot to an air freight company.

"Right where I left it," Mike breathed. "Okay, let's go."

I crouched in the trees just at the edge of the little lawn that surrounded the parking lot as Mike jogged to a silver 380Z parked at the far corner of the lot. I didn't know what the heck was going on and I was pretty sure I didn't want to know, but there was no turning back now, and I figured eventually Mike would fill me in on the details.

The Z roared to life and Mike zipped over, waving to me through the open window. I jogged out of the trees and into the lot as Mike slowed to a stop. He floored the gas as soon as my butt touched the seat.

Mike headed into the mountains, taking the Z up to eighty on the straightaways, maybe a little bit slower—but not much—on the curves.

We went through a couple of small towns in the foothills; then, right before the entrance to the national park, Mike turned onto a gravel road that seemed to wind straight up the side of a mountain. The little access road hugged the mountain on one side and a deep ravine dropped off the other. I happened to be seated on the ravine side. I closed my eyes and willed my heart not to leap out of my mouth.

Finally the car rolled to a gravel-crunching stop and I opened my eyes. We were parked in front of a log cabin sitting by itself in a clearing hacked out of the mature trees covering the mountaintop.

"Home sweet home," Mike sang out and stepped out of the car. "We're perfectly secure here. Nobody knows about this place, Al. Not even the Company, and the Company knows practically everything."

He came around to my side of the car and stood there, like he was expecting me to get out. I didn't.

"Get out of the car, Al," he said.

"I'm not getting out of the car, Mike," I said, "until you tell me what's going on."

"I think I told you. You've been extracted."

"Why?"

He smiled. "Get out and I'll tell you."

I thought about it. The leaves were gray in the dark, and the cold wind made a rattling sound as it moved through them. The lights were on inside the cabin, and the light looked inviting and warm.

"Why can't you tell me now, Mike?"

"Well, basically because of the car."

"The car?"

"It's brand-new." He pulled the gun from his belt and pointed it at my forehead.

"Out. Now."

I got out. Mike took a couple of steps back and gestured toward the cabin with the Glock.

"After you, Al March."

As I trudged up the hill toward the bright, warm lights, the hair on the back of my neck stuck up and I realized then what a terrible mistake I had made getting out of the car. *It's brand-new*, Mike had said. Why did that matter? Because he didn't want to mess it up when he shot me.

From behind me he said, "Okay, that's good." We were about ten feet from the front porch. I stopped. He stopped. I shivered in the cold air.

"Don't turn around, Al," Mike said softly. "It's better if you don't turn around. Maybe you should kneel."

To my left was the ravine, the deep gash in the side of the mountain. To the right the ground dropped off into a dense thicket of wild blackberry bushes and scrub pine.

"You know what the Company calls this, Al?"

"An extraction?"

"Right. But extraction comes in many varieties. This one we call an '*extreme* extraction.'"

"Can I at least know why you're going to extremely extract me?"

"For the world, Al. The welfare of humankind."

I heard him slide the bullet into the chamber. The wind sighed in the trees. I could see my own breath.

"I should tell you that I hate doing this, Al—you know, how I always liked you and respected you and all that, but that just isn't true. To be frank, you've always annoyed the heck out of me."

10

I waited for the bullet, but the bullet never came. Instead a gigantic white horse burst from the trees to my right, bearing a figure dressed entirely in black, down to the ski mask over its head, bending low over the horse's back as it came straight toward me. I heard Mike cry out, the sharp *pop-pop* of his gun, and then the rider was between Mike and me, and an arm swooped down and yanked me off my feet. Barely off my feet, because this rider was a lot shorter and thinner than I was, so my toes dragged the ground as the horse made straight for the ravine. I grabbed on to the back of the saddle and heaved myself up behind the black-clad rider as the horse swung around and headed back for the cover of the forest.

Mike had gone to one knee, holding the Glock with both hands as he fired, and a bullet tore through the back of my shirt as it fluttered behind me.

Then we were in the woods, plunging into the pines and oaks and maples, through thick undergrowth and hanging vines, and if we were following a path or trail, I couldn't see it—but I didn't see much because half the time my eyes were closed. When I did open them, I could see the rump of the white horse and the ground sloping down as we thundered toward the foot of the mountain, a descent that seemed to get steeper as we went. Any second I was sure the stallion would lose its balance and both of us would fly into a somersault, flipping end over end before a tree stopped us.

We zigzagged between the trees and scrub growth, occasionally becoming airborne as the horse leaped across ravines and deep gouges in the ground where tributaries of the Little Pigeon River ran.

Then we burst into a wide clearing maybe halfway down the mountain, a flat, treeless area, and the rider brought the horse to a snorting stop. I didn't dismount as much as slowly slide off the saddle onto the ground.

The rider fell to the ground beside me, and we lay there, contemplating the night sky. The rider moaned, one hand pressing against the dark fabric of the turtleneck sweater.

"I'm hit."

I rolled to my side. I recognized that voice.

She reached up with her free hand and pulled off the ski mask.

"*Ashley?*"

She tried to smile, but it was more of grimace. "Hello, Alfred."

"I guess you're not a transfer student from California."

"No."

"I knew it! Seniors don't eat lunch with sophomores. You're OIPEP, aren't you?"

She nodded, her eyes watering from the pain, I guess.

"Where are you hurt?" I asked.

She pulled up the sweater, exposing her rib cage. Mike's bullet had torn through the left side. She was bleeding pretty bad.

"Chopper's on its way," she gasped. Then she started to cough, and I saw blood shimmering in the starlight on the corner of her mouth.

"Got the lung," she whispered. "Alfred, strapped to my left leg . . ."

Her eyes rolled in her head. I reached down and pulled up her pants leg and saw a long knife in a black leather sheath strapped there.

Then I understood. I knelt beside her and yanked the knife from its sheath. My hands were shaking. I pressed the edge of the blade against my left palm. I hated knives, but I didn't see how I had a choice. Maybe the OIPEP chopper had a medic on board, but Ashley might not make it if we waited for them. She was bleeding to death.

I pressed harder and a thin line of blood welled up around the blade. I threw the knife into the grass and pressed my bleeding hand over the bullet hole. Ashley gasped. Her eyes came open.

"Alfred . . ." she whispered.

"It's okay," I said. "You're going to be okay."

Her breathing steadied and the wet gargling sound lessened, then faded away. She grabbed my wrist.

"I don't believe this . . ." she murmured.

"But you knew about it," I said.

She started to say something, but at that moment a black Apache helicopter rose above the trees, blotting out the stars as it climbed. A searchlight stabbed into the clearing.

I scrambled to my feet, running through the options in my head. I could run—I didn't know if Ashley would be able to stop me, but she had gone through a lot of trouble to extract me, so she would probably try. I could go with her, but so far I hadn't run into one OIPEP agent who hadn't lied to me at one time or another—so that might not be in my best interest either. She had saved my life, though, and running randomly through the woods didn't seem to be a very wise option, especially since Mike was still on the mountain, probably looking for me.

So when the helicopter set down, I scooped her off the ground and ran to it. The pilot, wearing a black helmet with a dark visor, met me there.

"What happened?" he shouted over the roar of the blades above us.

"She was shot, but she's going to be okay!"

He nodded and we got her inside.

I searched in vain for a safety belt, across the aisle from Ashley, who was sitting up, and her eyes were open as the pilot checked out her injury. He said something to her that I couldn't hear, and she nodded, waving him toward the front of the helicopter, making a twirling motion with her index finger as if to say, *Get us out of here!* The wind blasting through the open hold set my teeth to chattering uncontrollably. Then we were airborne.

Ashley smiled at me. All the OIPEP agents I had known had had great orthodontics. I wondered if that was a job requirement. Are people with good teeth more trustworthy?

"Where are you taking me?" I shouted over the wind at her.

"Airport!"

"Why?"

She shouted something back that sounded like *calcified*, but I figured I heard it wrong and probably what she said was *classified*.

"Why is Mike Arnold trying to kill me?" I shouted.

She just shook her head, looked at the luminescent dial of her watch, then slapped a headset on. Her eyebrows drew together and her smile faded away as she talked; it looked like she was having an argument. Then she ripped off the headset and stood up, legs spread wide for balance in the rocking hold, turned, and pulled down a black case from the compartment above her head. She dropped the case on the seat, her back toward me, and fumbled with the contents. Maybe, I thought, she was going to put a bandage on her wound.

Ashley swung around to face me, holding something that looked like a cross between a dart gun and a water pistol.

"What's that?" I shouted.

"I'm sorry, Alfred," she said. "I have orders."

And before I could move, she pressed the muzzle of the thing against my upper thigh and pulled the trigger. I felt something sharp plunge into my leg, and the world went black.

PART TWO
The Infernal Hordes

To: Aquarius
From: ChiCubsFan
Subject: Sub-Sub-Sec. Op Utopia

See attached report doc. S.S. A.K. now in Company control.

To: ChiCubsFan
From: Aquarius
Subject: Sub-Sub-Sec. Op Utopia

Unfortunate, but not necessarily world-ending.

Proceed posthaste to Nexus Point and execute Phase Three of Op Utopia. All third parties expendable. All Company personnel expendable.

Aquarius

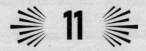

11

Every summer when I was a little kid, my mother threw me into our old Corolla and drove us down to Destin, a beach town in the Florida Panhandle. I loved those trips. We stopped at roadside restaurants to eat, greasy spoons with the vertical coolers that held the pies and cakes, and little one-story motels two blocks from the beach, like the Seabreeze Motor Court or the Conchshell Conclave.

The Seabreeze was my favorite, mostly because the beds had this vibrator built in: you dropped a quarter into the timer and the bed would vibrate for five minutes. Two quarters got you twelve minutes. As soon as we hit the door, I flopped on one of those beds, feeding it quarters. Mom wouldn't let me use the vibrating function at night, though. She thought the vibration while I slept would give me vertigo or bad dreams, or maybe both.

I woke with the name *Destin* on my lips. I could hear the

low, deep-throated hum of engines, one of those sounds that seem to come from everywhere and nowhere.

I started to notice other things too, things that came in flashes as I slowly woke up.

Crisp white sheets. The smell of lavender. Gray walls lined with rivets; even the floor was riveted. A round door with a ship's wheel for a handle. A porthole on the wall opposite the bed, nothing beyond the glass but darkness.

"Destin," I whispered again in the semidarkness of the little cabin.

Mom in her jean shorts and halter top, sunglasses covering almost her entire face, tiny beads of sweat on her forehead, a paperback novel resting on her stomach, calling to me, *Don't go out too far, Alfred! Don't go out too far!* Because I can't swim. She knew I wouldn't go far: there were scary things in the ocean, jellyfish and the sharp spines of dead horseshoe crabs and busted aluminum beer cans and sharks, of course. Swimming in the ocean is a little crazy when you think about it. The ocean is nature untamed, just like the woods, and who in their right mind would strip to their shorts and go running through the woods?

I remember wearing old bathing trunks with a starfish on the butt, faded from a bright yellow to a kind of dingy white, and a wide white stripe of sunscreen on my nose. I waded knee-deep in the languid surf of the gulf, kicking up little underwater puffs of sand, never worrying where she was, because I was sure she would always watch over me.

The wheel spun counterclockwise and the round door swung open. A big man dressed in black, with enormous ears and a face that reminded me of a bloodhound, stepped inside and looked down at me beneath the lavender-smelling sheets.

"Hi," I said. "I'm Alfred Kropp."

"I know who you are," he said.

"I know who you are too," I said. "Well, not your name, but I remember you. You came to my hospital room in London. Where's Abigail . . . I mean, Dr. Smith?"

As if on cue, Abigail Smith, Special Agent-in-Charge, Field Operations Division, of the Office of Interdimensional Paradoxes and Extraordinary Phenomena, stepped into the cabin and swung the door shut behind her.

"Hello, Alfred," she said.

She looked just like I remembered, her bright blond hair in a tight bun. But this time her three-inch heels were replaced with black lace-up boots and she wore a black turtleneck and pants.

"Where am I?" I asked.

"Aboard the jetfoil *Pandora*, somewhere off the coast of Oman," she answered.

"Oh." I had no idea where Oman was. "Why?"

"There has been a . . . development that has necessitated your extraction from the civilian interface," the dog-face man intoned.

"Huh?"

"What Operative Nine means is you were kidnapped for your own good, Alfred."

"Operative Nine?"

"Yes," she said, nodding toward Mr. Dog-Face. "Op Nine for short."

"What's his real name?"

"Whatever it needs to be," Op Nine said.

Abby said, "Only the director knows his real name."

"How come?"

"The nature of his work."

"And that is?"

"Classified," he said.

"That's pretty clunky, though, Operative Nine," I said. "Why don't you just use a code name like 'Bob'?"

" 'Bob' would be more an alias than a code name, don't you think?" Abigail was smiling.

"What's going on?" I asked, struggling to sit up, but my head was throbbing and the room was spinning, and I decided sitting up wasn't such a good idea at that moment.

"We don't know the answer to that question," Abby said. "It seems an odd turn of events, given what we know about Mike Arnold's plans."

"Maybe that's something you could share with me," I said. "Mike's plans."

"After he was terminated, Michael Arnold stole two very valuable items from the OIPEP vaults. We are on our way to intercept him before he can put them to use."

"What did he take?" I asked, and waited for the usual answer: *That's classified.*

Op Nine glanced at Abby, who gave him a sharp nod. He looked at me. His eyes were very dark, almost black.

"The Seals of Solomon," he said in that deep, undertaker-like voice. If he was waiting for some sign of recognition from me, he was going to be waiting for a long time. I just stared back.

"You have heard of King Solomon," he said.

"From the Bible, right?"

"Yes. In the days of his reign, Solomon possessed two items of great power, immeasurable gifts from heaven. The Great Seal and the Lesser Seal, also called the Holy Vessel.

These two charges he jealously guarded until his death three thousand years ago. The Great Seal was lost in antiquity, but the Lesser Seal was recovered from its hiding place in Babylon by an archeological expedition in 1924—"

Abby cut off the lecture. "The Greater Seal, or Seal of Solomon, is a ring, Alfred. The Company recovered it in the 1950s from a now-defunct apocalyptic death cult in the Sudan—"

"Wait a minute," I said. "Did you say the Seal of Solomon is a *ring*? Like a wear-on-your-finger-type ring?"

"Precisely.

"Have you paged Elijah Wood? I think I saw this movie."

She smiled. "The ring to which you refer is a product of art, a fiction. The Great Seal of Solomon is an artifact of history. It belongs to our world, not an imaginary one. Most significantly, Solomon's ring is not the creation of evil. Of course, in the wrong hands it could be used to that purpose, and that is precisely why we recovered it and kept it safe for the past fifty-five years—"

"Until Mike stole it."

"We have since launched a complete overhaul of our security protocols."

"Boy, that's a comfort. So Mike stole these two things from you guys . . . and then comes to Knoxville to kill me. Why?"

They looked at each other.

"We don't know," Abigail said. "We were hoping you might."

"Me? OIPEP's looking to me for answers? We're in bigger trouble than I thought. What about Ashley?"

Op Nine frowned. "What about her?"

"Why was she spying on me?"

Again they looked at each other.

"The Company often assigns operatives to keep tabs on Special Subjects."

" 'Special Subjects'? I'm a Special Subject?"

"How could the last son of Lancelot *not* be a Special Subject?" Abby asked tenderly. "Mike's entrance into your particular interface took all of us by surprise. Fortunately, Ashley was watching your house when Mike made his move."

"So you knock me out and bring me to this boat off the coast of Oman—where is that, Africa or something?—to do . . . what?"

"Intercept Michael Arnold before he can use the ring to open the Lesser Seal."

"Lesser Seal . . ."

"The Holy Vessel," Op Nine said.

"Why don't you want the Holy Vessel opened?"

For the third time they exchanged a glance. I was like the little kid in the room while the parents danced around the facts-of-life lecture.

"The ring, the Great Seal," Op Nine said slowly, "is the key. Without it, the wearer cannot control the . . . agents confined within the Vessel. Indeed, without the ring, the Lesser Seal cannot even be broken. One without the other is useless. With both . . ." He took a deep breath. "Catastrophe."

The door swung open and a guy in a black jumpsuit like Ashley's stepped in, carrying a tray with orange juice and two slices of toast.

"Ah," Op Nine said. "The food is here." He seemed relieved.

"Not much of it, though," I said, trying again to sit up.

Op Nine bent to help me. The room whirled around my head. I wondered why I felt so light-headed and weak. What was in that shot Ashley gave me on the chopper—and why had she given me a shot in the first place?

I drank the tall glass of orange juice down in three gulps. The toast was cut into quarters and that's how I ate it, stuffing a whole quarter in my mouth and barely chewing before I swallowed.

"Okay," I said. "Let me see if I have all this. After you guys fired Mike for trying to take Excalibur, he breaks into your vaults and steals the two Seals of Solomon. I'm still not clear on what they are or what they do, but anyway, after that you assigned Agent Ashley to keep tabs on me because now I'm a person of special interest or something. Mike shows up, kidnaps me, takes me up into the mountains to kill me—only Mike knows why—and Ashley rescues me in the nick of time. Now we're on a boat on our way to . . . where?"

"The nexus," Op Nine said.

"The what?"

"The center. The place of opening."

"Right. Gotcha. And the plan is to stop Mike before he can pull off this opening."

"Correct."

"Or else . . . ?"

"Catastrophe."

A bell went off, a blaring sound that seemed to come from everywhere and nowhere. Op Nine checked his watch.

"It's time for the briefing," he said to Abigail.

She nodded, then turned to me and gave my shoulder a little pat.

"We have to go, Alfred."

"When are you taking me home?"

They both looked away.

"You're not taking me home, are you?" I asked.

"You'll be safe here, Alfred," Abby said.

"I'd rather go home and take my chances."

Abby was looking at Op Nine. She pursed her fat red lips and for some reason I thought of goldfish, those big koi you see sometimes in little ponds outside Japanese restaurants.

He said, "Perhaps we will discuss it, once the Seals have been recovered."

They left, slamming the big round metal door closed behind them. The wheel turned and I heard a clanking sound, like a dead bolt sliding home. It hit me then that I had traded one kidnapper for another. OIPEP might not want to kill me like Mike did, but I was at their mercy just the same.

12

I don't know how long I lay there, waiting for them to come back. It seemed a very long time. There was really nothing to do, no magazines or books or a television or a radio, and I still felt light-headed and kind of hollow, like a scooped-out pumpkin. After a while I drifted off to sleep. When there's nothing to do, I sleep. I'm like a dog that way.

I had a horrible dream. First I was swimming, which wasn't so horrible, since I couldn't swim in real life. The sun burned high overhead, the waves rolled gently over my bare back, and the warm water seemed to buoy me up so swimming took hardly any effort. I was in the middle of the ocean, no shore in sight, and the water was this deep forest green and smelled rich, like fertile soil. Then I dived beneath the surface and things started to get freaky. I morphed into this scale-less fish, big-headed, with grayish skin, a white underbelly like a catfish, and a toothless mouth. I changed into this fish, and then I started to grow.

I grew till I was about the size of a whale shark, this gray and white behemoth of the sea, gulping hundreds of gallons into my wide, toothless mouth and shooting them out through my gills. I felt something pricking my fish-skin: hundreds of little silvery fish with suckers for mouths were attaching themselves to me as I swam. More and more of the little sucker fish appeared out of the depths and latched on to me, until thousands carpeted every inch, and I could feel them sucking the life out of me. I began to sink deeper and deeper as my life force waned, and the water began to turn black and very cold. I shivered. I'm not sure fish are capable of shivering, but in this dream anything seemed possible, even something like a white-bellied Kropp Fish.

I woke up and I was still shivering.

The porthole was shining brightly and light reflecting off the ocean was dancing on the glass. Right beside the porthole, Op Nine leaned against the bulkhead.

"What time is it?" I asked.

"We are two hours from the insertion point," he said.

"I love your super-secret-agent Tom Clancy lingo," I said. "Extreme extraction. Special Subject. Insertion point. What happens after we're inserted into the point?"

I sat up and a wave of dizziness swept over me. Someone, probably Op Nine, since I had a feeling he had been assigned as my minder, had brought me another big glass of orange juice. I gulped it down.

"Then we have approximately six hours," Op Nine said.

"Six hours to do what?"

"Stop the Hyena before he can unlock the Lesser Seal."

" 'Hyena'?"

"Mike Arnold."

"That's his code name, Hyena?"

"You don't like it? We thought it most apropos."

"It's okay, but my big problem with code names is why use one when everybody knows the real name?"

"Because that would offend our super-secret-agent Tom Clancy sensibilities."

He motioned toward the foot of the bed.

"Perhaps you would like to dress before we reach Marsa Alam."

"Huh?" I had no idea I *wasn't* dressed. Then I saw I was wearing a hospital gown. Why had OIPEP stuck me in a hospital gown?

I slid out of bed and grabbed the bundle of clothes. He just stood there, staring at me with those dark eyes. I hoped he didn't plan to stand there while I got dressed.

"Is there someplace I can maybe wash up and brush my teeth?" Running my tongue over them felt like I was licking carpet, and not the thin, worn kind in the Tuttle house, but something with a thicker pile.

"Of course. Left down the corridor, last door on the right at the terminus of the hall."

Terminus of the hall. He didn't have any accent that I could detect, but he talked like English was his second language. Who says "terminus of the hall"?

Op Nine opened the round door for me. I turned left, one hand pressing the clothes against my chest, the other clutching the gown closed behind me as I shuffled down the hall. In case you didn't know, hospital gowns are open in the back with just a little drawstring to tie them, and therefore my naked butt was flapping in the breeze. The hall was packed with agents hurrying up and down, and a few stopped and stared as I passed.

I thought I heard a couple of snickers and once the word "pimple," though it might have been "dimple," which made sense too.

I reached the terminus of the hall and went through the last door on the right.

I was in a tiny bathroom, maybe two or three times the size of an airplane bathroom. I barely fit in the shower, but it had one of those removable shower heads on a flexible tube with the adjustable sprayers for regular or massaging.

I stayed in that shower for a long time, leaning against the wall as the water pounded on my dimple, wondering what this dizziness was about and if it had something to do with jet lag. I found a sore spot in my left armpit and worried about that—I knew your lymph nodes were in your pits, and my mom had died of cancer. Cancer ran in families, though hers didn't start in her armpits.

I grabbed a towel from the peg on the wall and dried off, getting a little dizzy when I bent over to do my legs. I wrapped the towel around my middle, took a deep breath, and sat on the toilet.

I hadn't cried since this whole thing began back in Knoxville, but I finally had a little time on my hands and some privacy to get some quality crying in, so I started to cry.

Half a world away, kids were piling onto the school bus. Was anybody saying, "Hey, whatever happened to that big kid, Kropp?" Were any teachers looking at the empty desk and frowning, or was Horace camping out at the police station waiting for news? Was Kenny lying in his bunk, whispering in the dark, wondering aloud where Alfred Kropp had gone?

And in the afternoons the parks and practice fields would be packed with players, soccer and football teams wallowing in that sweaty camaraderie of jocks. Geeks would be playing the latest version of *Doom* and IMing each other with tips. The garage bands would be revving up the amps, moms would be sticking the chicken in the oven, and neighborhood streets would echo with the shouts of kids playing in the fallen leaves and soon it will be Thanksgiving . . .

I tried not to think of all those things, but the more I tried, the more I thought. Once, I thought normal life was boring and I hated it. Now I would give everything to go back.

But Thanksgiving made me think of food and food made me think of my teeth, and that brought me back to my senses. The thought of brushing my teeth calmed me down, I guess because it was an everyday activity that had nothing to do with biblical kings and extreme extractions and secret organizations with vaults filled with deadly artifacts that bring catastrophe if you mess with them.

I found a toothbrush still in its packaging and a travel-size tube of Crest in the cabinet mounted next to the mirror. No floss, but you can't have everything. I brushed until my gums bled and watched my pink spit swirl down the drain.

I dressed in the black OIPEP-issued jumpsuit. The underwear was boxers and I was a tighty-whitey man, but they were clean, so I wasn't about to complain. I filed the little fact that OIPEP men wear boxers; it might be useful later, but I doubted it. Most little facts aren't.

I decided not to go back to my cabin. I probably was

supposed to, but the crying had freed up something in me, like a lot of good cries will.

I walked back down the corridor to a stairway that wound upward, went up two flights, and stepped onto the deck, into brilliant sunshine. A stiff breeze blew from the stern, whipping my damp hair back from my face. I wondered if the *Pandora* had a barber on board.

I walked toward the front of the ship. To my left was the open water, but there was a dark line of land in the distance. Sunlight danced off the pointy tips of the waves, so bright, it left glittering spots in my vision. I passed several people in deck chairs or leaning on the railing, men and women dressed like tourists with cameras hanging from their necks and a dab of white sunscreen on their noses. I looked to my right and saw the upper part of the ship, where a sign was painted in big red letters: "Red Sea Adventures." There were more letters in another language right beside it; Arabic, I guess, with those funny curlicues and fat dots. So that was OIPEP's cover: we were happy Westerners on a jaunt before hitting the Pyramids.

I reached the front and leaned against the railing. I couldn't see any other ships. I looked straight down and saw how fast we were going. When Abigail called the *Pandora* a jetfoil, I wasn't sure what she meant. Now, leaning over the rail, I knew. The *Pandora* rode through the water on two huge fins, its underside about six feet above the surface. With this kind of setup, the *Pandora* could give a world-class speedboat a run for its money.

Op Nine appeared beside me. I was busted. To distract him, I pointed at the dark line on the horizon and asked, "What's that?"

"Egypt," Op Nine answered.

"So this is the Mediterranean?"

"No, this is the Red Sea," he said. Just five minutes ago I had looked at a sign that read, "Red Sea Adventures."

"I'm gonna need some shoes," I said. I'm a pretty tall guy, but this Operative Nine towered over me. Tilting my chin up, I could see the black tangle of his nose hair.

He didn't say anything, so I asked, "So what happens when we reach the insertion point?"

"We will wait for nightfall. Then the race for the nexus."

"Nexus—where in Egypt is that?"

"It is not a name of a place, Kropp. It is the nexus, the core. The nucleus."

"Oh, sure. The nucleus of *what*?"

"Reentry."

"Oh, boy. I don't guess you're ever going to tell me what's going on with these Seals, so I'm going to give it a shot. You don't have to say anything, just nod or twitch your mouth, some kind of signal I might be on the right track.

"This ring of Solomon's controls something that's locked up in the Holy Vessel. Like the name of this boat sort of implies, it's not something you want to be messing with. Mike got away with both of them, and he's hightailed it into the Egyptian desert, because he can't just open the Holy Vessel anywhere and, since we have five hours or so to get there, I'm guessing he can't just open it whenever he feels like it. Maybe the stars have to be in perfect alignment or there's some other criteria I don't know about, like Mars being in Sagittarius or something along those lines."

He didn't nod or twitch or move a single muscle. He just stared down at me. If I had some shoes, I'd be a little taller and might not be able to see so much nose hair.

"What's your name?" I asked.

"Operative Nine."

"No, I mean what's your *real* name?"

"Whatever it needs to be."

"I promise I won't tell anybody."

He was smiling. It wasn't a very natural-looking smile. He smiled like smiling hurt.

"I could tell you," he said. "But then I would have to kill you."

"That's a really old joke."

"I'm not joking."

He stepped back and motioned toward the bow. "Come, Kropp. We should not tarry. The sea has eyes."

13

I followed him back to my cabin. I told him my feet were cold and he just looked at me like I'd said something in Swahili, or maybe it was more like he spoke Swahili and I didn't.

"There are some matters I must attend to," Op Nine said. He left. I hoped one of those matters included socks and shoes. I sat on the bed. I picked at my toenails, which needed trimming. I was tempted to bite them down, but I hadn't done that since I was ten, and some things you should move past.

I wondered what happened to Ashley after the helicopter rescue in Tennessee. Was her injury completely healed now? I had mixed feelings about her. She had saved my life, but she had also lied to me about who she was and why she was "attached" to me. I wondered if my feelings were mixed because I thought she was a nice person or if it was because I thought she was pretty.

OIPEP agents fell into two categories, as far as I could tell: the preppie, grad student type, of which Mike Arnold was the perfect example; and the stoic, more menacing type like Operative Nine. That guy was so stiff and precise that I wondered if he was one of those "unacknowledged technologies" that Abigail mentioned back in London.

Maybe he was a cyborg, but that seemed far-fetched. On the other hand, I was chasing after a magical ring that once belonged to King Solomon from the Bible and I didn't seem to have trouble believing that.

The door swung open and a tall, tanned blonde with blue eyes about the size of quarters walked in, dressed in the standard-issue OIPEP jumpsuit. I stood up and we didn't say anything for a minute. Then she reached out and hugged me. Ashley smelled good, like lilacs, only I wasn't sure what lilacs smelled like; it was just the first word that popped into my head. She hugged me and I thought, *Lilacs*.

"I wanted to thank you," she said. "For saving my life."

"Okay," I said, because I didn't know what else to say.

"And I wanted to apologize."

"For what?"

"Tricking you like that in Knoxville."

"Well, that's sort of your job, isn't it?"

She nodded. "I guess."

"What's in the Holy Vessel?" I figured if anyone would tell me, it would be Ashley.

"I can't tell you."

"Do you know why Mike was trying to kill me?"

She looked away.

"Can you tell me why he stole the Seals?"

"We don't know why."

I was feeling light-headed again, so I sank back onto the bed.

"Is there a doctor on board?" I asked.

"Why, are you sick?"

"I feel really dizzy. Plus I found this sore under my . . ." I didn't feel comfortable for some reason using the word "armpit." "On my skin. I wouldn't care, you know, I'm a pretty tough guy, played football and everything, plus I've had my share of rough scrapes over the past year, including being killed, but my mom's cancer started with a sore spot and you know that runs in families. Not sore spots. Cancer. Well, I guess sore spots could run in families too . . ."

"Yes," she said. She was smiling for some reason. "There's a doctor on board. You want me to get him?"

"Maybe in a little while. It's better when I sit down."

She sat down next to me as if she needed to feel better too. Her hair fell across her cheek as she leaned forward, swinging her long legs against the bunk.

"I've been thinking about my mom a lot lately," I said. "After she died, things got really weird."

She nodded. She hooked a thick strand of her hair around her left ear and looked at me out of the corner of her eye.

"You probably know all about my mom," I said. "I bet OIPEP has a file on me and you had to read that when they, um, attached you to me. That's how you knew my blood had the power to heal."

"That's pretty smart of you, Alfred."

"So there is a file."

"The Company keeps files on a lot of people."

"How many people?"

"Practically everybody."

"Why practically everybody?"

"Because practically everybody has the potential to be important."

"Well, I never saw myself that way. I mean, I know I'm the last living descendent of Lancelot, and my dad was pretty rich and important, but it was mostly dumb luck how I saved the world."

She reached over and put her hand on the top of my hand.

"You're very special, Alfred. You have a very unique gift; don't ever forget that."

"I don't have any gifts."

That was sort of an invitation for her to list my gifts, but she didn't. For a tiny second I thought about putting my other hand on top of hers, but the second passed. She took her hand away.

"I have to go."

"You're on the team going in, aren't you?"

She nodded. Her expression told me she wasn't exactly thrilled she was on the team.

"Can I go too?"

She looked at me sharply. "Didn't they tell you? You don't have a choice."

14

At that moment, the door swung open and Op Nine walked in. He was carrying a pair of combat-style black boots and a pair of thick socks. Ashley jumped off the bed and I did too, as if he had caught us doing something we shouldn't. By the expression on his face, I figured maybe we had been.

"The rest of the team has already reported on deck," Op Nine said to Ashley.

"I was on my way."

"The deck," Op Nine said tightly, "is two flights above us."

Ashley left without another word.

I said, "Don't dock her pay or anything. She didn't tell me anything I didn't already know."

"It would be unfortunate, particularly for her, if she had," Op Nine said. He set the boots and socks beside the bed and stepped back.

"Well," I said. "She did tell me one thing. You're taking me with you to the nexus."

"It is unavoidable."

"And why's that?"

He just stared at me. I said, "I have this theory you might be a cyborg."

"You are making a joke."

"Half a joke."

"How does one make half a joke?"

"I've never really thought it through. What if I refuse to go?"

"I would be forced to compel you."

"I could fight you." One of his thick eyebrows rose toward his hairline. "I'm a biter. And a scratcher."

"I would immobilize you and carry you to the nexus over my shoulder like a sack of potatoes."

"That's a joke, right?"

"Half a joke."

He motioned to the boots and socks. He watched silently as I pulled them on.

"How do you feel?" he asked.

"Still a little dizzy."

"That will pass."

"How do you know?"

"I am a trained medic as well as a cyborg."

He opened the bulkhead door and jerked his head toward the corridor outside.

"After you, Alfred Kropp."

Something hit me then, and instead of keeping my mouth shut, which was probably the wisest thing to do at that moment, I blurted out, "I'm the bait, aren't I?"

"Bait?"

"Or ransom or something. Mike wants you to bring me to him."

"I doubt that."

"Then why do I have to go?"

"Because," Op Nine said calmly, "we say so."

Dumb, Kropp, dumb, dumb, dumb, I told myself, and walked through the door anyway.

15

We climbed the circular stairs two flights to the top, turned a corner, and suddenly we were in the open air. It was colder outside than I would have guessed, but I think I read somewhere that the desert gets cold at night. The *Pandora* had anchored about two hundred yards from shore. I could see lights there. Marsa Alam.

A group of agents was waiting on deck. I counted ten besides Op Nine and Abby, so that made me number thirteen, which seemed appropriate and ominous at the same time. When they saw us come up, the agents turned and stared at me.

"I'm Alfred Kropp," I said.

"They know who you are," Op Nine said.

I was about eight thousand miles from home, but some things you never leave behind, no matter how far you go, and right then, I felt like the big awkward dateless dork at the prom.

It was a young group, except for Op Nine. Nobody looked

over the age of thirty. The guys were all thick-necked and square-jawed, and their biceps bulged out the arms of their jumpsuits. There were two female agents, both blondes like Abby. They looked like fashion models with their oversized lips and very small chins and boyish hips.

Then I saw Ashley. She gave me a little smile. Op Nine cleared his throat, Ashley looked away, and then Abigail Smith began to speak.

"Well, we've come to it, folks. I don't think I need to remind you of the consequences should the Hyena succeed in opening the Lesser Seal—the greatest intrusion event in a hundred generations. For this reason, the director has invoked the First Protocol."

She paused to let that particular bit of news sink in with everyone—everyone except me, because I had no idea what she was talking about. The atmosphere got very somber.

"You understand what this means. You no longer exist—in the operational sense, of course." She took a deep breath. "You still have time to back out."

Nobody said anything. Abby nodded; I guess she was pleased that nobody was backing out. She asked if anyone had any questions. I had about a hundred. For example, what were an "intrusion event" and the First Protocol? The other ninety-eight were similar in that they were questions I probably didn't want answered. But the main question was why was everyone else allowed to back out but I wasn't?

Rope ladders hung over the railings, and we descended on them to the water below, where two speedboats bobbed gently, scraping against the hull of the *Pandora*. My butt had hardly touched the seat when we leaped forward and whipped hard to the left toward the lights of Marsa Alam.

The *Pandora* faded into the darkness, the darkest kind of dark, under a moonless sky, though the stars were very bright, much brighter than they appear in the States.

Two Land Rovers were waiting for us at the dock. Op Nine helped me out of the speedboat and I rode shotgun in the lead vehicle as he drove.

The roads in Marsa Alam were not up to American standards, and I was concentrating on keeping my tongue in the center of my mouth so I didn't bite it off as we jounced along. We didn't head for the lights of the town. Those lights stayed on our left and kept fading until the desert night closed around us and the only thing I could see were the twin beams of the headlamps cutting into the darkness.

After about fifteen minutes I saw a red blinking light against the backdrop of stars and other blue and yellow lights twinkling on the ground.

"Oh, great," I said. "This is just great. Where are we?" But I already knew the answer.

"An airstrip," Op Nine said.

Several men in black uniforms emerged out of the darkness as we got out of the Rovers. They carried automatic rifles and wore black berets. A man with dark skin, dressed in a very nice silk suit, separated himself from the soldiers and bowed to Op Nine.

"Dr. Smith," he said. "I am honored to make your acquaintance."

"I am Dr. Smith," Abigail said, smiling her brilliant smile and extending her hand. The man looked at her, startled. He wasn't expecting Dr. Smith to be a woman, I guess. He cleared his throat and made a show of pulling a sheet of paper from his coat pocket.

"I have a communication from His Excellency, the President of Egypt," the man said. He cleared his throat again and read very slowly, like he was translating Egyptian into English as he read, which maybe he was.

" 'As signatory to the OIPEP Charter, dated Copenhagen, 19 November, 1932, the Egyptian government pledges its full cooperation and support in this most urgent operation. Therefore, as President of Egypt and duly authorized signatory agent of the aforesaid Charter, I grant designated operatives of the Office of Interdimensional Paradoxes and Extraordinary Phenomenon, as determined by the director of said office, unconditional clearance in our airspace and any and all logistical support they may need for the successful completion of the aforesaid operation.

" 'We cheerfully place the fate of the world and its future generations into your hands. God be with you.' "

He cleared his throat a third time, carefully folded the communication, and handed it to Abby.

"Thank you, Ambassador," she said. "On behalf of the Office, I extend our gratitude and pledge our undying friendship to your government and all signatories to the Charter."

She bowed to him, he bowed to her, and then they bowed in unison.

He looked at each agent in turn, until he got to me, and the look became a stare.

"Hi," I said. "I'm Alfred Kropp."

"I know who you are," he said, and then he turned on his heel and strode toward a black Lincoln Town Car parked near the Land Rovers.

Op Nine said something to the soldiers in Arabic, which sounded very fluent to me, and at one point one of the soldiers laughed and clapped him on the shoulder like he'd gotten off a good joke. I tried to imagine Op Nine joking in any language, and couldn't. Over his shoulder I could see the dark hulk of a big plane. It looked like the same kind of cargo plane that had carried Bennacio and me over the Atlantic on my first globe-trotting secret mission last spring.

We walked toward the plane, the soldiers taking parameter positions around us. Op Nine led the way. I glanced to my right and saw Ashley walking beside me. Her hair was pulled into a knot on the back of her head, the same way Abby Smith wore her hair. Maybe it was a Company requirement, like a dress code. Three Egyptian soldiers kept pace about a dozen yards behind us.

"What's an intrusion event?" I whispered to Ashley.

She shook her head. "You don't want to know."

For the first time I noticed how different her voice sounded from when I first met her. I guess that was part of her transfer-student act. Her real voice was deeper and kind of raspy, the kind of voice you associate with smokers or female PE teachers. But I didn't think she was either one of those. I hadn't noticed the smell of smoke on her, and I doubted OIPEP recruited high school PE teachers as top-secret operatives.

I nodded toward Op Nine at the head of the pack.

"He kind of creeps me out. I was wondering if he was a cyborg."

She gave a little laugh. "A what?"

"You know, some kind of cybernetic robot or some-thing."

"He's human, as far as I know."

"Well, he doesn't act like any human I've ever known."

"He's sort of a living legend in the Company." She lowered

her voice, which made it sound even throatier. "He was in Abkhazia in eighty-three. The only one to come out alive."

We had reached the plane, which had no windows, and that was fine with me. Benches lined either side of the massive interior. We took our seats as the engines revved to life and I searched in vain for the seat belts. Ashley sat on my left and Op Nine on my right. Directly across from me sat Abigail Smith, who in the dim cabin lighting seemed to be smiling, but she might have just been gritting her teeth. Between us sat a half-dozen wooden crates bolted to the floor with heavy chains.

The plane began to accelerate, pressing me sideways into Ashley's shoulder. My stomach rolled, but things got a little better once we were airborne. Beside me, Op Nine reached under his seat and took out an oversized leather-bound book with funny triangular-shaped designs on the cover. Written in big letters the color of blood were the words "ARS GOETIA."

"What is that?" I asked him.

He cocked an eyebrow at me. *"The Ars Goetia,"* he answered.

"What's that mean?"

"It is Latin for *'The Howling Art.'* "

Then he proceeded to ignore me, burying his nose in the musty, parchmentlike papers of the old book, his lips moving as he read. I tried to think of something to say to Ashley, but I couldn't think of anything to say that didn't sound boring or stupid. Of course, I usually didn't let those considerations bother me, otherwise I'd never say anything.

"Do you know what's in the Lesser Seal?" I asked her.

She nodded, and her eyes were wide and wet-looking, and I wondered if that meant she was as scared as I was.

"Well," I said. "What is it?"

"The worst thing," she whispered. "The worst thing in the world."

At that moment Op Nine abruptly slammed the big book shut and stood up.

"We're at T-minus fourteen-thirty," he announced. "Insertion is approximately one hundred kilometers from the nexus. We will approach on sand-foils, since no doubt the Hyena is expecting an aerial assault. SATCON INTEL has identified Bedouin tribesmen recruited by our target."

"How many?" one of the guy agents asked. He had a great tan. I wondered if he was one of the people posing as a tourist above deck on the *Pandora*.

"Upwards of fifty, perhaps more, stationed as recons along approachable routes. Including, presumably, our route."

Op Nine opened one of the overhead compartments and pulled out something that looked like a cross between an elephant gun and a rocket launcher. It had a black strap for hanging it over your shoulder and a telescopic sight.

"Now," he said. "In the case of a full-blown intrusion event, this is the CW3XD." He held it high over his head so everybody could get a good look. "Obviously, it has never been field-tested."

"No time like the present," the tanned agent muttered.

Op Nine ignored him. "The magazine holds fifty rounds of ordnance." He pulled an oversized clip of bullets from the same overhead compartment. He ejected one of the bullets and held it up. It looked like an ordinary rifle round, except the tip was larger, about the size of an olive. "Be extraordinarily cautious with these. Loss of one into unfriendly hands could result in complete MISSFAIL."

"Mission failure," Ashley translated for me, but I had already figured that one out.

"The CW3XD is designed solely for containment of intrusion agents," Op Nine said, his tone becoming stern. "Under no circumstances is it to be discharged at the Hyena and his forces."

"Why?" another agent demanded. He was the biggest one of the lot; his thighs bulged in the shiny OIPEP jumpsuit and his biceps were about the size of my head, which, like too many people have pointed out, was large. "One round from this bad boy and they'll never find all the pieces."

"The ordnance is limited," Op Nine said.

"Extremely limited," Abigail Smith added, and for some reason she looked across the aisle at me.

"And it is specifically designed for operation against an intrusion agent," Op Nine said.

"So it'll kill 'em?" the big agent asked.

Op Nine gave him a cold stare. "What has never lived cannot be killed. Theoretically, the CW3XD will inhibit the IAs, giving us time to retrieve the Seals from the target."

Op Nine nodded to Abigail, who took a deep breath and rose from her seat with an air of weariness, like she could actually feel the fate of the world resting on her shoulders.

"Let's gear up," she said, and I thought her voice shook a little, and that wasn't encouraging, a senior OIPEP agent, afraid.

16

The agents stood up and popped open the overhead compartments, pulling out these yellow and orange bundles with white harnesses and clinking silver buckles. It took me a second to get it. This plane wasn't landing. Instead, we were jumping. My stomach did a slow roll.

Ashley touched me on the elbow. "You need some help with yours?" she asked.

"Yeah," I said.

"Turn around."

I turned my back to her and she slipped the harness over my shoulders. I turned again and she proceeded to snap the silver buckles closed. The top of her head was below my chin as she worked on the buckle at my waist, and her blond hair shimmered in the cabin lighting. I smelled lilacs. She gave each buckle a sharp tug before stepping back.

"The chute should automatically deploy after seven seconds," she told me. She touched a cord hanging over my left shoulder. "Pull the backup if it doesn't."

"What if the backup doesn't work?"

"It'll work."

"But what if it doesn't?"

"Then you hit the ground at five hundred miles per hour."

She turned away and rummaged in the overhead. Four agents fussed with the big crates in the middle of the hold, unhooking the heavy chains and checking the mattress-sized parachutes tied to them.

"When you say seven seconds, is that seconds like 'one-Mississippi, two-Mississippi' or 'one thousand one, one thousand two'?" I asked.

She turned, holding a gun and holster. She wrapped it around her slim waist and pulled it tight.

"It'll be all right, Alfred," she said. "Just don't stiffen up on the landing. Remember to bend your knees on touchdown; you'll be okay."

A bell rang inside the hold and a yellow light began to pulse over the cabin door. All the agents except two lined up for the jump. These two took positions in the rear on either side of the massive bay door; I guessed they were in charge of deploying the crates. I wondered who was in charge of deploying Alfred Kropp.

The agents lined up by the pulsing yellow light were hooking these long metal cords dangling from their chutes to a thin pole that ran the length of the cabin. I was wondering why, when the door swung open and a tornado roared into the plane. The wind kicked my feet out from under me and I would have smacked butt-first onto the hard metal floor, but a pair of huge hands caught me before I hit.

Op Nine shouted into my ear: "Be careful, Alfred Kropp! There may not always be someone near to catch you when you fall!"

He hooked me to the pole. I shivered in the howling wind. The temperature must have dropped about ten degrees when the door swung open.

One by one the OIPEP agents vanished through the opening. One second they were standing there, the next they were gone, like they were being sucked into the maw of an angry, screaming beast. Op Nine put one hand on my shoulder as we edged closer. My knees felt very weak and my throat very dry, but I didn't have a choice now—I couldn't turn back or change my mind, and sometimes that's better.

When my turn came, I put a hand on either side of the opening and stared into the dark Arabian night, unable to look up or down or unclench my cramping fingers from the cold metal. Op Nine bellowed in my ear, "Now! Let go, Alfred!"

That was it, the whole deal. I really had a problem with this letting-go thing. My mom. The truth about my dad. The loss of everybody who was close to me. I suddenly realized that sometimes the toughest thing is getting out of your own way.

I let go.

17

I spun and twisted and flipped as I fell, yowling my lungs out. The big plane appeared to shoot straight up toward the stars, and the world fragmented and refused to arrange itself into any kind of order: stars, earth, earth, stars, stars, earth, earth . . . and my mind fell apart with it. I forgot to count and by the time I remembered, I had no idea where to start—how many seconds had passed? Should I pull my cord just to be safe? Or would pulling my cord mess up the timing mechanism and tangle my chute? And, if my chute got tangled, would the desert sand break my fall? But if desert sand could break someone's fall, why use a parachute in the first place?

I hadn't been counting, but I figured I was way past the seven-second window, so I pulled the cord. Nothing happened. Stars, earth, earth, stars—and nothing happened. I yanked the cord again. I should know better than to jump from airplanes. In fact, with my track record, I shouldn't even indulge in something as commonplace as jaywalking. I pulled the cord a third time.

Nothing happened. Well, one thing happened: the rip cord broke off in my hand.

A few seconds later I was yanked about fifty feet straight up as my chute deployed and my descent slowed—but didn't seem slow enough. At least I was falling feetfirst. I could see one or two other OIPEP troopers silhouetted against the sky, dangling from their chutes like the toys I used to buy—the green army men with the plastic parachutes that you threw underhanded into the air. Half the time the kite string didn't unravel correctly and the army man crashed to earth or got hung up in a tree branch.

I looked down between my feet and saw the desert rushing up. *Bend your knees, Kropp, keep 'em loose,* I told myself, but I smacked into the ground with my legs as stiff as one of those army men's. My right ankle twisted in the sand. I pitched forward and the chute settled gently over my writhing body, the silky material wrapping tighter and tighter around me as I rolled in the sand.

Somebody pulled the chute off me and rolled me over. I looked up into Ashley's face—her red lipstick looked purple in the starlight—and said, "I think I broke my right ankle."

"Let's see," she said softly. She ran her fingers along the bones and then took my foot in both hands and gently turned it.

"Ouch!"

"I think it's a sprain. Let's see if you can put any weight on it."

She unhooked me from the harness and pulled me to my feet.

"Put your foot on the ground, Alfred," she said.

"Ouch!"

About a hundred feet away the agents were busy with the crates—or what was left of them. They had broken apart on impact; slats lay scattered in every direction.

Op Nine came up, frowning.

"Kropp is hurt?" he asked.

"Not badly," Ashley said. "A sprain, I think."

Op Nine said to Ashley, "Kropp rides with you."

He trudged toward the other agents gathered around the remnants of the crates. We trailed behind, my arm draped over Ashley's neck, my foot dragging in the sand. In every direction dunes marched like oceanic waves, disappearing into the horizon. I had thought the stars very bright on the shores of the Red Sea, but here in the desert they seared the blackness around them.

"Where exactly are we, anyway?" I asked Ashley.

"The Sahara."

The agents had pulled twelve snowmobiles from the shattered crates and were going down some kind of checklist, getting them ready, I guess, only there wasn't much chance of a snowstorm in the desert. One agent was handing out the CW3XDs and clip belts that they threw over their shoulders, reminding me of Mexican bandits. Abby Smith stood by herself a few feet away, holding some electronic gadget with a bluish LCD glimmering on her frowning face.

"What's the deal with the snowmobiles?" I asked.

"They aren't snowmobiles," Ashley replied. "Well, they used to be. They've been modified. We call them sand-foils."

Instead of the ski pads, these had thin metal blades, the

sharp edge facing down. Someone handed Ashley a helmet and she passed it to me.

"Put this on, Alfred. A sand-foil's top speed is a hundred and fifty miles per hour. Do you know what a single grain of sand can do if it hits you at that speed?"

"No, but I got hit with a baseball once that must have been going forty miles per hour; it hurt like heck."

I shoved the helmet down over my head. I could have guessed it would be too small, and it was. One of my ears was folded down.

Abby snapped her device closed and trudged over to us.

"We're approximately a hundred clicks due east of the target," she said crisply. Her voice sounded very far away inside my helmet. "Remember, no wake-riding and no unauthorized firing of the 3XDs. Op Nine and I are on the point. Any questions?"

Nobody had any questions or, if they did, they weren't going to waste time asking them. All the agents except Ashley flipped the big CW3XDs onto their backs. Ashley had to ride with hers awkwardly resting across her chest, since she had my big self awkwardly clinging to her back. Static popped in my ear and suddenly her purry voice seemed to enter my head and lodge in the middle of my brain. The helmets were outfitted with a wireless setup.

"You okay?"

"I guess."

She pressed a button on the console in front of her and indicator lights blinked on. I didn't hear the engine roar to life like I expected; the thing simply started to vibrate beneath me.

"Hang on!" she said. I wrapped my arms around her waist as the sand-foil leaped forward and accelerated, the blades rising out of the sand as it gained speed. These sand-foils were clearly not made for two riders. My butt hung about halfway off the back of the leather seat and I worried about a stray grain of sand embedding itself into the softest part of my body.

Looking over her shoulder, I could see the speedometer. The needle hovered just below the one hundred mark.

Abigail Smith had said we were due east of the target, which meant we must have been heading west, but the dunes ran roughly north-south, so our race across the Sahara was run half of the time in the air, as we crested one wave, became airborne, and then smacked back down in a trough before starting up the next dune.

The ride across the desert was like being on a roller coaster. Those rides always seemed to last longer than they really were. I raised my head and looked over Ashley's shoulder.

The other agents had already stopped. Straight ahead the horizon glowed a brilliant amber with little sparks flying around in the orange like sunlight reflecting off the tips of waves.

We slowed to a stop and I slipped off, fumbling with the chin straps of my helmet. I yanked it off, wincing as it scraped over my ears. I could see Op Nine standing a few yards in front of the rest of the group, studying the glowing horizon like he'd never seen a sunrise before.

"What's up?" I asked Ashley, but she just shook her head. I trudged through the sand toward Op Nine, dragging my bum foot. The glow on the horizon had deepened to an orangish red. But something about this desert sunrise wasn't right, and it took me the rest of the hike to figure it out: we were facing west, not east.

This was no sunrise.

Abby Smith was a few steps ahead of me and Op Nine must have heard her coming up, because she was still behind him when he turned his head and spoke.

And now the glow on the horizon looked like a wall of fire coming toward us.

"We are too late."

18

"How many?" Abby asked Op Nine.

"It's difficult . . ." He shaded his eyes with one huge hand and squinted toward the sparkling light. "Thirty, perhaps forty legions."

"Legions?" I asked. "What's a legion?"

Abby said to him, "Not all, then."

He shook his head. "A search party."

"A search party of what?" I asked.

"Can we outrun them?" she asked.

He said quietly, " 'Their horses are swifter than leopards, and are more fierce than the evening wolves: and their horsemen shall come from far; they shall fly as the eagle that hasteth to eat.' "

"I'll take that as a no," she said. "Then we engage." She started to turn away. He grabbed her arm and pulled her back.

"No!" he said in a fierce whisper. "Our mission is to acquire the target. There is still time."

"Time for what?" I asked, but I really didn't expect an answer by this point.

Now the orange on the horizon had deepened to a fiery red mixed with bright white sparks. The stars winked out as the burning light advanced, filling the night sky, and a breeze noticeably warmer than the cool desert air began to blow across our faces.

"We must take cover," Op Nine said. "Immediately."

Abby turned and started toward the others, making some kind of complicated hand signal as she went, and right away they opened the storage compartments on the foils and began pulling out what looked like brown tarps.

Op Nine had said we needed to take cover immediately, but he didn't move a muscle. He stood stock-still and stared at the flickering lights of white and gold. The breeze had turned into a full-fledged wind that grew hotter with each passing second. The ground started to tremble.

"Uh, Op Nine, didn't you say we had to take cover?"

He shook his head as if rousing himself from a dream.

"Yes. Come, Kropp."

He threw my arm over his shoulder and helped me back to the foils. The agents had spread the brown tarps over the vehicles and now were crawling underneath them. Ashley crouched beside one, motioning to us.

"Alfred," Op Nine said. "This is very important: do not look into their eyes. They will know what you fear."

He lowered me to the ground and I started to crawl under the tarp. He grabbed my arm and pulled my face close to his.

"And what you love."

He had to shout over the wind, which was howling by this point, spraying us with stinging grains of sand. He let the tarp fall and I felt someone's hand on my wrist, pulling me away from the edge.

"Don't move," Ashley whispered. "Don't talk."

The darkness under the tarp faded, or maybe I was getting used to it, because after a minute I could see her bright blue eyes darting back and forth. Ashley's hand was white-knuckled on the CW3XD that lay across her lap, her index finger caressing the trigger. Ashley was afraid.

The tarp rippled and snapped around us as the gale worsened and sand popped against the material, making this strange hissing sound like gas escaping from a bottle. I could hear something else too, as if the wind was a curtain rippling as this sound passed behind it. Voices, or maybe not voices but somehow the echo of voices, and I started to shake as the tarp around us began to glow red.

It was very close now, whatever it was, and the closer it got, the more I shook. It was hot and stuffy under the covering and I was sweating, but I shivered like I had a fever. Op Nine's warning echoed over and over in my head: *Don't look into their eyes! Don't look into their eyes!* My mind became like a slice of Swiss cheese, stretched thin, full of holes filled with darkness, and that darkness was full of horror.

Dimly, under the howling wind, I could hear someone screaming. *She needs to be quiet,* I thought. *Ashley, be quiet!* But it wasn't Ashley screaming, of course; it was me.

Then, as if it shot through one of those holes in my mind, a hand reached for me in the darkness, soft and warm, and without thinking I pulled her into my arms.

19

"Alfred, it's over."

She pushed on my chest and I unfolded my arms. Every inch of me ached. In the half-light beneath the tarp, I saw her brush back a strand of hair from her forehead.

"What was that?" I whispered hoarsely. My throat ached from the screaming. "What the heck was that?"

I flipped back the edge of the tarp without asking for permission. *Enough of this,* I thought. I was testy now. I wanted some answers. Everybody seemed to know what we were getting into except one key person.

Sand fell into a heap where I lifted the tarp. The winds had piled the sand all around us, like a snowdrift. I stood up and my knees popped. Twelve mounds of desert sand now stood where the foils used to be. And these twelve mounds were the only feature left in the Sahara. The desert was as flat and featureless as an enormous tabletop; the rolling dunes were completely gone.

But the night had returned and, with it, the brilliant stars and the cool air.

The others had already emerged from their hiding places and gathered in a circle around Op Nine. He saw me crawl out and waved me over. I waited for Ashley. Her cheeks were wet and her eyes red.

I grabbed her hand. She pulled it away.

"I'm okay," she said.

"I'm not," I said, and I grabbed her hand again and this time she didn't pull away.

We joined the other agents, who for some reason were kneeling in this circle, even Abby. Their eyes were downcast and their expressions somber, and I wondered why we were having a prayer meeting. Op Nine was the only one upright, standing in the center of the circle, arms folded over his chest, looking very grim. Even the big agent with the cocky, let's-mow-'em-down attitude looked like somebody had gut-punched him.

They adjusted themselves to make room for Ashley and me. Op Nine motioned for us to kneel. I don't know why, but I went down to my knees at once and so did Ashley. She pulled her hand free and this time I didn't take it back.

Op Nine said, "The worst has come to pass: the Hyena has unlocked the Seal. Yet Fortune smiles upon us, for we have escaped his minions' notice. We may assume he has divided his legions to search for us, thus exposing his position. A frontal assault will be the last thing he expects." He took a deep breath. "So that is precisely what we shall give him."

He reached into the pocket of his jumpsuit and pulled out

a small metal flask. He walked up to Abigail and stopped. He opened the flask, tipped the opening against the pad of his thumb, and then traced the sign of the cross on her forehead, muttering something I couldn't hear. He worked his way around the circle, wetting his thumb, muttering, making the sign.

Finally he came to me. He paused, staring down at me, and his dark eyes seemed even darker in the starlight.

"What?" I whispered.

"*Domine, exaudi orationem meam,*" Op Nine murmured, upending the flask. "*Et clamor meus ad te veniat.*" He pressed his thumb against my forehead and I felt the wetness there as he traced the cross. "*In nomine Patris, et Filii, et Spiritus Sancti.* Amen."

He stepped over to Ashley and I watched him bless her too, as a single drop of holy water (I guessed it was holy water—what else could it be?) trickled down my nose.

He capped off the flask and slipped it into his pocket. Nobody said anything as we pulled the tarps off the foils and folded them up. Ashley would pause every now and then to pull back the strand of blond hair that had fallen from her bun. Her fingers were shaking. I helped her fold the tarp.

"Okay," I said. "So what was that about?"

She shook her head, almost impatiently, like my question bordered on the cheeky.

"We're too late," she said. "Mike's unlocked the Lesser Seal. They're free."

"Who's free? What did Solomon keep in the Lesser Seal, Ashley? Why did Op Nine just bless us? Is he a priest or something?" I blurted out, though it was hard for me to imagine, a priest being an OIPEP agent. "What's his deal anyway?"

She grabbed the bundle and stuffed it back into its compartment on the sand-foil. She looked angry and frightened at the same time.

"Okay, I'll tell you. They brought you here, so you have a right to know. Let them fire me for it; I don't care . . . Op Nine's 'deal' is demons, Alfred."

"Demons?"

"He's a demonologist."

And that's how I finally discovered what had been imprisoned for three thousand years in the Holy Vessel of Babylon, the Lesser Seal of Solomon.

"Demons . . . ?" I said. "Demons. Well, that's great. That's just terrific."

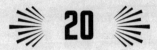

20

We climbed back onto the sand-foil and soon the speedometer needle was hovering near 110. We made better time now that the dunes were gone. We were crossing the Sahara, but it might as well have been the flats at Death Valley.

The speaker inside my helmet crackled with agent chatter, mostly from Abby as she reviewed the ATTPRO. I guessed it meant "attack procedure." It could also stand for "attitude problem," though I doubted it, given the context.

"Two groups!" Abby said. "First group will feint an attack on the Hyena's flank to draw off the IAs. Second group is the targeting force who will take out the Hyena and retrieve the Seal!"

Abby made it very clear that Operative Nine had dibs on Mike, I guessed because he was the expert in the group on handling these demons. It seemed to me what they really needed was an expert on handling Mike Arnold.

Then she called out the names in each group. ASSFOR-1

("Assault Force One," I was guessing, though the OIPEP shoptalk threw me for a second) would consist of Sam, Betty, Todd, Bill, Carl, and Agnes. All OIPEP people had names like that, never more than one syllable—unless you were a girl, then you got two or even three, if you were really important, like Abigail Smith.

The rest, Bert, Ken, Yule, Ashley, Abigail, and Op Nine, were ASSFOR-2. I assumed I was ASSFOR-2 too, since my big one was hanging off the backseat of Ashley's sand-foil.

After a while the horizon began to glow that sickening orange color and the chatter inside my helmet died away. My thoughts started to feel like Swiss cheese again, and I wondered how anybody, even a trained OIPEP agent, could fight in these circumstances, when absolute terror ripped through you like a buzz saw.

Ashley slowed the sand-foil and we fell back with the rest of ASSFOR-2. The first group roared straight toward the horizon with its sparks of white light that looked kind of like Christmas lights twinkling. They held the butts of their long 3XDs against their thighs, the barrels sticking up in the air at a forty-five-degree angle.

"Hold until they're engaged," I heard Op Nine say in my ear.

We came to a stop. Op Nine was right beside me, the visor on his helmet flipped up so I could see his face in the glow of the demon-fire.

"Where's mine?" I asked, nodding at the 3XD in his hand. "What's it shoot anyway—holy water?"

"Something far more powerful, I hope," he said. Then out of nowhere he added, "It has begun."

He flipped his visor down. I looked toward the orange glow and now there was red tracer fire from the group ahead arching into it, and when it touched the fire, a black tear or hole appeared, lingered for a few seconds, then closed back up. I didn't get a long look, though, because we leaped forward suddenly and my head snapped back. The needle jumped to 130 after we executed a hard left. Racing toward the battle, I could see over Ashley's shoulder that the orange glow came to a sort of point on the southern edge.

The orange had deepened to red when Abby Smith started yelling something over the speaker and we skidded to a stop. About thirty yards ahead I could see a sand-foil lying on its side and closer, crawling toward us, one of the OIPEP agents, clutching the 3XD in his right hand.

Ashley grabbed a satchel embossed with a red X, ripped off her helmet, and ran to the crawling man.

"Ashley!" Abigail called. "There isn't time!"

He had taken off his helmet. It was Carl, the biggest agent, the tough guy who talked on the plane about blowing Mike away. He was crying and slobbering and cursing, his face caked with wet sand. He cried out when Ashley touched him on the shoulder, cringing like a dog that's used to being beaten. As we got closer, I could see Carl had no eyes. There were just empty sockets where his eyes used to be.

Ashley realized it at the same time, I think, because she recoiled suddenly with a startled gasp.

"I do not, don't, won't—they come, they come, THEY COME!" he bellowed at her. He rolled himself into a ball and brought his hands to his face. When I first got a load of those empty sockets, I thought the demons must have torn out his eyes. But, as Carl clawed frantically into the spaces where his eyes used to be, the truth hit me: *Carl* had ripped them out.

Beside me, Op Nine said softly, "You see now why I warned you never to look into their eyes."

21

Op Nine grabbed the first-aid kit from Ashley's hand and pulled out a shiny instrument. It was the same thing Ashley had used on me in the helicopter.

"What are you doing?" Ashley asked.

"Sedating him," he answered. "Otherwise, he may literally tear himself to pieces."

He jabbed the needle into Carl's arm. In two seconds he rolled onto his back, out cold. Op Nine handed the kit to Ashley.

"Dress the wounds, quickly," he told her. He scooped the 3XD out of the sand and held it toward me.

I hesitated for a second, then took it from him. The rifle was lighter than I expected. It weighed about the same as a broom.

Op Nine kneeled beside Carl, pulled the sash of cartridges from his body, and handed it to me.

"Remember, Kropp, the ammunition is limited."

That's okay, I thought, *so am I.*

I threw the cartridge belt over one shoulder and slung the 3XD over my back. I trudged back to the sand-foil, dragging my aching right foot in the sand. Ashley trotted back after a minute, carrying the first-aid kit under her arm and pulling off bloody surgical gloves as she ran.

Op Nine took the point now, as we raced southwest.

His voice sounded tinny and distant over the speaker in my helmet: "If another operative flees the engagement, we do not stop."

It looked like the engagement was winding down. When it first began, the tracer fire lighting up the sky had looked like the climax of a Fourth of July fireworks show. Now the firing was sporadic and the black holes punched through the searing lights appeared less frequently. Either ASSFOR-1 was running out of ammunition or it was running out of personnel.

I blinked rapidly behind my visor, because the lights in the sky now reflected off the sand, like the battle was taking place over a vast lake.

Suddenly a ball of light separated itself from the main firestorm and came barreling toward us. We were going about 130 miles per hour; this thing came toward us at three times that speed.

"Engage, engage, engage!" a frantic voice screamed over the speaker. The agents brought the sand-foils skidding to a stop, angling them into a circle. They jumped off, fell to one knee inside the circle, and swung their 3XDs toward the sky.

I plopped down next to Ashley, swinging my rifle upward too, but feeling a little ridiculous, to tell the truth. I'd been to a carnival or two where you fire at the little plastic cutouts of ducks as they slowly roll along the track. I never knocked down a single duck. But maybe saving my own skin from being fried by demon-fire would focus my aim better than winning the kooky stuffed monkey with the disproportionately big head.

"On my mark . . ." Op Nine said.

I rested the pad of my index finger on the cool metal of the trigger. Sweat trickled down my forehead and burned my eyes, but I couldn't wipe it off because of the helmet, and I wasn't about to take my helmet off. The memory of Carl writhing in the sand was still fresh in my mind.

"Mark!" Op Nine shouted.

"Fire, fire, fire at will!" someone else screamed.

The 3XDs erupted all around me and the night lit up in a fury of red. My finger jerked on the trigger, which slammed the weapon hard into my shoulder as it recoiled, nearly knocking me onto my butt. I didn't aim, really—it was kind of a frantic repeat of my duck hunting at the carnival—but just jerked the barrel this way and that, firing randomly at any movement above me. Waves of furnace-level heat rolled down from the sky.

I could see them now, and the sight nearly made me throw down my gun and run in pure panic.

Thousands of demons—maybe tens of thousands—careened above us, diving, swooping, stalling briefly, then zipping away faster than you can blink, glimmering forms of men in flowing robes. They rode beasts with wings sparking with golden fire, the wings at least ten feet from tip to tip, with yawning mouths stuffed with fangs, hanging open as if frozen in midscream. I saw lions and tigers and bears and other beasts that I knew I should recognize. They reminded me of roadkill:

you knew they lived once, but now they were twisted and smashed into distorted versions of what they once were.

Their screams mixed with the roaring wind and the whispering of the damned.

But they didn't look like your typical comic book or movie demons—not like those hunkered gargoyles or the little grinning guys with pitchforks and horns growing out of their bald heads. These riders were seven feet tall at least. They wielded swords of fire, lances, or staffs that burned at the tips but weren't consumed. This close to them I could see now the source of the orange and red light was the demons themselves; it radiated from their eyes and their open mouths.

Some wore flaming crowns, and the light springing from their eyes was especially harsh, purer and brighter than the light of the crownless ones, which was flecked with black. The light made it impossible for me to see their faces—not that I really wanted to see their faces.

Abby's voice crackled in my headset, tinged with barely controlled panic: "Base One, Base One, this is Insertion Team Delta. We have a Level Alpha Intrusion Event. Repeat: confirm L Alpha Event! Request immediate air support at these coordinates!"

As I held down the trigger, the 3XD kept firing, and my shoulder began to ache from the kickback. I emptied my clip and fumbled at the belt for a fresh one, but then I couldn't figure out how to eject the spent cartridge, and I wasted a few precious seconds yanking on it, trying to pull it free from the rifle.

The noise was horrible, the screaming of the flying roadkill, the howling of the wind, the shouts and static over the speakers in my helmet, the booming of the 3XDs. When a round slammed into one of the demons, it blew apart in an explosion of sparkling light mixed with black, but only for a few seconds. I watched, horrified, as the thing reassembled itself and was whole again. I remembered Op Nine's words on the plane: *What has never lived cannot be killed.*

Holding them off was the best we could hope for, but our ammunition wouldn't last forever, and then what?

I finally found the release button for ejecting the cartridge. It plopped hissing into the sand as I slammed a fresh one into the slot and yanked the trigger. About that same time, the demon swarm leaped straight up, dwindling into the velvet blackness of the desert sky.

A voice shouted in my ear, "Hold your fire! Hold your fire!"

The noise died away until all I could hear was my own ragged breath inside the helmet. Even the whispering faded, but the memory of it lingered, like a slowly dying echo. We watched their shapes circle high above in concentric rings of fire, each ring turning in the opposite direction of the other one.

The eerie silence was shattered by a terrific roar, and my heart jumped. Ashley tugged on my sleeve and pointed toward the main body of demons about three football fields away. Something was coming toward us, moving slowly across the desert, bellowing as it came.

Beside me, Op Nine murmured, "'Behold the Ninth Spirit, Paimon, the Great King, second only to Lucifer, in the form of a Man sitting upon a Dromedary.'"

I didn't know what he was talking about, and I sure didn't know what a dromedary was, but whatever it was, it didn't sound good. Op Nine stood up and then everybody stood up and we waited for the bellowing thing to come.

It was huge, standing over ten feet from its hooves to the top of its slightly flattened head. Bulging red eyes, a neck thick and gnarled as a tree trunk, globules of slobber hanging from its open mouth.

"That's not a dromedary," I said. "That's a camel."

It stopped a dozen yards from our circle. It stopped, but the bellowing didn't. This perverted memory of an animal was in some serious pain.

A man-shape balanced on the forward hump, with a shining face like those of the demon-lords who circled high above us, lean and almost girl-like with its large eyes, delicate nose, and full, sensuous lips. A crown glittered on its head, spewing radiant light, red and gold and aqua and green, that shot out from its brow like laser beams.

A dark shape fell away from the rear hump of the monster camel and dropped to the sand. It walked slowly toward us, and beside me Op Nine whispered, "Hold, hold." He had pulled off his helmet, so the rest of us followed suit.

He was ordinary size, the man who now walked toward us, and he didn't carry a flaming sword or burning staff or anything like that. His head was bare. He wore a white robe that had come open, so beneath it I could see his khakis and white Lacoste polo.

And, of course, he was smacking gum.

"Hey, guys, how's it goin'?" Mike Arnold asked.

22

"Michael," Abigail said.

"Abby Smith—hey, it's pleasing as pickles to see you! I don't care what they said in headquarters, you're still a heck of a field agent in my book, and by the way you look just *fantastic* in that jumper."

He looked at Op Nine. "Figured you'd be here, Padre. Sort of the culmination of your whole career, huh. No thanks necessary."

Then he saw me. "Al Kropp! My God, is that you? Jeez, kid, you're like the Forrest Gump of supernatural disasters—you're always everywhere!"

He clapped his hands together. "So! This it? This all you brought for the greatest intrusion event in the past three millennia? I feel a little disappointed, to tell you the truth."

"You're not the only one who is disappointed, Michael," Abby Smith said.

"Well, like the old saying goes, you gotta crack a few eggs to make an omelet." He spread his arms wide, palms facing toward us.

I saw the ring then, the Great Seal of Solomon, shining on his right hand. Twice as thick as the average wedding ring, it shone with a reddish, coppery color.

"Tell us what you want, Michael," Abigail said.

"Oh, it's not what I want, Abby," Mike said. "Or what anybody wants, really. It's more of what we *need*."

Abby and Op Nine exchanged a puzzled look.

"Look, I'm not going to bust your chops," Mike went on. "It's a damned shame, but sometimes damned shames are necessary. Kind of like the demons here. That's my new best friend Paimon on the camel with the thyroid condition. I've freed all of 'em, down to the last demon, and they're all angry as hell, if you'll excuse the expression. They've been cooped up in a cell the size of a birdcage for the past three thousand years. Things got a little testy in there, as you can imagine."

"Enough," Op Nine said sharply. His tone was like a father who had run out of patience with a lippy kid. "What do you want, Arnold?"

"Oh, it's a little bigger than that, Padre. I'm just an insignificant blip on history's radar."

"Michael, we're willing to negotiate," Abby said. "But you are making that extremely difficult."

"This isn't a negotiation, Abby. It's a wake-up call. You know, like the Russians putting up Sputnik. Whether it likes it or not, the world's going to beat its swords into plowshares. Or else."

He walked back to the monster camel with the mouthful of slobbery six-inch fangs. He turned to King Paimon, and then jerked his head back toward us.

"Kill them, Paimon," he said. "Kill them all."

23

One of the agents—I think it was Bert—raised his 3XD. Paimon's right arm came up, the fingers spread wide in Bert's direction. I expected some kind of death ray or lightning bolt or maybe a stream of hellfire to shoot from its open hand.

Instead, the hand snapped closed into a fist, and Bert blew apart. I mean, his body twisted and bulged like he was made of Play-Doh and then just exploded.

The team's 3XDs opened up, and now this Paimon thing twisted and bulged as the rounds tore through its body, tearing it to pieces, but in seconds it was whole again.

I felt a blast of heat on the top of my head. The entire contingent of demons was descending on us.

I looked down and saw Mike hop onto the back of the camel and take off toward the mirage or oasis or whatever it was. I didn't even think about it, just jumped on the nearest sand-foil and took off after him.

Despite its massive size, that camel could move. I yanked back on the throttle and soon the sand-foil was clocking 140 and shaking like it was going to break—I figured maybe the foils themselves would snap off and send me straight over the handlebars.

The front edges caught on something hard and suddenly I was airborne, two feet off the ground, now smooth and shiny, not sand anymore, but more like ice.

I landed hard on my stomach and slid four or five feet before coming to a stop. I scrambled to my feet, my boots slipping on this strange surface, and looked around.

Mike was standing on a makeshift platform or altar, with about a dozen robed men gathered around him, probably part of the Bedouin tribe Op Nine talked about. The damned camel was gone.

In front of the altar, sitting on another wooden platform, was a lidless copper jar. It could only be the Holy Vessel, where the demons had been imprisoned for three thousand years.

I walked toward him, cradling the 3XD, still slipping and sliding a little on the glassy ground. Mike laughed when he saw me coming.

"You know what that is?" he shouted at me. "Glass! Heat from the demons' release fried the sand. Can you believe it?"

I didn't say anything. I didn't have anything left to say to Mike Arnold, who had literally dragged me into this whole thing and who was responsible for so many deaths.

I was going to get that ring from him or die trying.

I raised the 3XD—to hell with conserving ammo—and a dozen Uzis appeared from beneath the Bedouins' robes.

"Fortunately, the ol' Seal protects its wearer from a whole bunch of nasty consequences," he said.

He whispered something to one of the tribesmen, and I saw the muzzle of his Uzi flash before feeling the punch in my thigh. The round knocked my feet out from under me and I landed right on my tailbone, which hurt almost as much as the bullet.

I pushed myself up, rocking now on my heels. I could feel the warm blood running down my leg.

I gritted my teeth and took a step toward Mike, bringing up the 3XD a second time.

The next bullet hit me in the right shoulder, the impact flinging my arm away. The 3XD clattered to the ground. I fell to my knees, pressing the heel of my left hand against the burning spot in my shoulder.

"Stay down, Al," Mike said softly. "I promise it'll be quick."

I looked up at him, blinking back tears. Mike stepped off the platform, walked over to where I knelt, and pulled his 9mm Glock from his belt. He leveled it at my forehead.

"Good-bye, Al," he said.

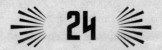

24

His finger tightened on the trigger—then suddenly froze. Something behind me had caught his attention. His eyes went wide.

"Awww, *darn* it!" he breathed.

I turned and saw two things: the sun rising in the east and something silhouetted against it—actually about fifty somethings, coming straight for us, flying in tight formation, their four low-hanging turrets flashing orange balls of light as they came.

They were Apache attack helicopters, the air support Abigail Smith had called in during the opening skirmish.

I lunged forward, slamming my weight into Mike's knees, knocking him backward, and he cried out when he smacked into the glass.

I threw myself on top of him and slammed my fist into his grinning, gum-smacking, wise-cracking mouth. Then I yanked the gun out of his hand and jammed the muzzle under his chin.

"Do it," he whispered. Blood ran out of the side of his mouth and trickled down his jaw.

I didn't pull the trigger, though. With my free hand I grabbed the ring and gave it a sharp yank, pulling it from his finger.

By then the Bedouins had reached us, shouting in confusion, some of them yelling at Mike and some at me, but it didn't really matter because I had the ring now.

I pushed myself off Mike and didn't bother trying to stand up. The ground was too slippery, plus I was losing a lot of blood and felt a little light-headed. I scooted back on my throbbing backside, putting some distance between us.

The Apaches swooped down into the swarming hornet's nest of demons, guns blazing, and the sun cast spinning bars of red and gold through the roiling haze.

I watched the demons adopt a Kamikaze mode of attack, gathering themselves into fireballs and ramming into the copters. At first, the Apaches seemed to absorb the blows, only to expand like overfilled balloons and blow apart, mini-suns going supernova against the indigo sky.

Then I slipped the ring onto my finger.

"Drop 'em!" I shouted at the Bedouins, even though I doubted the Seal of Solomon controlled anything but demon hordes. It worked, though. The Uzis fell out of their hands without a word of protest. Maybe I couldn't control them, but they knew what I could control.

I slid back around to face the battle and raised my fist, pointing the ring toward the demon hordes. I screamed at the top of my lungs: "STOP! QUIT IT! CUT IT OUT! I'M THE BOSS NOW! LEAVE US ALONE!"

Nothing happened. The battle went on. Maybe I put it on the wrong hand.

I yanked the ring off, and at that moment Mike Arnold jumped me.

He drove his knee into my back, throwing me forward. The ring flew from my hand and skidded across the polished glass. Mike landed on top of me, smashing my face into the ground.

"Oh, Lord," Mike breathed in my ear. I rolled him off me and scrambled after the ring.

I beat Mike to it, but only because he didn't chase after it. He had seen something that I didn't until it was too late.

The ring came to a stop at the feet of the seven-foot-tall demon king called Paimon, who picked it up just as I stretched out my hand to grab it.

Then I did an incredibly stupid thing: I looked right into its eyes.

PART THREE
The Hunt for the Hyena

To: Aquarius
From: ChiCubsFan
Subject: Sub-Sub-Sec. Op Utopia

See attached briefing memo. That damned kid has practically cost us the game! LS in my possession. Am now making for Barcelona via rail.

Request immediate recall.

Help.

ChiCubsFan

Attachment (SUBSUBSECOPUTOP.DOC)

To: ChiCubsFan
From: Aquarius
Subject: Sub-Sub-Sec. Op Utopia

Go immediately to ground until further notified. Situation is extremely fluid and IAs' intent not clear. I'll do my best from this end to manage interface with signatories. Hold for further instructions but under no circumstances make contact with anyone.

I suggest you sequester your loved ones to circumvent application of Section Nine protocols.

Aquarius

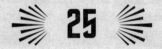

25

"Alfred? Alfred Kropp, can you hear me?"

"Yes."

"Alfred, I want you to do something for me. I want you to open your eyes, very slowly. Can you do that for me?"

"I'll try."

"There now. Is it too bright, Alfred? We can dim the lights."

"Do I have to leave them open?"

"Only for a few minutes, if you can."

"Okay."

"Can you see me, Alfred? Can you see my face?"

"Yes."

"Do you recognize me?"

"Yes."

"And do you remember my name?"

"I—I'm not sure . . ."

"It's all right. You're perfectly safe here. Alfred, my name is Dr. Abigail Smith. Do you remember now?"

"No. Not really. You look familiar, though. Why can't I move my arms?"

"We had to restrain you, for your own protection."

"What if I need to scratch my nose?"

"Does your nose itch?"

"No, but just in case . . . I'm not sure I remember your name, ma'am, but your face is familiar, or at least this fuzzy image I'm getting of your face. Where am I?"

"You are in Company headquarters, Alfred."

"What company?"

"OIPEP. Do you remember OIPEP?"

"Should I?"

"You should, though you might not wish to."

"Oh, well, I'd rather not remember anything I don't wish to. Who's the big guy standing behind you?"

"His name is Operative Nine."

"Weird. Why am I lying in this bed? Am I sick?"

"You have suffered . . . an attack."

"Like a seizure or something like that?"

"Something like that."

The lady called Abigail Smith smiled. She had very bright teeth. Mom always said you could tell a lot about a person by their teeth.

"Where is my mom?"

The lady glanced at the weird guy she called Operative Nine. "Alfred," she said. "Your mother passed away four years ago."

"She did?"

"I'm afraid so."

"I'm supposed to know that, right?"

"We're hoping your memory will return in time."

"How do I know you're not lying to me?"

The big guy stepped forward and I said, "You're probably the ugliest man I've ever seen in my life. What's the deal with the long earlobes?"

He didn't say anything. He just smiled.

"Your teeth aren't as nice as Dr. OIPEP's here. Are you both dressed in black because my mom died?"

"Alfred," he said. "I'm going to say a name to you now and I want you to tell me if you recognize it."

"Perhaps this is too soon," Abigail Smith said to him.

He ignored her. He bent very low over my face and whispered, "Alfred, the name is *Paimon*."

My arms jerked in their bindings. My fingers clawed at the metal poles of the bed, trying to reach my eyes. My mouth came open but no sound came out: the howl stayed locked inside my head. My gut heaved and I vomited greenish brown puke onto the crisp, white pillowcase.

Abigail Smith sighed. "I told you it was too soon. Get somebody in here to clean this up."

He left and she was leaning over me, cupping my face in her hands, forcing me to look into her eyes. Her breath was sweet-smelling, like licorice.

"Alfred, Alfred, it's all right. Everything's going to be all right. Stay with me, Alfred—I won't let you go, I promise. I won't let you go. Focus on my eyes, Alfred, *my* eyes. It can't find you now, do you understand? Do you understand me, Alfred?"

I nodded. I slowly relaxed, but the smell of my own puke was getting to me. She let go of my face long enough to grab a towel from somewhere. She lifted my head and wiped the pillowcase clean, then flipped the pillow over, puke side down. Then she lowered my head.

"You're safe now, Alfred, perfectly safe. It's not here."

I shook my head. "You're wrong. It is here. It'll always be here."

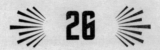

26

The big guy with the long earlobes came back with a fresh pillow, a man in a white lab coat right behind him.

"Another doctor," I said. "Great. How sick am I?"

Abigail Smith pulled out the pukey pillow and Operative Nine slid the new one under my head.

The doctor took my pulse and prodded my torso and stared into my cavities with a penlight. He measured my blood pressure and drew some blood. Except when he shone the light into them, he avoided looking into my eyes. He nodded to Operative Nine and left the room without a word. Abigail Smith came back to hover over me. I looked over her shoulder at the droopy-eared Operative Nine. "What's his story?"

"Op Nine is a demonologist, conversant in history, characteristics, classification, and possession. Best in the field."

"So that's why I'm here—I'm possessed?"

"Not precisely," he answered. "You have been—pried open. You cast your eyes into the very windows of hell, Alfred. Not the fabled or poetic visions of hell, of fire and brimstone and souls writhing in eternal agony, but the true vision of hell: the absolute and irreparable separation from heaven. What that experience is like I cannot say and hope you cannot remember."

Abigail Smith said to him, "Alfred told me it's still with him."

"Perhaps it is," Operative Nine said. "The Hiroshima bomb seared the very shadows of its victims into the pavement."

"This is not good," I said.

"On the contrary," he said. "This is extraordinarily good. You survived with your body and mind intact. That is more than can be said for the majority of our party."

"Well," I said. "Everybody's definition of the word may be a little different, but seeing that my memory's shot, I'm covered head to toe in bandages, tied down to a hospital bed, and talking very calmly about demons like they were the most natural thing in the world, like butterflies or Honda Preludes. I'm not sure I would call that *intact*."

"Your memory will return in time, I think, and your body will heal. The other person who met the Fallen's eyes is dead. He awoke in the desert and tore his own heart from his chest."

"So what's that mean? I'm gonna be tied to this bed for the rest of my life?"

Neither of them said anything, which I took as a *maybe* bordering on a definite *yes*.

"While they are free, no one who has gazed upon them

can be fully free themselves," Operative Nine said, choosing his words carefully.

"What's that mean, 'while they are free'?"

"They have taken the Great Seal of Solomon—and vanished."

"That would be a good thing, wouldn't it?"

"The Seal is the only thing that controls them, Alfred. Now Pai—now the demon itself commands. We must retrieve the Seal or watch all life submit to the will of the damned."

"I don't understand."

"In the beginning, there was a war, Alfred." He had a glassy, faraway look in his sad eyes. "Before there were men or green fields or the untamed sea. Before there was anything at all, before Time itself existed, there was a terrible war. A war that these beings you saw today lost. The Archangel Michael, with the Sword mortal men would name Excalibur, cast them down for their transgression against the throne of heaven. When the proper time arrived, they were sealed inside the Holy Vessel, to be ruled by the ring given to Solomon.

"After Solomon's passing, they slept for three thousand years, if such beings as these can said to sleep, safely imprisoned within the Holy Vessel. Before he bound them for the final time, however, Solomon commanded them using the gift of the Great Seal. Seventy-two lords, each with legions of minions under his rule, all conveying great wisdom and power to the one who wielded the Seal.

"Now they are free, for the first time answerable to no one but themselves. So you see the first war is not yet over; indeed, it may also be the last."

27

Operative Nine took a deep breath; he was going to go on, but at that moment the door opened and a short man wearing a tweed jacket walked in. He had a round face and pouty lips, with oval, wire-rimmed glasses perched on the end of his sharp nose. The most striking thing about him, though, was his hair: snow white, very fine, gathered around his round head like a crown of fluffy dandelion seeds. He looked like a cross between Albert Einstein and the inventor guy from the *Back to the Future* movies.

He was talking as he came in. At first I thought he was talking to himself; then I saw the wireless setup in his ear and the microphone dangling by a thin black wire near his mouth.

"Of course, Mr. Prime Minister, but it isn't my place to tell you what to say to the media. Perhaps you should confer with our MEDCON folks. . . . Media Control, yes. Excuse me, can I put you on hold? I have another call . . .

"Hello, Mr. President. How is the golf game? . . . Yes, it is quite an extraordinary development. . . . Well, that's very kind of you, Mr. President, but I don't think we need the U.S. military, not at this juncture. Would you excuse me for a moment? I have the British PM on hold . . . Thank you.

"Are you there, Mr. Prime Minister? . . . I would tell the media the current weather patterns are an aberration due to global warming and leave it at that. They adore global warming, you know. . . . What was that? . . . What's the size of basketballs? . . . Hail? Well, I would advise the public to stay indoors. Excuse me, can I put you on hold again?

"No, Mr. President, stealth bombers would be quite useless, I'm afraid. . . . Well, that depends on what you mean by the term 'contained.' SATCOM has them pegged in one location in the Himalayas. . . . Yes, of course we will keep you posted. . . . Thank you, Mr. President, I will . . . Yes, we do have a plan. . . . Would you excuse me for a moment?"

He stared at me through the entire conversation, tapping one foot impatiently as he talked, running a hand through his frizzy white hair. Maybe that's why it stood every which way.

"Mr. Prime Minister, are you there? I'm not going to argue with you. . . . Oh, indeed I think the public would accept the global warming cover, even if they are the size of Volkswagens—excuse me, did you say the size of *Volkswagens*? . . . Oh, dear. Well, it's rather like the Blitz, isn't it? Hello, hello? Damn, lost him. Mr. President, are you still . . . ?"

He shook his head in frustration, and the hair whipped about like a white tornado spinning around his head.

He ripped the headset off and shoved it toward Abigail Smith.

"Take this accursed thing, Smith. I'm sick to death of politicians!"

He stood over me, smiling down with teeth not nearly as bright nor as straight as Abigail Smith's.

"Alfred, this is Dr. François Merryweather," she said. "Director of OIPEP."

"I'm Alfred Kropp," I said.

"I know who you are. And I am more than relieved to know that *you* know who you are."

"That's about all I know," I said.

"Baby steps, Alfred! Baby steps! How do you eat an elephant? One bite at a time!"

"What's the matter with the weather?" I asked.

"They have drawn a shroud over the earth," Operative Nine said.

"Really, must you always be so lugubrious, Nine? Talk about drawing shrouds! My chest always hurts around you, the atmosphere is so thick with melancholy."

"I will strain to be jollier, Director."

"Jolliness cannot be strained at, Nine. Look at those abysmal circus clowns. So, Alfred, here you are, quite safe, though not quite sound. However, the doctor assured me we can expect a full recovery. If there is anything you need, anything at all, you must not hesitate to let us know. Is there anything you need right now?"

"Yes," I said. "My mom. I want my mom."

He looked at Abigail Smith, who shrugged.

"You said anything at all," I said.

"I'm afraid we're fresh out of mothers here. However, perhaps you might like something to eat? What is your favorite food? Pizza? Hamburger? Perhaps a taco? Or ice cream. What is your favorite flavor?"

"I don't want any of your freakin' ice cream! I want to go home!" I was starting to lose it again.

"Alfred," Dr. Smith said.

A loud buzzer interrupted her, followed by a man's voice from a speaker hidden somewhere in the room.

"Dr. Merryweather, I think you'd better get down here."

"Down where?" Merryweather asked.

"The morgue."

He exchanged a look with Abigail Smith and Op Nine.

"Can't it wait?" he asked.

"Uh, I don't think so. And I think you'd better bring Kropp."

"Bring Kropp?"

"Definitely bring Kropp."

"I'm not sure I'm ready for the morgue," I said.

"I'll meet you there," Merryweather snapped at us, and hurried from the room.

Operative Nine and Abigail Smith untied my arms and helped me to my feet. Pain shot up my leg and my knee buckled. Operative Nine caught me before I hit the floor.

"What's the matter with my leg?" I asked.

"You have been shot."

"Shot? What about my arm? What happened to it?"

"Shot."

"Two shots?"

He nodded. We were hustling down the corridor toward an elevator at the end of the hall. The walls were cinderblock, painted lime green, and the floor was gray. Abigail had one side of me and Operative Nine the other.

"What kind of guns do demons use?"

"You weren't shot by demons; you were shot by Bedouins."

Abigail punched the Down button.

"Bedouins! What do they have against me?"

"Nothing."

"So they shot me just for the heck of it?"

The elevator door slid open and they helped me inside. I leaned against the back wall, trying to catch my breath. Abigail pressed the button labeled "LL24" and we started to descend.

"They shot you because their master told them to," Op Nine said.

"Their master? A demon?"

"The Hyena."

"A hyena ordered some Bedouins to shoot me?"

"It is more complicated than that."

"How could it be more complicated than that?"

Abigail coughed.

The door slid open and we made an immediate right out of the elevator into a huge room with a metal floor and a bank of freezer-looking doors along the length of one wall.

Dr. Merryweather was there, and the same guy in the white coat who had examined me. He waved us into the room, a finger pressed against his lips. He then pointed that same finger at the bank of doors.

One of them was open and the shelf that had been slid out held a body bag. Half the bag lay on the shelf; the other half looked as if whoever was in that bag was sitting up.

"What is it?" Abigail whispered, clearly troubled by the sight of a dead body sitting up.

"Listen!" the doctor whispered back.

I couldn't hear anything at first, but after a second I did, a kind of hissing sound. After another second or two the sound took shape and I could make out a word.

That word was *"Kropp."*

"I come in to prep the body for autopsy and that's what I find." The doctor's voice was shaking.

Again, louder this time: *"Kropp!"*

"Open the bag," Op Nine said.

"You're kidding, right?" both the doctor and Merryweather said at the same time.

"Open the bag."

"Look," the doctor said. "I'm a civilian, a private contractor . . . I'm not a field operative. I've got a wife and family . . ."

"Open the bag."

"Do as he says," Dr. Merryweather said.

The doctor bit his lip, then walked over to the bag and slowly drew the zipper up and over the head inside. He stepped back quickly as the bag fell open, the material gathering around the body's waist.

The first thing I noticed was how ripped this guy was, a real Schwarzenegger type. The second thing was the gaping hole in the middle of his chest. And third, he had no eyes.

His lips barely moved, but the sound clearly came from his mouth, a hiss forming into the same word again.

"Kropp."

"Yes," Op Nine said loudly. "He is here. Kropp is here."

"Alfred Kropp," the dead man hissed. He had been a hairy guy, and the contrast between the pale, dead flesh and the coarse black hair was striking.

Op Nine gave me a little nudge and I blurted out, "Yes, I'm here."

"*We* know *thee*."

My knees started to give way, but not for the same reason they did back in my cozy, safe little room. I grabbed on to Op Nine's forearm and held tight.

"*As you now know* us."

I recognized its voice. I had heard it before, like a thousand years before, and it came back to me then: the little bedroom in Horace Tuttle's house, Mike dragging me through the broken window, Ashley rescuing me on the great white stallion, the *Pandora*, the race across the desert to find Mike before he could release the infernal hordes . . . everything, up to the moment when I looked into the demon's eyes—and that particular moment was a pit, a lightless hole with no bottom that I leaped across, bringing me here to this morgue deep in the bowels of OIPEP headquarters, where a demon spoke through a dead man's lips.

"What do you desire, O Great and Powerful King?" Op Nine asked.

The body's mouth moved, but no sound came out. Dr. Merryweather leaned over and whispered in my ear, "Perhaps you should ask him, Alfred."

"Me?"

He nodded to Op Nine, who repeated the question in my other ear.

My voice quivering, I asked, "What do you desire, O Great and Powerful King?"

"*The Seal.*"

Op Nine whispered, "But you have the Seal—do you not?"

"But don't you have the Seal?" I asked the dead guy.

"*The* Lesser *Seal, Alfred Kropp. The Vessel of our imprisonment. Bring it to us, last son of Lancelot.*"

"O Wise and Magnificent One," Op Nine whispered.

"O Wise and Magnificent One," I echoed.

"We do not possess the Holy Vessel."

"We don't?" I asked Op Nine. I was shocked. He jerked his head toward the body as if to say, *Don't talk to me; talk to the cadaver!*

I cleared my throat and said to the cadaver, "We, um, we don't have it."

There was a horrific screech like the sound of a car slamming on its brakes, the body on the slide-out tray jerked, and the head snapped forward, casting deep shadows over the empty eye sockets.

The head fell back, and the scream petered out into a soft hiss.

As I looked into those black holes, the blackness washed over me, and I went under, like a little kid in the surf. The blackness was as heavy as the weight of water all around me, and I could hear children crying, a million voices wailing in hunger and fear. I saw endless rows of bodies stacked like dried cornstalks in the autumn and a sky dark with roiling clouds. I saw the smoking ruins of cities and people scurrying everywhere, their clothes caked in ashes and dust, glass from broken windows crunching under their feet.

I saw the land stripped of green and all the other colors of life, pallid nameless things squirmed in the thick mud where the rivers used to run. And over all of it hung the sickly sweet stench of death.

From very far away I heard Op Nine's voice calling me. "Alfred! Alfred, what do you see?"

My mouth opened, but the only sound that came out was a wimpy echo of the hiss escaping Carl's blue lips.

"*Bring us the Seal, Alfred Kropp,*" the corpse hissed again, and then it toppled off the tray onto the floor, landing on its bare shoulder with a sickening smack, and lay still.

Op Nine strode over to the body and bent down, examining the face carefully. One of Carl's hands shot up and grabbed him around the throat. He tried to pull himself free, but the dead man's grip was too tight. Abby and the doctor rushed over and pried at the fingers until suddenly they relaxed.

Op Nine scooted back, clutching his throat and gasping for breath.

The doctor was staring at the body.

"Impossible!" he breathed.

"Oh, we're up to our hips in impossibilities," Merryweather said. He turned to me. "What did you see?"

I cleared my throat. It felt raw, as if I'd been screaming. "The end . . . the end of everything."

He turned toward Op Nine. "According to your briefing, Nine, the IAs had absconded with the Lesser Seal."

"That was the operating assumption," Op Nine answered.

"Clearly we must arrive at an alternative theory."

"The Hyena," Abby said suddenly. "He's taken it."

"Mike got away?" I asked.

"Both he and a sand-foil were missing after the battle," Op Nine said. "It is a reasonable assumption he did not perish after Paimon obtained the ring."

"Oh, another assumption!" Merryweather said crossly. "Your assumptions and a buck ninety will buy me a tall coffee of the day at Starbucks!"

Op Nine dropped his eyes and didn't say anything, though his lips tightened.

"So what do we do now?" I asked.

"Alfred," Merryweather said. "OIPEP is the only organization of its kind in the world, with practically unlimited resources and an intelligence network that spans every country on the planet. We shall do what any powerful, multinational bureaucracy would do in such a crisis: we shall hold a meeting!"

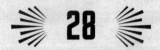

28

The meeting was held in a large conference room on lower level 49 of OIPEP headquarters. Lower level 49 looked just like lower level 24 with the windowless, institutional green walls and gray floor. A round wooden table dominated the room, surrounded by twelve soft leather chairs.

Me, Abby, Op Nine, and nine other Company personnel, five women and four men, sat around a few minutes waiting for Merryweather to come in. Like all OIPEP agents, they had names like Jake and Jessica, Wes and Kelly.

The men wore business suits with perfectly knotted neckties over starched white shirts. The women were in suits too, mostly navy blue, but a couple wore pinstripes, and all of them were blond like Abigail and Ashley, who wasn't there, and I wondered where she was, if she had been killed during the intrusion event. I remembered grabbing her beneath the tarp as the demons soared over us, the smell of her hair under my nose, and how the tears afterward seemed to make her blue eyes even brighter and more beautiful in a weird, sad way.

The door swung open and François Merryweather strode into the room, hair flying everywhere (if I were him, I'd cut it short or pull it back into a ponytail), carrying a stack of files under his right arm.

He slapped the files onto the glossy tabletop and said, "Well, folks, we've crossed the threshold, haven't we? Not since the signing of the Charter has there been an intrusion event of this magnitude, and so the day we have been waiting for, the day that demanded our existence in the first place, has finally arrived."

He stopped like he expected someone to say something, but nobody did.

"Whatever we decide today," he went on, "must be executed with the utmost haste—the United States has gone DEFCON-2, the European Union has activated its reserve, and I've just received a communiqué from our ops in China that half the Red Army has been mobilized to its border with Tibet. The world is itching to pull the trigger, which has the potential to be as catastrophic as the intrusion event itself."

He glanced at the ceiling and said, "Lights to half, please, and let's have SATCOM I-41."

The lighting dimmed and a three-dimensional image sprung up in the middle of the conference table. Dark clouds, their bellies full of flickering lightning, swirled over a mountain range, the jagged peaks snow covered and tinted red. The tallest peak was surrounded by a familiar orange glow flecked with bright white light.

"Everest, ladies and gentlemen," Dr. Merryweather said. "Unassailable by ground and nearly impregnable by air. Also,

I might add, for the literalists among you, the closest place to heaven on earth. Lights, please."

The image vanished and the light in the room went back to normal. I noticed my leather chair made that farting sound leather chairs make when you shift around in them. I glanced around to make sure nobody noticed and wondered why Alfred Kropp, the big trouble-making kid, was at this meeting cutting farts.

"Op Nine." The director nodded at him and Op Nine stood up.

"The wearer of the Great Seal commands seventy-two outcasts of varying ranks," Op Nine said. "Presidents, dukes, princes, counts, kings . . . but these are mortal designations, not their true titles, the hidden names spoken only once, and that by God. Each noble in his turn rules legions of lesser entities, some more, some less, according to his rank within the infernal hierarchy. For example, Paimon, the king to which the ring has fallen, commands two hundred legions."

"How many legions total?" the agent named Jake asked.

"Two thousand sixty-one."

Somebody whistled. Another asked, "And how many IAs per legion?"

"Six thousand."

Dead silence. Then Jake whispered, "Dear God, that's over fifteen million."

"Sixteen million, five hundred sixty-six thousand, to be precise," Op Nine said.

"That's twice the population of New York."

"Yes, yes," Dr. Merryweather snapped. "Or seventy-four percent of the total forces under arms in the world. Or sixteen times the size of the U.S. military. Or the entire population of

New Zealand, including women, children, and sheep. Continue, Nine." He was pacing around the room, rubbing his forehead. When he passed behind me, I could smell Cheetos. Cheetos have a very unique smell, so I was sure it was Cheetos. The crunchy kind.

"Each Fallen Lord has various powers or abilities at the disposal of the conjurer, some more . . . disturbing than others," Op Nine said. "Some have healing capabilities, some are builders—others are more destructive. There are givers of wisdom and slayers of reason. Those who control weather and those who are masters of the other earthly elements. Shape-changers, mind-readers, and mind-*benders*, all their myriad powers combine to serve the one who wears the Seal of Solomon."

"Now in the possession of this King Paimon," Merry-weather added. "Who is Paimon?"

"One of the Firstborn of Heaven," Op Nine answered. "Second only to Lucifer and the first to join the plot to overthrow heaven's throne. In the literature Paimon rides upon a dromedary, though there are other accounts that put it astride a great winged beast of monstrous appearance. Two lesser kings usually attend Paimon, Bebal and Abalam, with a host of other infernal beings, twenty-five legions or more, and Paimon commands two hundred legions.

"Paimon is a teacher, granting secret knowledge to the holder of the Seal, bestowing all the hidden arts and mysteries of heaven and earth. Paimon controls wind and water and can bind men's minds to the will of the conjurer. In short, of all the seventy-two lords, the Seal has fallen to perhaps the most powerful—and most terrible—of them all."

"In other words," the director said dryly, "the inmates have stolen the keys to the prison and for the first time since *before* Time, they answer to no one."

The whiff of Cheetos reminded me I couldn't remember the last time I'd had a meal. My stomach commenced to growling and continued to growl for the rest of the briefing. I also didn't know what time it was, what day it was, what month it was . . . although I was still pretty sure what year it was. What I needed, besides a meal, was something really ordinary, to remind me that I hadn't fallen down some gruesome rabbit hole where the mad tea party included sixteen million guests, all of whom could make you tear your own eyeballs from your head.

"Let's have SATCOM I-27S," Merryweather said toward the ceiling. The lights dimmed again and sitting in the middle of the table was the gigantic bowl of glass in the desert. This image was a still shot, and Merryweather directed a laser pointer at a tiny black dot at the edge of the shiny surface.

"This, we believe, is the Hyena, minutes after the Seal was lost. This"—and he moved the tiny red dot to another speck in the scene—"is the altar. Enhance to the third, please." The image grew, distorting slightly as it did, and now you could see the outline of the altar, though the edges were fuzzy. "The Vessel is gone. We *assumed*"—and here he cast a baleful eye in Op Nine's direction—"that the IAs had absconded with the Lesser Seal as well. Now it appears they did not. The key operational assumption we will make henceforth is that the Hyena took the Vessel in the confusion after the ring was lost."

"Why?" a lady agent named Sandy asked.

"Why what?"

"Why would Mike take the Vessel?"

"For protection, first," Op Nine said. "He has a bargaining chip, should they find him before we do. He may also approach us to broker a deal."

"I don't understand," Agent Jake said. "Why do they need the Vessel? We can't put them back in it without the ring."

"It is not a question of what they need," Op Nine said. "Without the Vessel, there will always be the risk, however small, that somehow they might be returned to it. Having the prison in their hands ensures their freedom from it."

"Their freedom to do *what*?" the agent named Greg asked.

"I don't know," Op Nine answered.

"Wait a minute, aren't you the demonologist here? If *you* don't know—"

"We do not need to know what they will do with their freedom," Abby interrupted. "All we need to know is what they will do if they do not obtain the Vessel."

She paused. Jake blew out his cheeks. Somebody coughed. Op Nine was staring at the tabletop. Finally, Sandy blurted out, "Okay, I'll bite. What will they do?"

Abby glanced over at me. So did Merryweather. I looked away. I didn't want to tell them what I saw in Carl's empty eye sockets. I didn't want to talk about it because I didn't want to think about it.

Op Nine spoke up. "Understand their hatred is beyond human comprehension. They abhor the Creator and so also the creation. Whatever brings joy, whatever brings peace, whatever redeems the dark deed or relieves the terrors of the night are their enemies. I do not know for certain what they intend to do, but I suspect it goes beyond our own pitiful comprehension of evil, our childlike notions of heaven's opposite. We must assume their goal has not changed since the beginning of time. What will they do? *They will consume us.*"

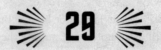

29

"I still don't get it," Jake said. "What's the point of pursuing the Hyena? Say we find him and get the Vessel—then what? We can't use it because we don't have the ring. We should be going after the ring, not the Vessel."

"Yes, well, we'll put you on that team," the director said. "You can lead the assault up Everest against the sixteen million fiends."

Jake ignored the sarcasm. "Maybe that's what we oughtta do. Take it to them!"

"We are still making modifications to the 3XD," Op Nine said. "As well as other applications for the active agent contained in the ammunition."

"I'm talking a small team, maybe two or three ops with a couple Sherpas. We draw this, what's-his-name, Paimon out and one shot to the hand does it."

Op Nine shook his head. "Perversely, the Hyena's instincts

to seize the Vessel were correct. Obtaining it strengthens our position. At the very least, our possessing it will give them pause."

"How so?"

"For the same reason they desire it. While it is outside their reach, they can never be assured of their freedom."

"Maybe not," Agent Jake shot back. "But they'll still be free and we'll still have no way of putting the genie back into the bottle. And you still haven't answered my question, so I'll ask it for, what, the third time . . . Let's assume we get the Vessel—then what?"

I guess nobody had an answer for that, because nobody said anything.

"Gee, this is terrific," Jake said quietly. "They better watch out, because we're gonna give 'em *pause*."

"Suggest an alternative," Op Nine said icily. He didn't like this Agent Jake, you could tell.

"Thought I already did."

"We pursue the Vessel because it is the only option open to us. Your suggestion is a futile gesture, doomed to failure, and we must not abandon the one thing that separates us from the Fallen."

"What's that?" Jake asked.

"Hope."

Dr. Merryweather clapped his hands suddenly and everybody gave a little jump. "So! We know where they are, we know what they want, and we know what they intend to do if they don't get it. The Hyena must be found and the Vessel secured, or we may expect all you-know-what to break loose. The question is . . . where is he?"

Nobody said anything. The director looked at Abby. She

stood up and Op Nine finally got to sit down. He didn't look good. He didn't look much better than Carl up in the morgue, and Carl was dead.

"All computer simulations return these ten locations as the most likely for target acquisition," she said crisply. "Based on prior associations, duration, and comfort level." She handed a stack of printouts to the person on her right, who took one and passed on the rest. The agent to my left took the last one, so I didn't get to see what was on the printout. "We'll dispatch teams of two to each location—"

"Why only two?" Jake asked.

"The smaller the team, the less likelihood of mission compromise."

"Also the less likelihood of finding the Hyena," Jake said. "I say we put as many boots on the ground as possible."

"Every signatory, with the exception of the Swiss, God bless 'em, has pledged full cooperation and logistical support," Dr. Merryweather said. "The locals will be available, if called upon."

"Again, Director," Op Nine said, studying the printout, "I would suggest sending a team to the Hyena's last known safe house."

I wasn't sure, but I guessed Op Nine was talking about the cabin in the mountains.

"Even Arnold isn't that foolish," Merryweather said. "Too obvious."

Op Nine started to say something, but decided against it.

Abby cleared her throat and said, "Make sure your people understand this mission is strictly voluntary. The First Protocol applies: no one with immediate family, mission objective deemed *Imperative*. The Holy Vessel of Solomon must be obtained. For this reason, the Hyena has been designated as a 'target' under the definition contained in Section 189.23 of the Charter."

"Good," Agent Jake said. "I hope my team finds him. I'm gonna take great pleasure putting a fat one right between that jerk's eyes."

30

The meeting broke up into little pockets of mini-meetings, with the director, Abby, and Op Nine huddled in one corner, whispering. All three would glance in my direction every few seconds, so I guessed they were trying to decide what to do with me now. I didn't figure they'd send me back to Knoxville: I knew too much and the encounter in the morgue with the devils' mouthpiece sort of indicated I was the only person the demons would talk to. I figured they would put me on ice here in OIPEP headquarters, where they could keep an eye on me and where I could do the least amount of damage.

Nobody had brought up that I was the reason we were having a meeting in the first place. I'd had the ring in my hands. All I had to do was get it to Op Nine. Instead I tried to play King of the Demons. Of course, it's hard to stay cool in the face of sixteen million spiteful spirits.

After a few minutes, Dr. Merryweather had to join a

conference call between the President of China and the Dalai Lama, so Op Nine and Abigail escorted me back to my room. My leg had gone stiff from sitting so long; I had to lean heavily against Op Nine on the way back. It took a lot out of me, and I sat gasping on the bed while Abby and Op Nine engaged in a whispering argument, probably a continuation of the one in the conference room.

"I'm hungry," I gasped. They kept arguing, so I said it louder: "I'm hungry!"

They stopped and stared at me for a second. Then Abby said, "What do you want?"

"Meat loaf, mashed potatoes, green beans, and some rolls." I was trying to think of comfort food, what normal people living normal lives eat. "And a slice of pizza."

"Pizza?"

"Pepperoni. Make that two slices. And some ice cream. Chocolate."

She was smiling now. "Anything else?"

"No. Yes. A peanut butter and jelly sandwich. With a pickle spear. Claussen."

"Claussen?"

"Or any crisp pickle, but Claussen's my favorite."

"Is that all?"

"Isn't it enough?"

She started out of the room. "Oh, and a bag of Cheetos," I called after her. "The crunchy kind."

She left. Op Nine studied me with his dark eyes. He wasn't smiling.

"What?" I asked. "Cheetos over the top?"

"Your appetite has returned. A good sign, Alfred."

"Not too many of those lately—good signs, I mean. What

happened in the battle, Op Nine, after I . . . ?" I couldn't finish. He didn't seem to mind.

"Once Paimon obtained the ring, it gathered the legions together and the battle was abandoned. They fled as fast as thought, Alfred."

"Mike too."

"Unfortunately, yes."

"How do we know he has the Vessel?"

"The area was searched thoroughly after the encounter. The Lesser Seal is gone, Mike has vanished, and Paimon now demands its return. I do not doubt Mike has the Vessel."

He took a deep breath and pressed his fingertips hard into the corners of his eyes.

"We lost forty-three of our helicopters and all but four of the insertion team."

"Ashley?" I asked.

"Fortunately, she survived with only minor injuries."

Hearing that made me feel better, but then worse for feeling better about her being alive when practically everybody else was dead.

"It's my fault," I said. "Once I got the ring from Mike I should have brought it to you. You would've known how to use it."

"Yes," he said. I didn't know if the *yes* was to it being my fault the demons had the Seal or to him knowing how to use it. Maybe both.

"So I blew it—again. And now the demons are free with no way to control them."

"No way that we can discern—yet. I have no doubt we shall find the way through our difficulties, Alfred."

"How come?"

"Because, as I said a few moments ago, the alternative is despair."

He excused himself after that, and I waited for my food. I was still waiting when Ashley stepped into the room. I sat up a little and ran a hand through my hair. I needed a haircut.

"Hi," I said.

"Hi." She was dressed in a pale pink cashmere sweater with a soft, high collar, jeans, and these pink suede boots with fuzzy fold-over tops. She looked like she was on her way to the ski lift.

"Well," I said. "I guess we made it."

She nodded. "I guess so."

She avoided making eye contact with me. Maybe she didn't want to look into the eyes that had looked into the eyes of a demon.

"Why are you out of uniform?" I asked.

"I'm leaving."

"To hunt for Mike?"

She shook her head. "No, I'm leaving the Company. I've turned in my resignation, Alfred."

"Really?" I was shocked. "Can you do that? Just quit like that?"

"There's no rule against it. But it's frowned upon."

"How do they keep you spilling all their secrets?"

"They know where I live."

"You're kidding."

"And where my family lives."

"You're giving me the creeps, Ashley. For months I've been trying to convince myself that OIPEP is one of the good guys, then you tell me something like this."

She shrugged. Most people don't look good when they

shrug. Shrugging makes their necks disappear, and nobody looks good without a neck—look at pro football players. But Ashley looked terrific when she shrugged. The blond hair bounced, one side of her mouth turned down, and a cute little line developed between her eyebrows.

"Sometimes good people have to do bad things," she said.

"But isn't that how you separate bad people from good? Bad people do bad things, good people do good things?"

"It's probably a little more complicated than that."

"Most things are. I can't figure out if I just want things to be more simple or things seem more simple to me because I am."

"Because you're what?"

"Simple."

She smiled. "You're anything but simple, Alfred."

I took that as a compliment, which I'm more likely to do when talking to a pretty girl.

"Why did you quit?"

She looked away. I said, "You quit because of what happened out there with the demons."

She didn't give a direct answer. She said, "I just . . . Sometimes you . . . sometimes things happen and you realize you've got your priorities all screwed up. I haven't seen my family in over two years, not since the Company recruited me out of college. I miss them. I miss my old life. I don't know if I can just pick it up after . . . after all that's happened, but I'm going to try. That's what they demand from you, Alfred: your life. And I'm not sure I can give it to them."

"The First Protocol," I said. She gave me a funny look. "That's the First Protocol, isn't it? Pledging to sacrifice your life for the greater good or something like that?"

She nodded. "Something like that, yes."

"Well, all I can say is I thought you did a great job out there, Ashley. Really. And, you know, I'm sorry about what happened under the tarp . . ."

"The tarp?"

"You know, grabbing you and everything."

She smiled and I could see the bright pink tip of her tongue.

"I was glad you did."

She said she hadn't seen her family in two years and the Company had recruited her right out of college. That would make her about twenty-four or twenty-five. Ten years wouldn't matter so much ten years from now, when she was thirty-five and I was twenty-five—those kinds of things happen all the time, especially among Hollywood couples, but right now it mattered a lot.

My timing always sucked. I wondered if I was attracted to her for the very reason that she was too old for me and that she was leaving.

"Anyway," she said. "I wanted to see you before I left."

"How come?"

"To see how you were. And to say good-bye."

She stared at me for a long moment, a moment so long, I began to feel uncomfortable—more uncomfortable than usual—and then she leaned over quickly and kissed me on the cheek. I smelled lilacs.

She whispered in my ear, "Be careful, Alfred. They lied to you and they'll lie again if they need to. They're using you."

The door sprang open at that moment and two guys rolled in a couple of carts with my comfort-food feast. Ashley pulled away quickly and she wiped away a tear.

"Good-bye, Alfred," she said, and then walked out the door. That's the last I saw of Ashley for a long time.

31

I wasn't feeling so good after my meal—go figure—and, as if on cue, the door opened and the doctor came in, the same doctor from the morgue. I never got his name, so in my head I called him Dr. Watson, after Sherlock Holmes's sidekick. I don't know why I chose Dr. Watson, except it was the first name that popped into my head after the word "doctor." I always thought those were two different kinds of doctors, those who worked on the living and those who worked on the dead. Maybe this doctor was both kinds, but still it made me feel a little creepy being examined by him.

He told me both bullets had been removed and he expected a full recovery. I told him, "Until the next time." Disaster had a way of following me around, like a faithful dog. You could forgive somebody maybe once for putting the world in imminent peril. Twice was really pushing it.

"You know what a dufus is?" I asked him.

"I know what a duffer is," he said.

"What's a duffer?" I asked. "Isn't that something you put on your bed?" I was getting sidetracked.

"It's a golfing term."

"Oh, sure. You're a doctor. Well, a dufus is somebody who can never get anything right."

"Very close to a duffer."

"Maybe dufus came from duffer."

"Oddly enough, the root word, 'duff,' is slang for the buttocks," said Dr. Watson.

"That is odd," I said. "Because an ass really doesn't have that hard of a job. Just sitting and—you know. There's one thing I've always wondered and maybe you could answer this, being a doctor. Why do we have a crack? I mean, what's the necessity of the dual cheeks?"

He thought about it for a minute.

"Basically, we need them for balance."

"Football players use them to express team spirit. I wasn't what you could call a star athlete, but when I was playing, I got my fair share of swats back there."

"I'm not sure I understand why we're having a discussion about buttocks."

"Well," I said. "That isn't *my* fault. But sometimes it's better to talk about things that are not what you don't want to talk about."

He stared at me. I asked, "Where are we, exactly?"

"OIPEP headquarters."

"I know that. I meant where is OIPEP headquarters?"

"I don't think I can tell you that."

"How come?"

"Because I can't tell anybody that."

He left the room and after a few minutes Op Nine came in, wearing a fur-lined parka over a tailored suit and a pair of snow boots. Ashley had been dressed for cold weather too, and I wondered if OIPEP headquarters might be at one of the poles.

"Well, Alfred, you've been given a clean bill of health. Or nearly clean," he said.

"That's like being nearly sane. Are you leaving too?"

" 'Too'?"

"Ashley came to see me."

"Ah. Yes, I am leaving."

"What about me?"

"That's the reason I've come. You have a choice, Alfred. You may stay here at headquarters or you may accompany me on the hunt for the Hyena."

"I don't like those choices. How about I just go home to Knoxville?"

"I'm afraid that isn't possible. It would not be safe."

"I figured that was the reason. They know I'm from Knoxville, don't they?"

"They know a great many things."

"How many?"

He sat beside me and put one of his huge hands on my knee. "There is nothing of you that is hidden from them, Alfred. Nothing. They know you better than anyone will ever know you. They have seen your secret face, the face you hide from everyone, even from yourself. All that you know, all that you remember—even those things you cannot remember—all that you desire, even those desires you hide from yourself, has been laid bare to their eyes."

"That doesn't sound good."

"Of course, there is no safer place on earth than here at headquarters. We can protect you here. I cannot guarantee any protection should you decide to come with me."

"So why would I decide that?"

He studied me for a long time, looking right into my eyes, but I didn't look away. I had looked into worse eyes than his.

"Can they see my future too?"

He shook his head. "No one knows the future, Alfred, save one, and that secret is safe with him."

"You know what I'm going to say, don't you? You already know what my choice is going to be."

I pushed myself off the bed, wincing as my right foot hit the floor and the pain shot all the way up my leg.

"Okay," I said. "Where's my parka?"

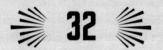

32

I followed Op Nine through a maze of corridors, into two separate elevators, past unlabeled doors with security keypads, some with armed guards stationed next to them, struggling to keep up with my bum leg as he strode down the lime green hallways, silent for most of the way, but sometimes, like in one of the elevators, he would turn to me and say something.

"Do you know you are the first civilian to set foot inside headquarters since its founding? Few know of its existence and none know its location, but these are extraordinary times, Alfred Kropp."

And, while we marched down yet another corridor, he said, "You are in an underground city roughly the size of London. And, like a city, there are shops and restaurants, a postal center, movie theaters, places of worship for all the major religions. Lecture halls, research facilities and a library that would be the envy of the world—if the world knew of it."

"Sort of like OIPEP University," I said.

He frowned. "There is no university here."

"I was making a joke."

"I see."

"You know, only about two percent of the human population lacks a sense of humor, Op Nine."

"Indeed. Then I am in a select group, yes?"

My stomach was bothering me before my feast because it was empty; now it bothered me because it was full. Next time, I promised myself, I wasn't mixing pepperoni pizza, Cheetos, and a pint of double-chocolate-fudge ice cream.

We finally stopped at an unmarked door. Op Nine swiped the pad of his thumb over a sensor and the door swung open. We stepped inside a room that looked like a dry cleaners, with clothes hanging on poles that ran the entire length of the room. A round little man wearing a tweed vest appeared.

"Yes? What do you want?"

"Something appropriate for him," Op Nine said, nodding at me.

The little guy stared at me.

"Hi," I said. "I'm Alfred Kropp."

"I know who you are," he said. He looked at Op Nine. "Define 'appropriate.'"

"Private school, weekends in the Hamptons, old money," Op Nine said.

The little guy looked at me, pursed his fat lips, and said, "If you say so, but it's gonna be a stretch. Nationality?"

"American."

He disappeared into the couture forest.

"We're going undercover?" I asked.

"We've ruled out running ads and printing flyers," Op Nine said. His eyes sparkled. "No humor."

The little vest-wearing man came back with a stack of clothes—sweaters, shirts, pants, mostly khakis. For the next twenty minutes I tried on different combinations. Op Nine finally settled on a blue pullover sweater with khakis and brown loafers.

"It would work except for the hair," vest-man said. "The hair's all wrong, and the face."

"What's the matter with my face?" I asked.

"Pores too big. You're supposed to be rich. Rich kids get dermabrasion and those zit pills."

"We'll risk it," Op Nine said.

"Teeth are nice, though."

"Yeah," I said. "But you should see my toenails."

"I don't want to see your toenails."

I also got a fur-lined parka identical to Op Nine's and big snow boots that fit over my loafers.

Vest-man called after us as we were going out the door. "I'd take him over to Cosmetics if I were you. Get something for those pores!"

On the way to the elevator, I said, "You know, I never would have guessed headquarters looked like this."

"Like what?"

"Like a very old high school or hospital ward. I thought it would be all glass and shiny metal and people-movers like at airports and digitalized—you know, monitors and gadgets all over the place."

"There is all of that," Op Nine said. "We just have cleverly disguised it all to look like an old high school or hospital ward."

"This is about the humor remark, isn't it? You're trying to prove you have some."

We stepped into the elevator. We were on LL56. He pressed the button labeled "S" and the elevator started up. I had the sensation of great speed as we rocketed upward, I assumed, fifty-six stories.

"And a logo," I said.

"Logo?"

"Sure. The OIPEP logo. Every big spy outfit—well, every spy outfit period, even the small ones—has a logo. Where's your logo? I didn't see one in the conference room or anywhere else."

"We have no logo."

"How come?"

"Why would we need one?"

"Well, logos aren't something you absolutely need, I guess. They're just something you have."

"Like a name," he said.

The doors opened into a tiny space about the size of a hall closet. Stepping out, I realized it *was* a hall closet. The elevator doors opened just behind a row of winter coats. Op Nine parted them, opened the closet door, and we came into a small, sparsely furnished living room.

An old couple was sitting on the ratty sofa watching a television with a screen about the size of a postage stamp. They didn't look up or move when we stepped out of their closet. It was like we weren't there. It was cold in that little living room and I thought what a lousy job that would be for a super-spy, bundled up in old clothes watching television, providing cover for agents coming and going on exciting missions. Maybe they took turns taking the old-couple-just-watching-TV duty.

We stepped outside into a world of gray sky and white earth. The clouds hung low over a landscape of clapboard houses hunkered in four-foot-deep snowdrifts. Past the cluster of houses, the land was flat, featureless, a desert of ice for as far as the eye could see.

"Where are we?" I asked, pulling the hood of my parka over my head with its too-shaggy-to-be-rich haircut. There was nothing substantial in this winter wasteland to block the wind blowing directly into my face, so cold, it made my snot freeze.

"The entrance to headquarters," he answered, which was no answer at all, of course, but what did I expect by this point? A black Land Rover idled at the end of the frozen walkway. A big man in a gray overcoat opened the back door for us and I slid in first.

We drove for about thirty minutes, first down the narrow streets that wound between the little houses, then onto a larger road, where we picked up speed, but too much speed, in my opinion, for the conditions. I looked up at the clouds and saw lightning flickering deep within their dark bellies.

At the edge of town I saw a group of kids playing soccer on a solid sheet of ice, which must make for some interesting bounces and slide tackles. I would remember them when I came to that place my father had written about, the spot between desperation and despair.

I turned to Op Nine and said, "I've been working on a theory that this whole thing with the Seals and the demons and OIPEP and all that is just a dream. You see it in movies and books all the time. You know, where the main character has all these awful things happen to him and then he wakes up and realizes none of it was real."

He stared at me and didn't say anything.

"It's just a theory," I said.

The kids and the soccer field without the boundary lines, which kind of made the whole world their field, were far behind us by this point. There was just gray sky, white earth, and the black ribbon of the road between the two.

"If you're Operative Nine, what happened to the first eight operatives?" I asked.

"The 'Nine' doesn't refer to a sequential number."

"I'm no math whiz, but I thought nine *was* a sequential number."

"It refers to a section of the OIPEP Charter."

"Lemme guess. Section Nine."

He nodded. I asked, "So what is Section Nine?"

"I can't tell you that."

"And if you did . . ."

"I would have to kill you."

"I think we're really bonding here. Establishing a rapport. Have you ever had to? Kill somebody, I mean."

"Only once. In Abkhazia."

"Abkhazia. Ashley mentioned you were in Abkhazia. What happened in Abkhazia—or can't you tell me that either?"

"I shouldn't tell you."

"It's classified?"

"It's painful."

"Well, maybe you should tell me to get it off your chest. You know, to help with the bonding, since we're partners now and everything."

"I do not need it off my chest."

" 'And we're not partners.' You were about to say that."

"I was about to say Abkhazia is something you may want to hear now but would regret hearing afterward."

"I can take it," I said. "I'm tougher than I look."

"Oh, you are many more things than how you appear, Alfred Kropp."

"You're talking about the whole Lancelot thing, I guess, and the fact that Bernard Samson is my dad. But the thing with that is it's not anything I did. I mean, it didn't require anything special on my part."

He leaned his head back and closed his eyes. His eyelids were the color of charcoal. He must have been one of the homeliest people I had ever seen, with those long flappy earlobes, the droopy cheeks, and raccoon eyes that reminded me so much of a hound dog. But you shouldn't judge people by appearances—the credo I lived by.

"Padre," I said softly. Then louder: "Back in the desert, you blessed us with holy water and later on Mike called you 'Padre' . . ."

His eyes stayed closed. "I was a priest—once."

"What happened?"

"My particular theological views made the church uncomfortable."

"I guess they would," I said. "I mean, not even the church buys into demons these days, does it?"

He didn't answer. So I went on. "So that's the deal with the holy water and all the Latin and praying. I haven't been to church since my mom died. You think that's part of it, Op Nine . . . um, Father?"

"Do not call me that, Kropp."

"Well, what do I call you then?"

"Operative Nine."

"No. What's your real name?"

"Whatever it needs to be."

"If I guessed your real name, would you tell me?"

"No."

"Adam."

"You are wasting your time."

"Arnold."

"Enough, Kropp."

"Alexander. Axelrod. Benjamin. Brad. Bruce. What about the first letter—can you give me that?"

He didn't say anything. I didn't see what the big deal was about his name. Maybe he was somebody infamous or wanted for some terrible crime, like maybe what happened in Abkhazia had something to do with it, but OIPEP protected him.

"Okay, forget it. I was going to ask if you thought everything that's happened has something to do with me not going to church since my mom died."

He opened just his left eye and looked at me with it.

"You know, these world-threatening disasters I keep causing. You think maybe God's mad at me?"

His left eye slowly closed. He said, "Isn't it odd, Alfred, how often we attribute the terrible things that happen to us to God, and the wonderful things to our own efforts?"

I thought about it. I wasn't sure, but I think he was accusing me of being egotistical. Me!

"Do you think I'm a bad person, Op Nine?" I asked.

"I think you are a fifteen-year-old person."

"What's that mean?"

"The angels were fully formed in an instant. We human beings take a bit longer."

"That's good. And bad too, I guess, from my point of

view. One thing is for sure. This whole intrusion event is going to make believers out of a lot of people. I know your plate is kinda full right now, but maybe if you have a couple extra minutes you could say a prayer for my mom?"

"I am not a priest anymore, Kropp."

"I know, but it couldn't hurt."

He didn't say anything. His eyes were closed, so he might have been saying one or he might have just fallen asleep.

33

Soon I could see an airstrip, the runway a thick black scar in the pristine snow. We stopped at the edge of the tarmac and I hopped out without waiting for our silent driver to open my door. The force of the wind nearly knocked me over, and I wondered how we were going to take off.

Op Nine joined me and I pointed at our ride sitting at the end of the airstrip.

"What the heck is that?"

It didn't resemble any plane I had ever seen. It looked kind of like a paper airplane, with sleek wings that started near the front and gradually widened as they went back toward the tail fin, which seemed small for a plane about the size of a 747. The fuselage came to a sharp point at the cockpit, as if a giant had taken a normal plane and stretched it, creating an elongated teardrop shape. It looked like a gardening trowel with wings.

"That is a specially modified version of the U.S. Air Force's X-30 aircraft, the fastest plane on earth," Op Nine said. "It skims along the very edge of the atmosphere at four thousand miles per hour."

"Wow," I said. "I've always wanted to do that."

"Which means we should reach our insertion point in under an hour."

"Terrific. What's our insertion point?"

I expected him to name some exotic locale, a place Mike Arnold visited on one of his missions for the Company, like Istanbul or Sri Lanka.

Instead, Op Nine said, "Chicago."

I didn't see a pilot or any crew onboard the X-30. We stepped into the main cabin, Op Nine closed and locked the door, and we took our seats. Everything looked brand-new, down to the plush carpeting and the first-class-sized leather seats. We buckled up and Op Nine pressed a button on his armrest. The plane immediately began to accelerate, and I felt my big body being flattened against the backrest. Then I found myself lying at a forty-five-degree angle as we roared upward, bouncing some when we hit the low clouds, but only for a second or two, and then the sun burst through the window beside Op Nine as we lifted over the clouds and kept climbing.

I turned my head slightly to get a better look, but the turning took a long time, because we must have been going close to Mach 2 and that makes turning your head a matter of willpower as much as strength.

The scene outside was breathtaking: the sun above the rim of the horizon, illuminating the solid cloud cover beneath it, painting the ridges gold, the bright unmarred blue of the sky. I thought of those kids playing soccer on that barren snowfield.

Don't forget, Kropp, I told myself. *It's beautiful. Don't ever forget that.*

The plane climbed until I could see the horizon begin to curve away from us, until I could see the actual curvature of the earth, and the sky darkened from bright blue to smoky violet to glimmering black.

Op Nine leaned over and raised his voice to be heard over the roar of the engines. "We have reached the edge of the atmosphere, Kropp! Approaching Mach 6!"

Normally, Op Nine was about as joyful as an undertaker, but now he was grinning like a kid on a theme park ride. We leveled off and the noise settled some, which is more than I could say for my stomach.

"What is it, Kropp?" Op Nine asked. Maybe he noticed that my face was the color of the snow about a mile below us.

"I'm not sure this was such a great idea," I said. "The last time I got on a plane I deboarded the hard way."

He reached under his seat and pulled out that same oversized leather-bound book I saw on the flight into the Sahara.

"What is that, anyway?" I asked.

"*The Ars Goetia . . . The Howling Art.*"

"What kind of art howls?"

"The title refers to the method with which the conjurer controls the Fallen. Said to be written by King Solomon himself, *The Ars Goetia* contains descriptions of the seventy-two lords, their symbols and powers, and the incantations to bring them forth from the Holy Vessel and control them. The conjurer is instructed to 'howl' the incantations, hence the name."

"So it's kind of a manual for fighting demons?"

He winced. "No, it is a guide for using them to the master's purpose. The Great Seal is useless unless the wearer speaks the incantations as written by Solomon, word for word, with no variation."

"I get it. That's why the demons ignored me even though I was wearing the ring. I didn't know the spells."

He grimaced again. "I prefer not to call them demons. It demeans their nature."

"But isn't that what they are?"

"We should pity more than fear them, Alfred. They were angels once."

"Yeah, but didn't you say they rebelled against God? They got what they deserved."

"Perhaps." He sighed. "Yet do we not all hope and pray that we ourselves escape what we truly deserve? None have fallen as far or as irrevocably as the outcasts of heaven. Did you not find them beautiful?"

"Well, yes and no. They sure didn't look like I thought demons or, um, outcasts, would look. But they were . . . it was . . ." I searched for the right words. "Almost like looking too long at the sun." But that really didn't come close to describing them. They *were* beautiful, but their beauty was wrapped in terror and despair, kind of like that sick feeling in your gut when the prettiest girl in school finally notices you . . . but that really didn't describe it either. A pretty girl doesn't push you to the point of tearing your own eyes out.

"Their essence—the truth of what they are—has not changed since their creation, Alfred. How could it? No matter how far they have fallen, they are the first fruits of the divine imagination. They have gazed upon the very face of God, the face they will see no more for all eternity—and so I pity them." Tears welled in his eyes. "Even as I envy them for having seen it."

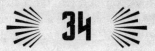

34

We landed in Chicago at what looked like an old military base. The flight had lasted about fifty minutes, so I figured at four thousand miles per hour we had traveled maybe three thousand miles. That meant OIPEP headquarters probably wasn't in North America. Antarctica seemed too far away, so maybe it was somewhere in the Arctic Circle, though I didn't see any polar bears or walrus or Eskimos, which I figured were plentiful in the Arctic.

A sheet of gray clouds hung low over us, moving rapidly as if a giant unseen hand was pulling it westward. The absence of the sun seemed to bleed all the color from the world; the grass was the same dull gray color as the hangars. I heard thunder rolling deep in the cloud cover.

"The whole world is covered?" I asked Op Nine as we walked toward a blue Ford Taurus parked by one of the hangars.

"Yes."

He popped the trunk and unzipped a large canvas bag that sat inside. Op Nine took a quick inventory as I looked over his shoulder. The bag contained maps, a couple of wallets, two semiautomatic handguns, socks, underwear, some shirts and pants, a laptop computer, two other pistols that looked like flare guns, the *Ars Goetia*, and a roll of toilet paper.

"Toilet paper?" I asked.

"One never knows."

He stuck one of the semiautomatics behind his back. Then he took the flare gun and ejected the clip from the handle to check the bullets. The bullets had a slightly flared head; they looked like a miniature version of the bullets for the 3XDs.

"What is that?" I asked.

"My life's work."

He stuck this pistol into some hidden pocket in the lining of his parka, and then turned to me, holding one of each type of gun in either hand.

I would have preferred my sword, the blade of the Last Knight Bennacio, but that was back in Knoxville and I didn't figure we had the time to get it, although the X-30 could probably get us there in about ten minutes.

He tossed the weapons back into the bag, slammed the trunk closed, and we climbed into the Taurus. He pulled down the visor and the keys fell into his lap.

"Not exactly James Bond," I said, looking around the ratty interior. The seats were stained, the floorboards crusted with mud, the lining on the roof coming off in one spot and hanging down.

"This is a covert operation," he reminded me.

"Where's the button to convert it into a submarine?"

"You've seen too many movies, Alfred."

"You're right. I'll try to stay grounded in the real world of demons zipping around Mount Everest plotting the end of human existence."

He turned off the access road onto a two-lane highway, then jumped on the interstate. Directly ahead I could see the Chicago skyline on the shores of Lake Michigan.

"So why do we think Mike might be in Chicago?" I asked. "I mean, I figured he was from here; he always wears that Cubs cap and he mentioned the Natural History Museum, but if I was going to hide somewhere, I wouldn't go to the most obvious place people would look."

"He may not be here, but he may have come seeking his comfort zone, the place with which he is most familiar—and his pursuers not."

I watched as the speedometer leaped to 110.

"Aren't you afraid we'll be pulled over?"

"We won't be."

Ten minutes later we were downtown, parked in front of the Drake Hotel. The wind was ferocious, howling like something alive as it roared between the skyscrapers—a beast—not just a beast, though, but a beast that hated you. I pulled the hood of my parka over my head as Op Nine got the bag from the trunk.

At the check-in desk Op Nine went British.

"Good afternoon!" he said in a perfect accent. "Lord Polmeroy and nephew to check in, please."

I looked over at him, startled. Not only had his accent changed, but everything about his voice: the pitch higher, the modulation a little quiverier. Even his face looked different somehow, as if he had the ability to control his facial muscles to achieve different looks.

We took the elevator to our room on the sixteenth floor.

"Nephew?" I asked.

"Preferable to son. Not enough of a resemblance."

"Thank God."

In the suite, he took out the laptop and booted it up on the kitchenette table. I opened the refrigerator, half hoping it would be fully stocked, but it wasn't. I pulled back the curtains and looked out at Lake Michigan, as gray and drab as the low-hanging sky.

Op Nine was typing something. Maybe an e-mail to head-quarters: *Arrived at insertion point. Proceeding to acquire target. Kropp still mildly annoying.*

I let the drapes fall—the view was too depressing—and turned on the TV. CNN was running a special report called *Crisis in the Sky,* and two talking heads occupied a split screen, a meteorologist and some guy from the government, arguing whether global warming was responsible for the fact that clouds now covered ninety-eight percent of the planet. That was more depressing than the view, so I flipped to the next channel. Its special was called *Recent Storm Terror— The Al-Qaeda Connection.* It looked like OIPEP's MEDCON was executing OP-FOOL'EM. I turned off the TV.

Op Nine was still typing away.

"I feel weird," I said.

"Hmmm." Some kind of satellite image occupied the top half of his screen; the bottom half contained the text of what-ever he was typing.

"Maybe I've got jet lag. You know, flying all the way from the North Pole in an hour . . . that'll kill you."

"Hmmm-mmm."

I was fishing with that North Pole remark, but he didn't bite. I yawned. Some hunt this was turning out to be.

"Maybe I'll take a nap."

He didn't say anything. I went into the bedroom, kicked off my snow boots, and threw the parka onto the chair beside the bed. The room was stuffy. A radiator hissed under the window. The *click-click-click* of his typing continued. I closed my eyes.

When I opened them again the radiator was still hissing, but the *click-clicks* had stopped. I sat up and looked at the clock. It was a little after three in the afternoon when I lay down; now it was a quarter past six.

I got up and went into the other room. Op Nine reclined on the sofa, long legs stretched out, one arm thrown over his eyes, breathing deeply.

He had left his computer on.

I stared at the dancing Microsoft flag for a few seconds, chewing on my bottom lip. What was the protocol if I got caught? Would Op Nine be compelled to shoot me? I couldn't picture Op Nine shooting me, but that may have been just a failure of my own imagination.

I could always say the thing was making a funny noise and I was just checking it out, making sure it was okay. Ashley told me they had lied to me and maybe this computer held the evidence to that.

I touched the touchpad and the desktop screen lit up. There were only three folders besides the recycle bin: one labeled "SATCOM Hookup," another called "Dossiers," and the bottom one, "Chart."

I dragged the pointer to the one labeled "Dossiers." I'd

seen enough spy movies to know what a dossier was, and I wanted to see if he had one labeled "Kropp, Alfred." But after I double-clicked on the folder, a message popped up asking for a password. I closed the box.

Same thing with the SATCOM folder, the one I figured he was working on when I went to bed, since I saw the satellite image on the screen. I closed the password box, and almost didn't click on the third icon, figuring it would demand a password too.

But I did click on it, and up popped a Word document with this title page:

OFFICIAL CHARTER

OFFICE OF INTERDIMENSIONAL PARADOXES
AND
EXTRAORDINARY PHENOMENON

Copenhagen
19.11.32
[As Amended 05.10.78 & 04.05.01]

I glanced over my shoulder at Op Nine, who hadn't moved a muscle. I started to scroll through the big blocks of text, single spaced, with all sorts of acronyms and code language so it read like those tiny disclaimers they flash on the screen during car commercials. I looked at the bottom of the screen. The OIPEP Charter ran over two thousand pages.

I wasn't going to find any lies in this file or, if I did, I wouldn't be able to tell they were lies. There was one thing I was curious about, though, so using the edit function I searched for these words: "Section Nine."

And this is what I got:

SECTION NINE

9.1 At the director's discretion, one or more Company personnel may be designated as "Superseding Protocol Agent(s)" (SPA(s)). All Protocols relevant to protection of third parties, signatories, noncombatants, or informants as defined under Section 36.718 of this Charter *do not apply* to SPA(s).

9.2 SPA(s) are authorized under this Section to take any means necessary for mission success. For purposes of this Section, "any means necessary" is defined as not only the superseding of Company Protocols, but *all* law, international as well as the laws of the signatory and nonsignatory nations, including those relating to homicide and other serious offenses as defined in Section 2.34 of this Charter (e.g., theft, willful destruction of property, torture, etc.)

9.3 The Company and signatories to this Charter agree to hold harmless SPA(s) who commit acts that, in any other circumstances, might warrant the ultimate penalty, as long as those acts were performed with due diligence and in the SPA(s)' official capacity as Company operatives. No SPA(s) will be prosecuted for any act committed under the auspices of this Section and all signatories agree to harbor and protect any operative acting under this Section from hostile parties or nonsignatories who seek retribution, whether legally or illegally . . .

There was more; Section Nine ran on for twelve more pages, but I had seen enough. I closed the file, turned around, and saw Operative Nine sitting up on the sofa, watching me.

35

I broke the awkward silence first.

"You're a SPA."

"And what does that mean?" he asked quietly. He didn't sound sarcastic.

"It means OIPEP's rules don't apply to you. *Nobody's* rules apply to you."

"You're forgetting the natural ones."

"Natural ones?"

"Gravity, for example. Gravity applies to me."

"I'm not trying to be funny here, Op Nine."

"Neither am I."

"Is that why nobody can know your name? So when you're done murdering, raping, and pillaging, there's nothing to hang on you because you don't officially, like, exist or something?"

"That much is true: I do not officially exist. There is no birth certificate, no hospital record, no valid driver's license, no passport, no Social Security card, no fingerprint record, no document—or witness, for that matter—of any kind anywhere that establishes or confirms my existence. Whole weeks pass, months even, when I forget what my name used to be, when I forget I even *had* a name. I am no one, Alfred, and my name is whatever it needs to be."

I backed up as he spoke, right into the door leading to the hallway—and freedom.

He stood up. "Alfred, listen to me. There is a very old saying: 'If it is necessary, it is possible.' Our organization is tasked with an extremely delicate and dangerous mission, making many distasteful things necessary, and I am the designated agent of necessity. I am the one who does that which *must* be done. That is all Section Nine means. I am the sole operative in the Company fully authorized to do what must be done, even if what must be done falls outside the normal boundaries of acceptable behavior."

"Oh, well, that's a nice way to put it!"

"It is the best way. The Operative Nine cannot hesitate to do what must be done to achieve the objective."

"It's a rotten job, but somebody's gotta do it?"

"Something like that."

"That's a phrase that applies to garbagemen, Op Nine! Garbagemen don't murder people!"

"Neither do I."

"That's not what you told me. You told me you murdered somebody in Abkhazia."

"I never said I murdered them."

"You said you killed them."

"So I did."

"So you said it or so you killed them?"

"Both."

"Since when is killing somebody not murder? What if I get in the way of the mission . . . you'd kill me too, wouldn't you? Is that what they did in Abkhazia? Got in your way?"

"I'm not going to talk about Abkhazia."

"Why not? You said it wasn't classified."

"You asked if it was classified and I answered that it was painful. That is not the same as saying it wasn't classified."

"So it *is* classified? Why do you talk in circles like that? Look, I'm going to be honest with you, Op Nine. I'm a little freaked out right now. I've been lied to . . . ."

"By whom? Who has lied to you?"

"I—I'm not sure, but somebody has."

"I don't know what you're talking about, Alfred."

"Well, of course you're going to say you don't know what I'm talking about! Even if you did know what I'm talking about, you're authorized to say you don't, and you probably would even if you weren't."

"Alfred, I think you still may be suffering from some lingering effects of the—"

"Oh, you bet. I've got lingering effects out the yin-yang! Kidnapped, nearly drowned, thrown from an airplane, shot, and my brain scooped out by something I don't even believe in! From the beginning you people haven't leveled with me. Mike didn't and you're not now. For all I know you lied to me about my mom."

"About your mom?"

"About her being dead. Maybe she really isn't dead. Maybe she's as alive as you and me and King Paimon."

"Alfred, your mother died when you were twelve years old, before any of—"

"I know that! Or I knew that! I don't know what I know anymore. I don't even know what I don't know! The inside of my head feels all crumbly, like stale birthday cake left out too long."

"I see," Op Nine said. He was frowning, staring at me intensely, which didn't help matters. I wasn't crying, but his face was distorted, like a reflection in a funhouse mirror; the earlobes looked particularly long and Goofy-like.

I went on. "But one thing I do know is that you people are hiding something. Something doesn't add up here."

I rubbed my temples. The room spun around my aching head. Now it was as if my brain were made of broken glass, like the glass in Betty Tuttle's hand that fell when Mr. Needlemier said I was worth four hundred million dollars, shattered into a thousand pieces, then slapped back together with glue.

"It doesn't add up. There's something you're not telling me, which is a kind of lie even if you're not telling a lie lie."

" 'Lie lie'?"

"None of it makes any sense. Why am I here? Why did you bring me, a fifteen-year-old kid with no qualifications whatsoever in the covert op department, on your big mission to find Mike and the Vessel? Tell me why I'm here, Op Nine. Give me one good reason and I'll shut up and we'll go get Mike, which there seems to be a very mysterious lack of, the getting part, since that was the reason we flew four thousand miles per hour in the first place to get here. Why are we hanging out in this hotel room? That's my question."

"We were waiting for nightfall."

"Well, it's almost seven o'clock. It oughtta be fallen by now."

"Then we ought to be going."

"You didn't answer my question."

"You offered to come."

"I did?"

He nodded. I thought about it. "I don't remember offering that."

I slid down the door until my butt hit the carpet, dropped my head into my hands, and closed my eyes. I could smell something foreign, a sickly sweet odor like rotting fruit. I sniffed my hand. It came from me. I smelled like a rotten banana. It wasn't a stench like BO (though I couldn't remember taking a shower since that day on the *Pandora*—not that my not being able to remember meant anything), so what was it? I'd heard gangrene can stink to high heaven as your flesh rots right off your bones. Did I have gangrene? Had one of my long toenails cut into my toe, causing an infection? Why was my flesh rotting off? Maybe it was all in my head. Maybe something was leaking from the splintered glass of my mind, and that leaking something smelled like rot.

I felt him touch my shoulder.

"There's something wrong with me, isn't there?" I whimpered. "There's something very bad happening to me."

"I think so, Alfred."

"Because I looked into its eyes." I remembered Carl writhing on the desert sand, screaming gibberish as he tore at his own face.

"It could be."

"Well, is it or not? Aren't you the demonologist?"

"Alfred," he said softly, patting my shoulder. "Alfred, it will soon be over," he said.

"That's what I'm afraid of."

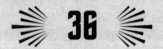

36

Op Nine changed his clothes before we left, putting on a rumpled jacket and a tie with a mustard-colored stain on it. He looked like your typical high school assistant principal or a salesman at a low-end used car lot.

We went downstairs and the valet pulled the Taurus around to the front of the hotel. I saw Op Nine slip him a fifty-dollar bill. That seemed excessive for somebody supposedly traveling incognito and didn't match his getup or the vehicle we were driving. After getting a tip like that, the valet was sure to remember us.

Op Nine jumped back on the interstate and we headed north. A light, freezing rain was falling and we passed a couple of cars that had spun off the slick road, the flashing of their hazard lights sparkling red and yellow in the frozen condensation on the windshield.

"How do you feel?" he asked.

"Shaky."

He just grunted back. His whole being seemed focused on the road or what lay at the end of it.

"Where are we going?" I asked.

"Evanston, just north of the city."

"Mike lives in Evanston?"

"His mother does. Everyone, Alfred, without exception, has a . . . vulnerability. A pressure point, if you will. For the Hyena, that point is his mother."

"What are you going to do to his mother, Op Nine?"

"I didn't say I was going to do anything to her."

"I read Section Nine. You're allowed to do anything you want to her, aren't you?"

He didn't say anything.

"You could kill her if you wanted."

"I would not want that. Alfred, simply because I have certain . . . latitude doesn't mean I take pleasure in it. It is a great responsibility and burden."

"Yeah. Playing God usually is."

"I did not volunteer to be a Superseding Protocol Agent."

"That's not the point," I said. "The point is if you had to hurt her or even kill her to get Mike, you would. An innocent old lady. Not that you *could*, but you *would*."

"If the world were at stake—wouldn't you?"

I had to think about how to answer that, but thinking was becoming increasingly difficult for me. My head had not stopped hurting since I woke up in OIPEP headquarters. I felt a little better since my breakdown in the hotel room, though. The rotten fruit smell wasn't as bad, but the inside of my head still felt fragile.

We took the Evanston exit and soon Op Nine was cruising

down tree-lined streets with brick sidewalks and quaint little storefronts, their display windows decked out for Christmas. Strands of white lights decorated the bare branches of the trees. I'd had no idea it was the Christmas season. Somehow I had completely missed Thanksgiving.

"Mom was a terrible cook," I said as Op Nine drove us out of downtown and into a neighborhood of big houses set far back from the road, with those light-up deer and spiral Christmas trees and walkways lined with candy canes. "Every Thanksgiving she made this casserole out of sauerkraut and brown sugar."

"That seems odd."

"It wasn't odd; it was awful, but every year I ate a plateful of that crap—you know, so I wouldn't hurt her feelings. The turkey was always dry, the mashed potatoes lumpy, and when you sliced into the pumpkin pie, all this brown liquid ran out and filled up the plate. I'm not sure what the brown liquid was about."

Op Nine had cut the headlamps and slowed to a crawl down the street, lined on either side with huge oaks and maples that must be breathtaking in the fall but now loomed like many-armed monsters reaching over the dark road.

"Sometimes I thought maybe she was cooking that way on purpose, so I'd lose some weight. 'Why don't you ride your bike, Alfred?' she'd ask if she caught me inside reading a book or watching TV. Or she'd go, 'What's Nick doing? Maybe you could invite him over to play some basketball.' She would snack on rice cakes. I don't think she liked rice cakes, but she ate them in front of me all the time, like every time I saw her she was munching on a rice cake, I think maybe the idea was to make me curious about rice cakes and eat them too. I've been meaning to see if there's been any research into rice cakes as a possible carcinogen, like maybe there's a connection between all those rice cakes and her cancer. Then I could sue the rice cake people. I don't really need the money and I know it wouldn't bring Mom back, but it would send a message and maybe even shut down the whole rice cake industry, so nobody else dies from eating too many rice cakes."

"What kind of cancer did she have?" he asked.

"Melanoma. Skin cancer."

"I doubt it was the rice cakes, then."

He pulled to the curb and cut the engine. We were parked in front of a handsome two-story Colonial with a brick walkway and big columns on the front. Unlike most of the houses on the block, this one had no lights on.

"Doesn't look like anybody's home," I said.

"I would be surprised if she were. The Hyena was a Company operative, Alfred. He understands better than most the pressure point theory."

"So she's not here. Doesn't that mean we're wasting our time?"

"I prefer to believe he is wasting his time."

He stepped out of the car and after a second I got out too. The rain had stopped. It was bitterly cold, a dead cold with no wind, but I could hear the wind, high in the cloud cover above us. I looked up where the light from the streetlamp bathed the underside of the clouds, but they weren't marching across the sky.

"Do you hear that?" I asked Op Nine.

He nodded. "Yes."

"It's not wind, is it?"

"No."

I heard voices whispering, but I couldn't make out the words, like hearing someone through a wall as they talked in another room. It got under your skin, a maddening itch you couldn't scratch.

"Are they here?" I asked. "Did they follow us here?"

He started across the street, toward the house directly across from Mike's mom's.

"What are we doing?" I asked, trotting to keep up, although my trot was thrown off by my injured leg.

"Say nothing. Follow my lead."

He rang the doorbell. Our breath fogged and swirled around our heads.

A middle-aged lady with dark bobbed hair opened the door. Behind her, in the foyer, were two little kids, staring at us.

Op Nine went Midwestern. "Evening, how are ya? I'm Detective Bruce Givens with the Evanston PD." He flashed a badge at her. I looked at him. His face had changed again. He didn't quite look like Op Nine or the face he used for Lord Polmeroy; he looked just like a police detective should look. My opinion might have been influenced by the fact that he just identified himself as one, though. If he had said *I'm Bob from Lucky's Used Cars*, I probably would have thought, *Yep, that's Bob*.

"Hate to bother you," he went on. "But I'm wondering if you could tell me if you've seen this kid before?" He jerked his head toward me.

The lady squinted at me. "I don't think so, no."

"We've had a couple calls, some vandalism with the yard decorations. Found him wandering around the Arnold place just now."

"Agnes's?" She looked over his shoulder at the dark house across the street.

"That's right. Says he's selling magazine subscriptions."

"Well, I don't know about that. But Agnes is out of town."

"He didn't try to sell you a subscription?"

"No. I've never seen this boy before."

He turned to me. "Thought you said you stopped by this house."

I shrugged, rolled my eyes, and tried to curl my upper lip like a hoodlum. A prep school hoodlum, judging from my clothes. I didn't say anything. I was a lot of things, but actor wasn't one of them.

"That's what I thought," Op Nine said. "Okay, let's call your folks." He nodded to the lady with the saucer-eyed kids hovering behind her. "Sorry to bother you. Have a good evening."

He took me by the elbow and walked me down the drive.

He stopped at the road, as if he had just thought of something. He turned back toward the house. She was still standing in the doorway, watching us, a faceless silhouette.

"Agnes is out of town, you said?"

"For two weeks. Her son sent her on a cruise."

"He's house-sitting, then?"

"No. I think he went with her. Early Christmas present."

He nodded. "Maybe I'll just take a look around over there. Just to make sure everything is okay."

He turned me back around and marched me across the street to the car.

"She's watching, Alfred. Get in the back."

He opened the back door and I slid inside. He got behind the wheel and closed his door.

"What now?" I asked. "She isn't here."

"Perhaps. Perhaps not. This is a subtle game, Alfred. No doubt he has anticipated this move and also anticipated we would understand his anticipation, and therefore would not pursue him here, thus there would be no need to move his mother."

I thought about it. Then I said, "Huh?"

"Like Poe's purloined letter, he hides the object in plain sight."

"Like whose what?" I looked out the window. The neighbor had closed the door, but I thought I saw a shadow in the window next to it.

"Mike took her on a cruise," I said.

"Unlikely."

"Why are we just sitting here?"

"I'm interrogating you."

He pulled a thin black object from his pocket and held it toward me. I thought it was a pen.

"You want me to write something?"

"It is a communication device," he answered. "Press the red button to speak, release to listen."

"Oh. Walkie-talkies, I get it." I had seen one of these before. Ashley had it in the woods outside Knoxville. I took it from him. "In case we get separated."

"We will be separated," he said. "You're staying here."

"I am?"

"The neighbor is watching," he said. He reached into his pocket again. This time he offered me the modified flare gun, the mini-3XD loaded with anti-demon ordnance.

"They're here?" My heart fluttered with budding panic. I

thought of the strange whispering I heard high above the clouds.

He shrugged. I said, "I don't want that thing. I'll probably just shoot off my foot."

"It may buy you a few moments. If anything happens, hit the blue button on top of the communicator."

"What happens when I hit the blue button?"

"It will send a signal to me that you're in trouble."

"Like a panic button?"

"Yes. Like a panic button." He dropped the mini-3XD in my lap and put his hand on the door handle.

"It's a poor design, if you ask me," I said, looking at the communicator. "Red to talk and blue to panic. Panic buttons should be red."

"I will speak with R and D about it." He gave me one of his rare smiles, and I had a sudden, nearly overwhelming urge to snatch the demon gun from my lap and blow his head off with it. It was so vivid, I shivered and shoved away the image of his head exploding. The shove caused a shock wave of pain behind my eyes.

"Don't worry, Alfred," he said. "Just a quick look around. He had to remove her quickly and he may have gotten sloppy. No more than fifteen minutes, I should think."

He got out of the car, slammed the door, and I was alone. I watched him walk up the drive to the dark house. He stood on the front stoop for a minute. I couldn't really see what he was doing; a hedge blocked my view. I looked to my left and noticed he forgot to lock the doors. I leaned over the front seat to hit the automatic lock button, and when I sat back, Op Nine was gone.

I guessed he used some high-tech gizmo to get in the house. I didn't have a watch on, so I would have to rely on my own interior clock, which had never been that great. I was always late for class, for example. The bell would ring and I would think, *Okay, I got five minutes.* Then after only two minutes of Kropp-time, the tardy bell would ring.

A light rain began to fall again, rain mixed with little pellets that I figured was snow but maybe I had some Volkswagen-sized hail coming my way. I looked at the Christmas lights on the lawns, distorted by the wet glass of the car window, blurry-edged and dreamlike, and I remembered my "catch Santa" phase when I was a kid in Ohio. I was nine and determined to get a look at the jolly ol' elf with my own eyes. I drank four cans of Coke in an hour, and I really had no idea that caffeine was a laxative as well as a stimulant. I spent half the night on the john, doubled over in pain, afraid to call Mom for help, because I'd have to reveal my scheme.

The rain started coming down harder, and the ice pellets pinged on the roof and tapped on the windows. How long had he been gone? I could hardly see the house anymore for the rain. I began to imagine all sorts of horrible things happening to him in there. Had Mike anticipated this move (Op Nine had said he would) and was he waiting inside, crouched in the dark? Maybe Op Nine was already dead and Mike was sneaking up behind the car . . . I jerked around in my seat and peered out the back window, one hand gripping the gun, the other clutching the OIPEP communicator. I didn't see anything, but that didn't mean there wasn't anything, so I hit the red button and said loudly, because I didn't know where the mike was on the thing, "Op Nine, Op Nine, this is Alfred Kropp. Come back." I released the button, realized I made a mistake, and pressed it again. "Uh, Op Nine, this is Alfred again. 'Come back' means 'please answer,' not literally 'come back.' Sorry about that. Come back. I mean, over."

Silence. I examined the sleek metal body of the communicator, but didn't see any controls besides the two buttons, no on/off switch and no volume control. Maybe there was a wireless earpiece that went with it and Op Nine forgot to give me that one little bit of essential equipment. Whatever was wrong, no sound came from the communicator.

Now what do I do? Wait here for him? I didn't think it had been fifteen minutes. Ten, tops. Maybe twelve. Twelve and a half, no more than that. Do I go in? And do what? If Mike was in that house, he'd take me out easily, probably much more easily than he took out Op Nine. Okay, so I stay in the car. Thirteen minutes now. Maybe. I could just hit the blue button. If Op Nine didn't come out, that meant something really bad had happened. If he did, I'd just apologize and say I hit the button on accident. He'd believe that after all the accidents I was responsible for. If Op Nine got killed in this operation, it would be my fault for losing my head in that battle and trying to take on those demons myself. I thought of Carl, or rather Carl's animated corpse in the morgue, the empty eye sockets and the hole where his heart should have been, and that was my fault too . . . but no, that really wasn't my fault; why did I think that was my fault? Carl got demon-fried before I laid hands on the ring. So I wasn't to blame for that, was I? All that happened before I got the Seal, didn't it? I tried to remember, but my memory was as fuzzy as the Christmas lights through the wet windows. Again I caught a whiff of that odd rotten smell, distinct as when you eat too much garlic and a half hour later you can smell it oozing from your pores.

I pressed the red button again. "Op Nine, Op Nine, this is Alfred. Answer if you can hear me. It's raining. Over."

I counted to five, and then tried again. "Op Nine, really need to talk to you. This is Alfred, over."

Nothing. Not even static. Maybe it was defective or maybe the batteries were dead. You would think highly specialized operatives—particularly a SPA like Op Nine—would check their equipment before a covert op like this one.

There was only one way to test it. Technically, I wasn't in a panic—not yet—but I was about as close as you can get. I decided I could always tell him I hit it accidentally.

I pressed the blue button. ·

I counted to ten. Nothing happened. He didn't come bursting through the hedges, gun drawn, to my rescue. He didn't come at all, even after I reached sixty and then gave up counting, slipped the mini-3XD into my coat pocket, and eased out the door that faced away from the street, so the mother of the saucer-eyed kids wouldn't see me. I ran bent over to the hedge, then ducked around it, putting it between me and the road. Now maybe if I stood up and walked casually toward the front door she might mistake me for Op Nine—or Detective Bruce Givens—though that seemed unlikely, since he was about three inches taller and twenty pounds lighter. Sometimes you have to go with all that's left, even if all that's left is foolish hope.

I sauntered up the walkway to the front door. I didn't see how Op Nine got in, but I figured I'd start with the door. The concrete was slick with ice and I had to walk very slowly. At the bottom of the steps leading up to the porch was a flower bed filled with leafless shrubs and a small figure standing guard, just to my left.

A yard gnome. I had a thing about yard gnomes, like I told Dr. Benderhall; I'm not sure why. I put them in the same class as clowns: something that's supposed to be funny but really is kind of scary. This particular yard gnome had seen his share of winters. The paint on the face was flecking off and the paint that remained had faded to various hues of gray.

I dropped to a crouch and shuffled to the door—I wasn't sure if I could be seen over the top of the hedge. I could hear the neighbor now: *Quick, call the cops! It's that huge-headed hooligan!*

So how did he get in? The front door was locked and the two windows on either side were closed and latched down. Maybe he could melt through walls, like a phantom. First I had him pegged as a cyborg; now he could melt through walls.

So I froze up again and tried the blue button one more time while I leaned against the front door.

At that moment, I heard the dead bolt slowly pull back. I scrambled to my feet, turned, and watched as the front door creaked open about two inches.

"Op Nine?" I whispered.

Nothing. So I took a deep breath, pushed open the door, and stepped inside my own personal house of horrors.

37

The first thing I noticed was the smell of cat. It's an unmistakable odor and also unavoidable, no matter how often you change the litter box. If this was a movie, the cat would leap out of the dark at me, I would scream, the audience would jump, and then both of us would go "whew!" right before the slasher came barreling out of the shadows with the butcher knife. I should probably neutralize the cat before proceeding.

The second thing I noticed was the yard gnome.

Was it the same gnome from outside? In semidarkness almost everything took on shades of gray, so I couldn't be one hundred percent positive, but it could have been the same gnome, now standing a few feet inside the entryway. Same height, same rubbed-out face, same creepy ambience that all yard gnomes have.

Cold air blew through the open door behind me, so I

pushed it closed, keeping my eye on the gnome. It didn't move. Well, I didn't really expect it to come to life, did I? Yard gnomes don't come to life, not in the real world. Then I thought, with a pang of sadness, that the real world was gone, the world I knew before Bernard Samson, OIPEP, the Sword of Kings, and the Seal of Solomon came into my life.

That world was gone and never coming back, even if we somehow got the genie back in the bottle. Like Dr. Merryweather had said, we had crossed the threshold into a new reality, and maybe it wasn't looking into the demon's eyes that had me so screwed up—maybe it was the loss of everything that made sense to me.

"Okay, look," I said to the gnome. "I'm not afraid of you." Probably the first time in the history of the world anyone had said that to a yard gnome—also probably the first time anyone had ever lied to a yard gnome.

He just stared back at me wearing that sly little grin.

To heck with it. "Op Nine!" I shouted. "Op Nine, where are you?"

The lights in the entryway blazed on and the floorboards creaked behind me. I whirled around, jamming my hand into my coat pocket, fumbling for the mini-3XD Op Nine had given me in the car.

An old lady stood by the front door, wearing purple house slippers with a flowery print that matched her robe. On her left hand she wore an oven mitt. In her right, she held a gun, pointed directly at the center of my forehead.

"If you move, dear, you're dead," she announced.

"I'm going to take my hand out of my pocket," I said. "Okay?"

She nodded. "Slowly, dear. It's late and I'm jumpy."

I slowly brought my right hand into view and then raised both into the air.

"I'm not a burglar," I said.

She smiled. I got an eyeful of large, sparkling white teeth with oversized incisors, just like Mike's. She had a small head and a wide, round face, crisscrossed with wrinkles and deep creases, her eyes bright blue and kind.

She dropped the gun into the pocket of her robe and I took that as a signal I could lower my hands. We stood there for a second, staring at each other.

"I'm Alfred Kropp," I said.

"I know who you are, dear," she said. "Michael said you might show up. Well, not you specifically, but someone from his company."

"That's actually who I came in looking for," I said.

"Well, you won't find him here. I sent him on his way. Police detective!" She trilled a little laugh.

"That's good," I said. "I was afraid maybe you shot him."

I was trapped between her and the yard gnome by the stairs. Why would someone put a yard gnome by their stairs?

"I've baked an apple pie, Alfred. Would you like a slice?"

"I'm not really that hungry."

"I insist."

"I guess I am a little hungry."

"After you, dear. To your left."

I walked through the formal dining room and into the kitchen, which was decorated in a country theme, rooster figurines and Jersey cow kitchen doodads and a red and white checkered tablecloth on the table.

The pie was sitting on the sill over the sink, and steam still rose from its golden brown lace crust. My stomach rumbled. I was starving.

"Please sit down, Alfred," she said, waving me toward the table. "A few more minutes to cool and it's ready to slice. A la mode, dear?"

I cleared my throat. "Just the pie, ma'am. That's fine."

I wondered where Op Nine was. Probably scrambling around outside, looking for me, though I wondered how I missed him. Most likely he was beside himself, while I sat in Mama Arnold's kitchen, eating pie.

"How do you know my name?" I asked.

"Michael's told me all about you."

"Where is Mike?"

"I have no idea, dear."

She pulled a gallon of milk from the refrigerator and poured a big frosty glass. She set it on the table in front of me. She smelled of vanilla.

"Somebody told us you were on a cruise," I said.

"Mike made up that story. He wanted me to leave, of course, but why would I leave? I may be old, dear, but I can take care of myself. I go for target practice twice a month."

"Well," I said, because I didn't know what else to say. "Everybody needs a hobby."

Right by the litter box stood another gnome. And there were gnome refrigerator door magnets and gnome figurines standing like little guards around the pie pan on the sill.

"You like gnomes," I said.

"Gnomes keep evil spirits away."

"You're worried about evil spirits?"

"Aren't you?"

"Mike's told you what happened?"

She was standing on her tiptoes by the sink—she was only about five feet tall—sticking her nose near the pie.

"I had to know why he was so desperate to get me out of this house."

She put on another oven mitt and picked up the pie. She set it on the counter and shook off the mitts. Her hands were very small, but her knuckles were big, from arthritis, I guessed, and mottled with age spots. She grabbed a big knife and cut a fat slice that she slid onto a little plate with a picture of a gnome painted in the middle.

"He's a good boy, but he associates with the wrong sort of people—not you, Alfred. You're a wonderful child with great potential. I hate to see you squander it on people like those Mike used to work with."

She cocked her round little head and her voice dropped. "Listen to that!"

It was the freezing rain, the little pellets smacking against the roof and the kitchen window.

"I do hope something can be done soon," she said. "I'm worried about my spring bulbs."

"That's why it's real important we find Mike, ma'am," I said. "We can't do anything about it till we find him."

She placed the pie in front of me and stood back, folding her arms across her chest and just beaming down at me.

"Taste it, Alfred," she said. "I am the best baker in the tri-counties."

"Maybe just a bite," I said. "But then I have to go. Op— my friend's probably wondering what happened to me."

But I figured I might be able to worm some clues out of

this old lady. I didn't believe she didn't know where Mike was. Maybe if I was nice and ate some of her pie she would let down her guard some and tell me where he was hiding.

I took a big bite of pie as she stood over me, smiling sweetly, and I have to admit there was a little pain in my heart because everything seemed so normal. You don't realize how much normal, boring things like eating pie late at night in a warm kitchen matter until those things are taken from you.

Something crunched in my mouth. Thinking I must have bitten into a piece of stem, I reached in and pulled out a long gray stick. It didn't look like wood, though. It was jagged on one end and dangling from the other by a glistening piece of tissue was a partially chewed eyeball.

I dropped the small bone onto the table and shoved myself away, knocking the chair over, my stomach heaving as I spat and gagged and tears burned in my eyes. My tongue was covered with fuzz and I frantically scraped it with my fingernail, bringing out tufts of orange and white fur.

"What's the matter, Alfred?" she asked. "Don't you like cats?"

There wasn't time to indulge myself in nausea. I ripped the mini-3XD from my pocket and took aim at her round, doll-shaped head.

"Where is he?" I demanded in a loud, high-pitched voice. "Where's Op Nine?"

"Why, he went upstairs, dear."

I started to back out of the room, keeping the gun pointed at her. "You're not Mike Arnold's mom," I said.

She didn't say anything. Her blue eyes danced and behind those eyes I recognized something. Something I had seen in the Sahara. Something that *knew* me.

"There are many rooms upstairs, Alfred," she whispered. "One door but many rooms. A person should be careful which room he enters."

She made no move to stop me. I turned and ran through the formal dining room, whipping around the corner toward the stairs where the yard gnome still kept guard. I kicked it as hard as I could and started up the stairs. Then something grabbed my pants leg. I felt long claws or nails sinking into my ankle, and I didn't have to look to know it was the gnome or something posing as a gnome, and I thought that was particularly fiendish and nasty, posing as something that was supposed to protect people from evil spirits.

Op Nine had told me back in the desert that if you looked into their eyes they would know what you feared and loved.

I was about to find out exactly what he meant.

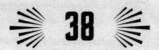

38

I took the stairs two at a time, hardly feeling the gnome's claws digging into my flesh. I stopped about halfway up and, holding my breath, aimed at the little grayish green cap near my leg. I fired the 3XD, certain I was going to lame myself. But my shot was true—the muzzle was only a few inches from its head—and the thing blew apart into flecks of black and orange and gold.

I started back up. At the top of the landing the very thing I expected to find was there: another yard gnome.

I didn't hesitate. I pointed the barrel of the demon blaster right at its enigmatic little smile and wasted it.

Behind me I could hear little scratching noises and tiny voices whispering, though I couldn't make out the words. More gnomes. I didn't want to use up the entire clip on gnomes, so I made a beeline toward the end of the upstairs hallway.

She had been telling the truth about one thing, at least. There was only one door up here, at the end of the hall, which

I knew wasn't the normal setup in house plans, and I remembered Op Nine saying in the briefing at headquarters how some demons can alter reality.

The old Alfred Kropp would have hesitated at that door. Maybe even under these very weird circumstances I would have knocked, but the old me had been scooped out hollow by a demon and the new me wasn't about to let the same thing happen to Op Nine.

"Saint Michael," I whispered softly. "Protect me."

Then I kicked the door right off its hinges.

I whipped the 3XD in an arc, like I'd seen on a hundred cop shows and movies, my left hand gripping my right wrist.

I was standing in a hospital room. The room was empty, the bed neatly made, and the only sound was the TV on its wall mount opposite the bed. *The Price Is Right* was on. I had been in this room before, and my first thought was, *It's a lie. Don't panic. It's another lie.* I didn't know what the deal was with this room, but I didn't have time to puzzle over it. I had to find Op Nine. I turned, and when I turned she called out to me.

"Alfred."

I froze. I knew that voice. It had been a long time since I had heard it, but since it was the first voice I had ever heard, I recognized it immediately.

It was a trick. I knew it was a trick and I knew Op Nine was still somewhere in the house and his only hope of survival lay in Alfred Kropp keeping his focus, but something made me turn back. I guess it was hope that made me turn back. I was about to find out they could use that against you too.

The bed wasn't empty anymore.

"Ah, come on," I said to the person in the bed. "This isn't fair."

"Sit down, Alfred," Mom said. "We need to talk."

"I'm not going to sit down," I said. "I need to find Op Nine."

"There is no such person. Now stop being silly and sit down."

"If there's no such person," I said, "then how'd I get this?" I showed her the 3XD. My hand was shaking.

"Alfred, you know how."

I lowered the weapon. I knew the smart thing to do at that point. And the longer I let her talk, the harder the smart thing to do would be, but how does anyone in his right mind blow away his own mother?

I swallowed hard. "You're going to tell me I'm dreaming."

"You are dreaming."

"It's all been just a horrible dream."

"Well, of course it has. You fell asleep, Alfred, sitting right in that chair."

"And I'm really twelve years old and you're still alive."

"Of course, my darling."

Tears shone in her eyes and I looked away. I always looked away when she cried. I couldn't take it.

"That's mean," I whispered. "That's really mean. That's stepping over the line."

I sank into the chair beside her bed and leaned over, my elbows on my knees, the 3XD now hanging loosely in my hand.

"Alfred, I'm all you have."

"Stop it," I said.

"All you have in the world. Of course you would dream of being a hero, a brave knight riding to my rescue. But you know such things don't really exist, don't you, baby? Holy swords and demonic yard gnomes, Alfred? You know it can't be real."

I nodded.

"Alfred, your father wasn't a business tycoon or the last son of Lancelot. He was a big-headed, long-haul truck driver named Herman."

"My dad . . . my dad was a trucker?"

"Watermelons. Doesn't that make more sense than what you've been dreaming?"

I nodded. "You bet it does."

"And isn't that what you want most of all, Alfred? For everything to make sense?"

I lifted my head and looked at her. The same skeletal face, the same deep-set, black-ringed eyes, the same yellowish skin and thin gray lips pulled back from her teeth. Just like four years ago (if it really was four years ago), it was Mom and it wasn't Mom.

"So what do I do now?" I asked.

"Wake up, honey. That's all. Just . . . wake up."

She smiled at me, and it was *her* smile, my mom's smile.

"It isn't right," I mumbled. "It's not *fair*. You're all that I had—why did you leave me alone? I'm so sick of being alone—I don't want to be alone anymore!"

"Alfred, I know, I know," she cried. "But you have to be strong for me, baby. I need you now. All we have is each other, and I need you to be strong for me now."

I nodded. "Okay. Okay, Mom. I can . . . I can be strong . . ."

"Then you have to wake up, Alfred."

"How—how do I do that? How do I wake up?"

"Look."

She pointed toward the door. I had kicked it off its hinges—I distinctly remembered kicking it off its hinges—but now it was whole again and closed, and sprawled on the floor with his back against it was Op Nine, his chin against his chest so I couldn't see his face.

"These are the dreams we dream," Mom whispered. "The worst that come before waking."

"I don't understand," I said. But I did understand. I stood up and walked over to him. I saw his chest rise and fall. He was alive.

"You must choose now, Alfred," she said behind me. Her voice was sad and soft and sounded very far away. "Between the waking and the dream. I know you don't want to wake up. Waking up means you have to face the fact I might die—but I need you now. Please don't abandon me, Alfred, my baby. Please wake up and take care of me."

I raised the 3XD that didn't exist and pointed it at the top of the head of the OIPEP operative, the Superseding Protocol Agent, who also didn't exist. It wasn't murder. How could it be? He didn't exist. None of it did. I was just a twelve-year-old kid who couldn't face the fact that his mother was dying. Enough fooling around. I needed to wake up.

"Well," she said sharply. "What are you waiting for, Alfred?"

"That which must be done," I whispered. I took a deep breath, pivoted around, and swung the barrel of the demon-blaster toward the face of my mother.

"If this is just a dream—if this isn't real—then this won't hurt at all."

I squeezed the trigger.

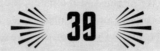

39

There was no blood, just a blinding flash of white and orange, flecked with black, and a huge distorted face shot out of the fireball, zooming across the room toward me, its mouth a yawning blackness, an abyss that swallowed me and a roaring voice boomed inside my head, *THOU CANNOT ESCAPE US, FOR WE ARE INSIDE THEE ALREADY!*

I heaved Op Nine to his feet, pulling his arm around my shoulders. He moaned against my chest. I pulled him into the hallway, my body turned at an angle so I could point the 3XD into the hospital room—only it wasn't a hospital room anymore but a maelstrom of interlaced spinning wheels of fire. I wasn't sure what *that* was about.

I headed toward the stairs, then stopped. A wave of twisting, squirming black creatures about the size of my fist was barreling toward us.

A wave of scorpions, millions of them, their three-inch tails hissing and whipping, smashed against our ankles and rose to our knees. Their barbs stabbed through my pants again and again as I pushed Op Nine through the undulating river of their swarming bodies. The pain was excruciating, but I told myself they weren't real; that if my mind held we'd make it out okay.

Then the river parted and the scorpions disappeared into the cracks and crevices of the walls. We were halfway to the stairs when the walls began to sag as if they were melting, and faces began to emerge in the undulating plaster. I saw my mother and Bernard Samson, Uncle Farrell, and Lord Bennacio. I saw the faces of all the people who died because of me and they didn't say anything, but their eyes were sad and filled with the loss of betrayal. I lowered my eyes and kept moving.

I came to the head of the stairs, but the stairs were gone. We were teetering on the edge of a black chasm and I could actually see rivulets of light pouring down into it, like water over falls, and something very hot was bearing down on us from behind. I felt the hairs on the back of my neck curl and singe, and tasted acrid smoke on my tongue. I shook Op Nine as hard as I could and shouted in his ear, "This would really be a good time for you to wake up!" But he didn't.

"Not real," I muttered. "Not real."

I couldn't go back, but this was the worst thing yet, so I couldn't go forward either. We teetered on the edge while the heat grew more intense behind us. Something told me if I turned around to face it, we were lost. I closed my eyes, took a huge breath, and whispered, "Let go. Let go. *Let go.*"

I wrapped both arms around Op Nine and jumped into the chasm.

We tumbled into the utter darkness until we smacked at the bottom of the stairs.

Looming in the open doorway was a ten-foot-tall being of shimmering golden light, a demon without the masks of my mom or Mike's mom. It had assumed its true form, and its face was more beautiful than anything nature gave us ordinary people, only the eyes were black pits, black as the chasm I just fell through, as if something had torn or burned them away.

"We're leaving," I gasped at it. "Let us pass."

It didn't move. I felt something squeezing the inside of my head, like when Paimon raised its fist and popped the agent named Bert like a human grape.

Then its voice: *Bring us the Seal.*

I emptied the clip as I rushed it, holding the trigger down as I moved forward, pulling Op Nine along with me. I ducked my head, clinching my eyes tightly closed, and felt some kind of membrane stretching over my entire body, and then we popped through it into the night, into the storm of pelting, freezing rain.

I dragged Op Nine over the frozen walkway to the Ford, yanked open the passenger door, tossed the empty 3XD into the backseat, and slung Op Nine into the car. I raced around to the other side and threw myself behind the wheel. A hunk of ice the size of a baseball smashed into the windshield, sending cracks racing toward the four corners. I jammed the car into reverse and slammed down on the accelerator. I whipped the wheel hard to the right and we spun around, the tires screaming on the slick pavement.

"Hold on, Nine!" I shouted, throwing the Ford into drive. Huge hunks of ice rained down, smacking into the roof and the hood, only now it was burning, and big globs of fire dotted the pavement. I roared out of the neighborhood while fire rained down from the sky with no idea where I was going but determined to get there as fast I could.

40

By the time I found the interstate I was shaking so badly, I could hardly keep us on the on-ramp. The pain in my head blurred my vision, but I could see streaks of black and gold as the burning hail hurtled down from the sky, and the tires went *whump-whump-whump* as we drove on the fiery hunks.

This wasn't illusion created by the demons to drive me mad; this was real and, looking to my left as we flew into the southbound lanes I saw orange and black everywhere, and the flashing red and white lights of fire engines. Chicago was burning.

"Op Nine!" I screamed. "Op Nine, wake up! You gotta tell me what to do!"

His head leaned against the window. His eyes were closed, but I could see him breathing, so he wasn't dead.

The interstate was deserted except for some cars that had either pulled into the emergency lanes or had been run off the road by the firestorm. I pushed us up to ninety-five, heading south, formulating the beginnings of a plan that probably wouldn't save the day but might save me and Op Nine long enough to fight tomorrow.

I looked into the rearview and saw a mass of black shapes, a flying wedge of short, fat creatures with soft, pointy hats rippling straight back as they raced toward us. I did a double take because it isn't every day you look in your rearview mirror and see a squadron of yard gnomes mounted on vampire bats the size of rottweilers, wielding lances tipped with fire and flaming swords, bearing down on you.

I pushed the accelerator all the way to the floorboards and kept pressing till the pressure made my knee ache. The old Taurus rattled and shook as the needle leaped to 110 and wavered there.

But I knew I could be flying the X-30 at Mach 6 and I wouldn't outrun these nasties. Op Nine might be a SPA, answerable to no laws except the natural ones, but these things answered to no rules period. They came before *any* of the rules had been written.

They swarmed around the car, and little flaming darts smacked against the windshield, the hood, and the trunk, exploding with firecracker-loud pops. The gnome riders were smiling and the bats' razor-sharp fangs were about four inches long, dripping goo and glimmering in the streetlights. It was all I could do to keep us from skidding off the road and slamming into the concrete barrier separating us from the northbound lanes.

Four gnomes dropped off their mounts onto the hood. They attacked the windshield with flaming axes, hacking at the cracked glass with those ironic little smiles frozen on their faces. I heard more smacking and cracking behind me, and figured more gnomes were skittering around on the trunk, chopping at the back window. Red and orange tracers lit the night sky as the flaming ice boulders rained down. Great hunks of concrete spun into the air with each impact. We roared by a car balanced on its roof and another one that had burned down to its axles.

I yelled at Op Nine to wake up. I yelled at the bat-riding gnomes to cut it out. I yelled at myself for looking into the demon's eyes and then I yelled at myself for not giving the ring to Op Nine when I had the chance.

And when my throat was raw from all the yelling at everybody, I figured enough was enough and, if I didn't do something drastic, the hell that had broken loose because of me was going to get a lot hellier, and "hellier" wasn't even a damn word.

So I slammed on the brakes. The gnomes on the hood lost their footing and slapped into the windshield, then slid out of sight. The rear wheels locked and the car went into a skid. I actually laughed aloud at that point and shouted at them: "Ha! Guess you bats don't got brakes, do ya? Do ya?" The Taurus careened sideways and that's how we came to a stop, with fiery ice balls zipping and popping on the road all around us. I didn't stop to think. There wasn't time. I got out of the car and waited.

It was very quiet, except for the ice hissing on the pavement and the distant sirens of the fire trucks.

It came alone, three feet tall, wearing a pointy red cap, a green shirt, blue suspenders, and brown shoes, with a smile frozen on its face, and I knew without knowing how I knew that this was the same creature that had posed as Mike's mom and my mom. The same eyeless creature that had blocked my way out at the front door.

I held up my hands.

"I'm unarmed!" I called over to it. It stopped about fifty feet away and cocked its little gnome head at me.

"I've had enough!" I continued. "You win. I'll get you the Vessel, but you gotta stop harassing me like this!"

I paused, waiting for the gnome to say something. It didn't.

"Just tell me where to find you once I have it."

The lips didn't move; I heard the voice inside my head.

Meet us at the gate.

"The gate?" I shouted. I wasn't sure why I was shouting. "What gate?"

The gateway to hell. The devil's door.

"And where's that? Where's the devil's door?"

Two days, Alfred Kropp.

"Two days or what?"

It didn't answer. It didn't need to. Op Nine had already told me: *They will consume us.*

"Okay," I said. "Okay. But I'm not sure where—"

And then the gnome disappeared, vanishing with a loud *pop!* and I was alone on the highway.

Well, not completely alone. I took a deep breath and hopped back into the car. Op Nine hadn't moved, but his jaw muscles were working overtime and his eyes were rolling behind his charcoal-colored eyelids. Maybe he was dreaming. I had hoped I was dreaming back in the Arnold house, and that's what will get you in trouble. Not the hoping. The dreaming.

41

I managed to get us off the interstate and back to the Drake in one piece. It wasn't easy. The highway was littered with chunks of asphalt and abandoned cars, and once I got off the interstate I inched along, weaving through a massive traffic jam, every street clogged with cars and bicycles, and people dodging between them carrying suitcases. I passed broken storefront windows and could see people milling about inside, looting.

I didn't see any valets in front of the hotel, so I double-parked about two blocks away. The wind howled and swirled and little flecks of burning ice stung my cheeks and I worried one would land in my eye and blind me. Op Nine's head lay in the crook of my neck as I dragged him into the lobby. Nobody paid any attention to us because the place was crazy, the front counter packed ten people deep and cell phones ringing and people mingling about either talking very fast or talking not at all but walking around with dazed expressions, and I thought, *Hang on, people, 'cause you ain't seen nothin' yet.*

Back in our room, I threw Op Nine on the bed and pulled the covers up to his chin. He was shivering pretty badly, muttering under his breath, and his right eyelid twitched. I'd figured out by this point what was wrong with him, so I grabbed a towel from the bathroom, rolled him onto his side, and tied his hands behind his back. The towel was too thick and the knot too big to hold him for long, but it might give me a few seconds to get to him once he woke up.

Then I searched his pockets.

A handkerchief, a travel-sized plastic bottle of Visine, nose spray, a comb, and a crucifix. Then I found his cell phone and clicked through the address book. I highlighted the entry called "HQ" and was rewarded with a recording that all circuits were busy and to try my call again later. I didn't have much "later" left, nobody did, but I slipped the phone into my pocket to try later or in case it rang.

I went into the main room and booted up the laptop. This time I tried to crack the code, but nothing worked, including such attempts as "SPA," "NINE," "9," and "OUR FATHER."

I went back into the bedroom and sat beside him.

"The phone lines are out," I told him as he lay there, muttering and sweating. "I can't get into your computer and we have forty-eight hours till they consume us. Well, more like forty-six hours. I know you're hurting right now, but sometimes you have to suck it up and just push through. Take it from me; I've done more sucking it up than your average NFL quarterback.

"I need the access code to your computer, Nine. We've got

to get in touch with headquarters, let them know what's happened, and come up with some kind of plan. It would also be helpful to know what and where the devil's door is, and you're the expert. I'm just a kid mucking around with these demons, and I'm losing my grip. I mean, I think I'm going insane. I've been having these hallucinations about killing you, so I'm starting to not trust myself when it comes to homicidal impulses. I've got to get a grip on this situation because right now it's got a grip on me—both of us, I guess."

He probably couldn't hear a word I said. I got a wet washcloth from the john and wiped his face with it and shouted right in his ear, but nothing worked.

Back in the main room, I opened up the minibar (I figured we were traveling on the corporate tab) and ate a chocolate bar, drank a Coke, then brought a bottle of Evian back into the bedroom and dumped the contents over his hound-dog head. He still didn't wake up. I felt pretty bad about doing that, so I fetched a towel from the bathroom and dried him off the best I could.

"They get you with the worst thing," I told him. "For me it was my mom. What are they doing to you? What's the worst thing, Nine?"

I had a feeling I knew, and that gave me an idea. I sat back down in front of his IBM ThinkPad and typed in "ABK-HAZIA."

A box popped up on the toolbar: "WELCOME NINE."

I clicked on the SATCOM folder. The screen flickered, then another message box popped up: "SATCOM DOWN." Below it was the little e-mail icon, so I clicked on that and his in-box popped up. There was only one message.

From: Aquarius
To: Nine
Subject: RE: OPREQ

As you predicted, Research advises active agent cannot be cloned or synthesized. What an annoying habit you have of always being correct. Accordingly, unless conditions on the ground warrant otherwise, protect at all hazards the AC-TAGE carrier. Do not put him in harm's way unless absolutely necessary.

Aquarius

I read this twice. What was "OPREQ"? Operational Requirement? Operative Request? "ACTAGE" must be short for "active agent," but what was the active agent he was talking about? Then I remembered the briefing, and Op Nine talking about the 3XDs and the active agent, the whatever it was that gave the ammo its bite. And I remembered asking him in the desert if the bullets were loaded with holy water and him saying no, it was something he hoped was more powerful.

Then I remembered my dream, of the gigantic Kropp Fish and the little suckers all over my body, and how when I first woke up on the *Pandora,* I was dizzy and drank those big glasses of orange juice. I remembered the soreness under my arm, and suddenly it all came together. The sore spot must have been the insertion point for the needle they used. The needle to drain my blood.

I read the e-mail again: ". . . protect at all hazards the AC-TAGE carrier . . ."

I clicked on the other boxes: Sent Mail, Trash, Drafts, but every file was blank.

So I clicked on the Compose button and wrote:

To: Aquarius
From: Nine
Subject: Help

I'm not sure who you are, but I guess you're Director Merryweather. This is Alfred Kropp. I broke into this computer bcuz Op Nine is hurt. Still in Chi. City burning. Two days to get Vessel or world ends. Need help here. Send help.

AK

I hit the Send button and the message vanished. Then a dialogue box popped up.

Message Undeliverable: Unknown Recipient

"Wuddya mean?" I yelled at the computer. " 'Unknown recipient'?"

I hit the Compose button again.

To: Aquarius
From: Nine
Subject: Help

This is Alfred Kropp. We need help. No Hyena in Chi. Raining fire. Op Nine very hurt. 2 days or else. Send help!

AK

I hit the Send button and again the little box popped up. I clicked on his address book and a long list popped onto the screen. So I wrote a third e-mail to everyone on the list, a kind of bulk mail SOS.

To: ALL COMPANY PERSONNEL
From: Nine
Subject: Help us

This is Alfred Kropp. Op Nine very hurt. 2 days to give them Vessel. Don't have Vessel. Don't have Hyena. Where is devil's door? Please send help.

AK

I held my breath, my index finger hovering over the touch pad. I clicked, waited, and then a box popped up.

Message Undeliverable: Unknown Recipients

I gave a yell of frustration and pushed back from the table. From the bedroom Op Nine moaned loudly, as if in answer.

His body jerked on the bed and his head lolled back and forth on the pillow. His color, never very healthy looking, now looked even worse, a kind of burnt orange, and spit rolled from his open mouth. I went into the bathroom for a fresh washcloth and caught my reflection in the mirror.

I froze. Red spots with white centers the size of nickels had appeared all over my face and neck. I touched one on my cheek. It was like pressing the head of a hot match against my skin, and I yanked my finger away. What now? What the hell were they doing to me now? I pulled the sweater off and lifted the shirt underneath. The marks were there too, and on my back. I was covered in boils.

"Okay," I muttered, dropping my shirt and ducking my head over the sink as I wet the washcloth. "Okay. Pustulating boils. That's fine. You wanna play hardball. I can take it."

I returned to the bed and wiped Op Nine's face.

"I can't get through," I told him. "I don't know, maybe headquarter's been destroyed or something. We're on our own and since I can't get through to you either, I guess that means I'm on my own. Not a happy development in terms of MISS-COMP."

He moaned, eyes jerking behind fluttering lashes.

"You guys did lie to me," I went on. "I'm the carrier. My blood is the active agent in the 3XD ammo. You must have taken a couple pints from me on the ship to put in your guns, and that's really low. That borders on the despicable. You could have just asked. But I guess being a SPA means you never have to ask. No wonder Ashley told you to take a hike. You're gonna have to answer for that, but you're not going to have a chance to answer because they've scooped you out too, and you can't help me find Mike or the devil's door and so everything's screwed. Game over."

His arms began to pull against the knotted towel, his fingers clawing in the air. I didn't have much time before he went for his eyes. I went back into the bathroom and smashed one of the drinking glasses in the sink, picked up the longest shard, and without even a second of hesitation cut my left palm open and walked back to the bed, my hand raised over the level of my heart, palm upward, cupping the blood.

I sat on the edge of the bed, dipped two fingers into the blood pooling in my palm, and smeared the blood over his eyelids, saying the whole time, "Now in the name of Saint Michael, I order you to be whole—though I oughtta . . ." Then I stopped, because a healing was no place for bitterness. "So be healed, Operative Nine, be healed."

I traced a cross on his forehead with my blood and then took my hand away. The moaning stopped, the eyes went still, and the hands relaxed. I gave his shoulder a little poke, but he didn't wake up. Something had happened, though.

I wrapped a hand towel around my left hand, dragged myself into the main room, collapsed on the sofa, and lay there for a few minutes before I got back up, went into the bathroom, and trimmed my toenails.

Then I went back to the sofa, threw an arm over my eyes, and fell asleep. It would be the last sleep I got for a very long time.

42

I don't remember what I dreamed during that last bit of sleep before my final showdown with the demon king. But when I woke up I knew my next move.

Op Nine was still flat on his back, but his eyes were open, staring at the ceiling. The towel must have come loose at some point while I slept, because his arms were crossed over his chest, the way they arrange dead people in caskets, and that unnerved me, like a portent of things to come.

"Op Nine?" I said softly.

His eyes rolled in my direction, but his head didn't move. The dried blood on his eyelids and forehead had turned a rusty red.

"What," he croaked, "is an 'Op Nine'?"

"That's complicated," I said. "But don't worry, your memory will come back. Mine did, so I don't see any reason why yours wouldn't. Here's the deal: we're in Chicago right now, but we won't be for very long. We've lost contact with HQ and so we're going solo. You've been attacked by demons, only you don't like that word, but sometimes you gotta call a spade a spade. My name is Alfred Kropp."

"Alfred Kropp!" His eyes widened. "I know that name!"

"I'm going to order some room service because I haven't had anything except a Snickers and a Coke—not counting the dead cat, which I'd rather not."

"Dead cat?"

"You want anything?"

He swallowed. "Perhaps some water."

"Bottled or tap?"

He didn't answer. I fetched a bottled water from the minibar and held it to his lips while he drank. He emptied it in about four swallows.

"Okay," I said. "I gotta make a phone call. Try to remember what you can."

I picked up the phone and dialed room service. It rang about fourteen times before somebody picked up.

"What?" they shouted.

"I'd like to order some breakfast," I said.

"Kitchen closed!" And they slammed the phone down.

I got up and looked in the bathroom mirror. The boils had popped open during my nap. I splashed some warm water on my face and yelped, clawing for a towel. The water burned like acid.

I came back to the bed.

"You know, I sat in that briefing listening to everybody discuss where Mike might have gone, and it never occurred to me that I might know exactly where he's gone. It's the obvious place, like Director Merryweather said. Too obvious, and that's why he went there. He knew it was obvious and he knew *you* knew it was obvious, so he went there knowing its obviousness was what made it un-obvious. So I've got one more call to make. You okay? You need to go to the bathroom or anything?"

He shook his head.

"Okay."

I dialed 411 and got the number I needed. Then I dialed the number and told the person who answered that I needed to talk to Mr. Needlemier right away. They put me on hold. The Beatles were singing "Yesterday."

"I am a priest," he said suddenly.

"Not anymore," I told him.

"No?"

"Now you're a demonologist working for OIPEP."

"OIPEP?"

"The Company. Only you may be unemployed because I'm not sure OIPEP exists anymore. I'm not sure what exists anymore."

The music stopped and the line crackled with static.

"Hello? Hello?"

"Mr. Needlemier," I said. "This is Alfred Kropp."

"Alfred Kropp!"

"You know, Mr. Samson's son."

"I know who you are, Alfred . . . Alfred, where have you been? And where in heaven's name are you now?"

"Chicago, but not in heaven's name."

"Chicago!"

"Mr. Needlemier, I don't have time to explain everything, but here's the important thing: I need to get a plane back to Knoxville ASAP."

" 'Giddyyap to Knoxville'? Alfred, I can barely hear you . . ."

"I said I need a plane! Pronto!" I shouted into the receiver.

"Tonto?"

"Pron! Pron! Not ton!"

"Not on? What's not on?"

"Plane!" I yelled. "Chicago! Can you get me one?"

"No planes, Alfred. All planes are grounded!"

I walked to the window and pulled back the curtains. The world was gray and shadowless, except for the orange flickering of the fire-rain and the fires that seemed to burn on every block.

"A car, then, the fastest you can find," I said. "I'm at the Drake Hotel. Did you hear me?"

"Yes, yes, Alfred. I'm writing this down. What kind of car did you say?"

"I didn't say. Just the fastest you can find. The fastest car in the world. And I need it in the next thirty minutes."

"Thirty minutes! Alfred, I don't know if that's possible—"

"*Make* it possible!" I yelled.

"All right. Fastest car. Thirty minutes. Drake Hotel. Anything else?"

"No. Yes. I need to know where the devil's door is."

"Devil's door?"

"Or the gate to hell. It might go by either name, or both. And I need the answer by the time I get to Knoxville."

"All right, all right. Devil's door. Hell's gate. What else?"

"Nothing. Wait, there is something." I told him what that something was, gave him the number of the hotel, and hung up.

I plopped Op Nine's bag on the bed, pulled out the

semiautomatic, and dropped it into my pocket. I opened one of the maps and spread it out over the bed while Op Nine watched.

"Are we fugitives?" he asked.

"More like refugees."

He sighed. "We are at war, then?"

I nodded. I was trying to use the key on the map to figure out how many miles lay between us and Knoxville. The last time I had tried something like that was in the third grade, but I figured five hundred and fifty miles. I folded the map and jammed it into my back pocket.

"What is in Knoxville?" he asked.

"A certain Hyena that I'm gonna pop in the nose when I find him."

He frowned. "A hyena?"

I nodded. "And the Holy Vessel of Solomon, I hope, because if I'm wrong and it isn't, this war is over and the world is toast."

43

Op Nine said he had to use the john, so I helped him into the bathroom and averted my eyes while he leaned against me and peed. Then he collapsed back onto the bed, breathing hard.

"I am too weak to travel," he gasped. "Leave me."

"Don't think I'm not tempted," I told him. "You pulled a fast one on me, Nine. You lied to me and used me, I guess because you're a SPA and you figured that gave you the right, but I don't care what's written down in your precious Charter, some things are just wrong and the whole world signing off on it doesn't make them right."

I shut down the laptop and stuffed it into the bag. My whole body felt as if it were on fire, and every time I moved, my clothes rubbed against the boils, which now itched as well as burned, making it very hard to concentrate, something I'm not that great at even in the best of circumstances.

I decided we should go on down to the lobby to wait for the car. That worked better in theory than in practice. I had Op Nine on one shoulder and the big duffel on the other, and it felt like any second I was going to topple over and land smack on my pustulating face.

The lobby seemed even more crowded and noisy than before. I managed to get us close to the revolving door so I could check out the street. I looked at my watch. Forty-five minutes had passed. I dialed Needlemier's number on Op Nine's cell phone and, after counting fifteen rings, hung up.

Five minutes later, a man in a gray suit with dark shiny hair appeared beside me and touched my elbow.

"Excuse me," he said.

He drew back a little when I turned to him. I guess he wasn't expecting Weeping Boil Boy.

"I'm Alfred Kropp," I said.

"I know who you are. My name is Gustav Dahlstedt, with the Koenigsegg Corporation."

"You're the car guy."

He nodded and smiled. "Alphonso Needlemier sent me. He said it was urgent, yes?"

"Urgent, you bet."

He touched the strap of the duffel. "May I?" I nodded, he shouldered the bag, and I followed him through the revolving door. Revolving doors are tough enough, but try doing it with somebody the size of Op Nine draped all over you.

It was freezing outside, but the tall buildings blocked most of the icy fireballs falling from the sky. We followed Mr. Dahlstedt into the alley beside the Drake. Parked beside a Dumpster was a low-slung sports car the color of a smoky sunset.

Mr. Dahlstedt's chest swelled a little as he said, "The Koenigsegg CCR, the fastest production car in the world, Mr. Kropp. Note the boldly shaped side air intakes and the front splitter, designed to optimize high speed aerodynamics."

"That's fantastic," I said. "Can you pop the trunk for me?"

He blinked. "There is no trunk."

He had the key ring in his hand. He pressed a button on the remote and both doors slowly rose and rotated forward. I lowered Op Nine into the passenger seat, grabbed the duffel from Gustav, and stuffed it into the little space behind Nine's head.

"The engine of the CCR is boosted by a bicompression Centrifugal Supercharging System," he went on, as if I wasn't fully appreciating my good fortune. "With twin parallel mounted Rotrex compressors, generating the one-point-four bar boost pressure needed to create the colossal output."

"Colossal output, gotcha," I said. On the hood of the CCR I noticed a silver logo of a ghost floating inside a circle.

"Ah, you have discovered our ghost. It adorns all our CCRs. An homage to the Swedish Fighter Jet Squadron Number One."

"I'm not too crazy about spirits," I said. He trailed after me, speaking rapidly now, like the spiel came with the wheels.

"Eight hundred and six horsepower extreme peak value at six-point-nine rpms. Zero to sixty in three-point-two seconds. Three-point-two *seconds*, Mr. Kropp."

I dropped my boil-covered butt into the driver's seat and put both hands on the tan, leather-covered steering wheel.

"How fast does it go?" I asked.

"Oh, now that is something we do not advertise," he said,

beaming. "We tell our customers 245 plus. The 'plus,' of course, relies upon road variables and your own conscience."

So Mr. Needlemier had taken me literally: I was behind the wheel of the fastest car in the world.

He handed the keys to me and I started the car. The thing woke up and growled.

Mr. Dahlstedt held out a credit card.

"At the direction of your company, for gas and incidentals," he said. I took the card. Platinum AMEX in the name of Samson Industries.

"Thanks, Mr. Dahlstedt," I said. "Thanks a bunch. How do I close these doors?"

He showed me the button and kept talking as the doors rotated shut.

"We appreciate your business, Mr. Kropp! My card is in the glove compartment. Do call if there is any—"

The doors snapped shut, cutting him off. I gingerly pressed down on the accelerator and the car leaped forward, like some kind of beast being let out of a cage. I made a hard left out of the alley, back wheels screeching and sending up twin plumes of white smoke.

Damn the road variables. And damn my conscience too. I was going to find out how much "plus" there was in 245 mph "plus."

44

Orange and white barrels blocked the on-ramp onto I-90. I didn't let the barrels concern me. Op Nine jerked in his seat when I took them out at sixty-five and his jaw clenched as I hit the interstate at ninety-seven. Then we really booked. After twelve minutes and taking out another set of barrels, we were on I-65 heading south toward Indianapolis pushing 240 miles per hour.

It was about ten o'clock in the morning, but it seemed like twilight under the low gray clouds spitting burning chunks of ice. The hell-storm was beginning to slack off though. I didn't know what that was about but maybe the demon hordes were honoring my request to back off so I could deliver the goods.

"There are faces in the clouds," Op Nine murmured. "Do you see them?"

I could see them. Distorted human faces that bulged and receded, some laughing, some snarling, some with hooded eyes and crooked noses and some blank as masks, which was scarier in a different way.

"Does the name Abalam mean anything to you, Alfred?" he asked, staring into the clouds.

"It sounds familiar."

"Is it my name?"

"I think it's the name of a demon. One of the lackeys to Paimon."

"Paimon?"

"He's the one who took the Seal."

He looked over at me. "The Seal?"

"The Seal of Solomon. This ring you use to control the demons. Only Paimon has it now, so he's in control."

"In control . . . of Abalam?"

"Of all of them. There's about sixteen million. Abalam's probably the one we met at Mike's house, and that's why you remember its name."

He shook his head. "This is all very strange. Very strange."

"You're telling me."

"We are two—against sixteen million?"

"More like one against sixteen million: You're at half speed right now and I've always been, so that's the math. Not very good odds, but you gotta hope. You told me that once. Do you remember?"

"I wish I could. But I am somewhat glad I can't."

I nodded. "Dude, I know the feeling."

The interstate was deserted. Occasionally we roared past abandoned cars parked in the median or in the emergency lane. The only moving vehicles I saw between Chicago and Louisville was a convoy of National Guardsmen, the soldiers crammed into the backs of canvas-covered trucks, and they craned their necks to stare as I barreled past them.

I turned on the radio. I expected every station to be talking about this first phase of the last war, but only the talk stations were jabbering about the crazy weather that had brought the entire world to a standstill. The music stations stayed with their programming, like the dance band on the *Titanic*. I found a PBS station out of Chicago where somebody from the government droned on about how the latest "meteorological crisis" demonstrated we still have a long way to go in our understanding of global atmospheric phenomenon. I laughed out loud.

"What?" Op Nine asked. "Why is that humorous?"

"Well," I said. "At least your personality's still intact."

I turned off the radio. He said, "What did you say my name was?"

"I didn't because I don't know. Your code name was 'Operative Nine.'"

"Why did I have a code name?"

"Because you're a Superseding Protocol Agent."

"And what is that?"

"It basically means the rule book's out the window."

"What rule book?"

"Every rule book." It felt strange to me, being the one in the know. "You work for a super-secret agency called OIPEP. Right now we're hunting down a rogue agent named Mike Arnold. Mike stole the Seals of Solomon from the OIPEP vaults or whatever you call them, and then he tried to kill me, I guess because he knew my blood was the only thing that could do some damage to the demons. But he lost the ring—I mean, *I* lost it—to King Paimon, and now Paimon wants the Vessel basically to avoid ever being shut up in it again. So you and me went to Chicago to hunt Mike down and to get the Seal from him—the Lesser Seal, not the Great Seal—only the demons got there before we did and they were waiting for us in Mike's house. You left me in the car and went in alone and I guess Abalam got hold of you and made you look into its eyes."

"I should not have done that?"

"Oh, you most definitely shouldn't have done that."

"I remember a whirlpool of fire and, in the center, utter darkness." He shook his head. "But that is all I remember."

I pulled off at the next exit for gas and to pee. There were three stations at this exit, but only one was open, manned by a very nervous clerk who kept playing with the metal stud in his bottom lip. He told me he was shutting down the station as soon as his girlfriend got there with the car and he didn't care if they fired him. Then he asked what happened to my face. I paid for the gas and some munchies with the company credit card and dropped Op Nine's snack into his lap.

"What is this?" he asked.

"A corn dog."

"Why a corn dog?"

"It's for luck."

He peeled off the yellow wrapping paper and took a bite, chewing it very slowly.

"Corn dogs are lucky? Is this something else I've forgotten?"

"I had one the last time I saved the world. Or actually, come to think of it, I had two."

He glanced at me. "You are an agent for this OIPEP?"

"No, I'm just an oversized kid whose hobby happens to be riding to the world's rescue."

"You are being facetious."

"I'm working on laughing in the face of despair."

I jumped back on the interstate and we drove in silence for a few minutes. The speedometer went up to 250, and the needle hovered just above the number. My driver's ed teacher had talked about "acceleration desensitization," the phenomenon where you get used to the speed you're going and are lulled into a false sense of security. But I didn't think there was any danger of my developing a false sense of security in this situation.

"So we still pursue this Mike Arnold?" he asked.

"You bet."

"To gain the—what did you call it?—Holy Vessel."

"Right."

"That we may do what with it?"

"Well, I've got about thirty hours left to rendezvous with Abalam and his boys at the devil's door."

"Devil's door?"

"Wherever that is."

"And there we will imprison them in the Vessel?"

"We can't. Nobody can without the Great Seal, and they have that."

"Then why do we bring them the Vessel?"

"So they won't consume the world."

"What is to stop them once they have it?"

"Nothing, I guess."

He was silent for a couple miles.

"This mission does not make sense to me," he said.

"Well, I'm doing the best I can. I don't have a choice now but to get the Vessel. If I don't get it, we don't have a prayer."

"We seem not to have one either way."

"We're smack dab in the middle of it," I admitted.

"The middle of what?"

"The place between desperation and despair. That's where my father told me Fortune often smiles."

I saw it then, a gray wall of smoke or fog looming up ahead. I eased up on the gas, but still we plunged into the fog at over two hundred miles per hour. Suddenly I couldn't see two feet in front of the headlights.

"This is quite dangerous," Op Nine said.

I ground my teeth and didn't say anything, gripping the wheel hard with both hands.

"Alfred," he said. "We must slow down."

"I'm not slowing down," I hissed between my grinding teeth.

With no points of reference, we hardly seemed to be moving at all. Of course, Op Nine was right. If I hit something going two hundred miles per hour, we'd be vaporized, but what choice did I have?

Mixed now with my fear was an expanding pocket of rage. What did they hope to accomplish with this? Did they want me to get the Vessel or not? My jaw was aching by this point and my fingers cramping from gripping the steering wheel so hard.

"Alfred, I really must insist—"

I lost it. "Look, buddy, you're not in the position to insist on *anything.* I've been literally put through hell because of you people and I think I'm doing pretty well considering I'm completely cut off from any help whatsoever, plus the fact that I'm slowly being driven mad with cracks in my brain and weeping pustules and the knowledge that when it really comes down to brass tacks, *there is no hope.* That's how they get you in the end, with hope, don't you understand? They dangle it in front of you and yank it away again—until you can't take it anymore."

He stared at me for a second. "In the medieval renderings of hell, the souls of the damned writhe in eternal agony as demons prod them with flaming brands."

"That's right! You got it!" I was sweating by this point, and the salt in my sweat burned in the open sores covering my body. I wanted to leap out of my own skin. "Flaming freakin' brands of fire!"

"Or the Greek story of Tantalus," he went on, "who in Hades suffered of starvation while a bunch of grapes dangled just beyond his reach."

"Damn straight!" I shouted. "Flaming brands up your ass, the itch you can't scratch, the grapes you can't reach!"

"Perhaps they torment you because it is already too late, Alfred. The day is lost and it delights them to torture you with hope."

"I'm not dead yet," I breathed. Then I shouted it at the top of my lungs. "I'M NOT DEAD YET, YOU HEAR ME? YOU GOT THAT? SO BRING IT ON! BRING! IT! ON!"

I shouldn't have said that.

45

I looked at my hands gripping the wheel and noticed the sores there had crusted over and were pulsing to the rhythm of my heart. A huge one on my knuckle itched horribly, and I started to scratch it, out of defiance, I guess (I'll show them I can scratch the itch!). My nail barely nicked the surface and the scab tore off. Clear liquid seeped from the wound and my heart quickened, not from the sight of the pus, but from the squirming gray-bodied, black-headed creature that rose from the little pool, twisting this way and that in the air, as if shaken from a sound sleep. I watched it in horror for a second, then took my hand off the wheel and held it under Op Nine's nose.

"What is that?" I asked.

"A maggot, I believe."

I could taste the corn dog on my tongue as I yanked the

rearview mirror toward my face. Fighting the nearly over-whelming urge to throw up, I gently ran my fingertips over my cheek.

The scabs burst open and a stench crowded my nostrils, that same smell I had noticed in the hotel room, the smell of decay—I was rotting from the inside out.

I screamed and Op Nine shouted, "Alfred!" as I slammed on the brakes, sending the car into a spin, until our rear wheels hit the grass on the edge of the road, which slowed us down enough to keep the car from flipping.

As soon as the car stopped, I hit the button to raise the door. I fell out onto the moist grass, on my hands and knees, retching. The fog wrapped itself around me and the car looked ghostlike in the shroud of mist.

I felt a hand on my shoulder, pulling me back.

I leaned against Op Nine's chest, crying and cursing. My hands flailed at my face until he grabbed my wrists and forced my arms down.

"Alfred," he said into my ear. "Alfred, tell me what to do. Just tell me what to do."

They will consume us, Op Nine had said in the briefing. *They will consume us.*

I looked into his face, the kindest, ugliest face I think I've ever seen. "Home," I croaked. "Get me home."

46

He helped me back to the car, but it was hard going because he was weak, I was big, and neither of us looked forward to hitting the road again. I sank into the passenger seat and he took the wheel, while I sat on my hands to keep myself from tearing open any more boils.

I glanced at the speedometer: forty-five mph.

"Faster," I murmured. The rank smell rising from my pores was making me dizzy and it took every bit of willpower I had to keep from giving in again to the nausea.

I watched the needle creep up to sixty.

"Faster," I said.

"Alfred, in these conditions . . ."

"We're running out of time!" I shouted. "And time's the only condition that matters now!" Then I shut up because the screaming hurt my throat. The needle hit eighty-five and kept inching higher. He squinted through the windshield, as if his squinting would somehow penetrate the white cloak around us.

My right arm twitched as I fought the urge to reach into my pocket, pull out the semiautomatic, and blow his hound-dog head off. It was like the feeling I had in the Taurus that night outside Mike's house, but ten times stronger and I fought it in silence for a few miles.

"There's something I need to tell you," I said finally. "Something you should know."

He nodded.

"I've been getting these urges to, um, hurt you. Kill you. It's almost more than I can stand."

He glanced at me.

"It's not me," I went on. "At least, I'm pretty sure it's not me. I didn't have homicidal urges before they got into me—at least, not like these. I guess it crosses everybody's mind and that doesn't make it right, just normal."

He nodded. "I have had similar thoughts."

"About me?"

He nodded again. "Since I woke in the hotel room. I came close to leaving you back there by the roadside. The urge was almost overwhelming."

"I can still tell which ones are their thoughts and which ones are mine. But the line is getting thinner between them. I'm scared that I'll reach the point when I can't tell the difference."

I pulled the gun from my pocket. He looked at it, and then looked quickly away.

"It would be useless against our enemies, would it not?" he asked.

I nodded. It comforted me in a strange way, holding it.

My head hurt and my vision began to cloud. *Kill him. He betrayed thee and lied to thee. Kill him!*

I rolled down the window and wind whipped into the confines of the little cockpit. He wasn't looking at me. His whole body tensed, waiting.

I threw the gun out the open window.

For the rest of the drive, I spoke only to tell him to go faster, because without realizing it, I think, he would slowly back off the gas, and I would say, "Faster, faster."

There was fire in Louisville and Frankfort; we could see the fuzzy orange glow of it burning through the fog. I had lost all sense of time. When we were about a hundred miles north of Knoxville, I dialed Needlemier's number on Op Nine's cell phone.

"Hello, Alfred." The line was staticky, but I could hear the tremble in his voice behind the pop and crackle. "Everything's been arranged."

"About an hour," I said. "Meet us at the airport."

On impulse, I hit the speed dial for headquarters. I didn't get a recording. I didn't get anything. The line just went dead without ringing.

The fog was so thick on Alcoa Highway that Op Nine missed the airport entrance, and we had to pull a U-ie to get back. A silver Lexus was the only car in the parking lot. I wondered what Mr. Needlemier thought when he saw us stumbling toward him, two broken-down, slumping shapes, leaning on each other as they emerged from the fog.

"Alfred . . ." He took a step forward. "Dear Lord, what has happened?"

"Practically everything," I said. "Mr. Needlemier, this is—"

And Op Nine said, "Samuel." He looked as startled as I must have looked. "Yes, I remember! My name is Samuel."

"Great," I said. "Now you'll have to kill me."

"The first order of business is getting the two of you to a doctor," Mr. Needlemier said.

"No," I said. "There's no time."

He opened the door to the backseat and we slid inside.

"There's a duffel bag in the CCR," I told him. He left to fetch it.

"How much farther?" Op Nine asked. His face had gone the milky white color of the fog.

"He's in the mountains south of here," I said. "About a thirty-minute drive."

"You are certain of this?"

"I'm not certain of anything anymore."

Mr. Needlemier dropped the duffel into the trunk. He came to my side carrying a long thin box.

"You got it," I said.

"I got it. But faced many uncomfortable questions while getting it. Horace Tuttle is not a trusting fellow."

"Horace Tuttle is a jerk," I said.

"What is it?" Op Nine asked.

I opened the box and drew it out. "The blade of the Last Knight of the Order of the Sacred Sword of Kings."

47

Of course, we had to rely upon my memory to reach Mike's hideout, and my memory wasn't great, plus the fog had thickened and Mr. Needlemier crawled along, even when I yelled at him to speed up.

"Where is Hell's Gate?" I asked him.

"Ah, I've done some research on that," he answered, and passed a folder back to me. Inside were several pages printed from the Internet.

"The first Hell's Gate we found is in Kenya," Mr. Needlemier said. "There is another Hell's Gate located in British Columbia and a third in New York City. However, the only mention we could find of a 'hell's gate' that is also called 'devil's door' is in Florida."

"Florida?" I asked. I turned to the last page in the file.

"Called 'Devil's Millhopper,'" Mr. Needlemier continued.

"What's a millhopper?"

"A place where corn is held before it is ground into meal."

"A grinder?" I studied the picture. Shot from the top of a winding wooden stair leading to the rim, the picture showed a black hole about five hundred feet across, rimmed by tangled undergrowth and the tops of trees growing in the bottom of the pit. "You grind things up in it?"

"Yes. The oldest legend surrounding the millhopper concerns an Indian princess who was sucked into the hole by the devil. It is well known in the literature for, and I quote, 'devouring sinners.' Of course, geologists believe it is actually a sinkhole."

"That's it," I said, slapping the file closed. "That's the one they mean."

"How can you be sure?" Op Nine asked.

"It's the only one that goes by both names. Plus the grinder reference. It's their style."

"Whose style?" Mr. Needlemier asked.

"The demons," Op Nine answered.

"The demons! Alfred, what have you gotten yourself into?"

"Well," I said. "At least it's not something really bad, like drugs or alcohol."

A sign materialized in the swirling mist. It was the sign for the park entrance.

"There!" I said. "Right before the sign, that gravel road."

"That road?" Mr. Needlemier asked. "Alfred, that road appears to go straight up."

But he turned onto the road, and the gravel crunched beneath the tires of the Lexus. I sat holding the sword between my legs and it comforted me somehow. We crawled up the side of the mountain, the needle on the speedometer barely register-ing. I could see sweat shining on the back of Mr. Needlemier's bald head.

"What is our plan?" Op Nine asked.

"I don't have one," I said.

"Perhaps this is the time to develop one."

"It was hard for me to plan even when I wasn't slowly go-ing mad."

Mr. Needlemier looked at me in the rearview mirror.

"Is this Mike person armed?" Op Nine asked.

"Oh, you can bet on it."

"But we are not."

"Just the demon blasters. They'd blow a hole in him the size of Nebraska."

"Do we wish to do that, though? Blow a hole in him the size of Nebraska?" Op Nine asked.

"Timing's everything," I said. "First we get the Vessel; then we blow a hole in him the size of Nebraska."

"To what purpose, if we have the Vessel?"

"He's the cause of it all," I said, my face growing hot. "He's responsible."

"I still do not understand. Why do you need to kill him, Alfred?"

"One word," I said. "Maggots."

We reached the final crest before the road leveled off at the top of the mountain. I ordered Mr. Needlemier to stop the car. We got out. It was very cold. The fog of our breath mixed with the fog that had wrapped itself around the world.

We gathered around the open trunk. I loaded fresh clips into the 3XDs and handed one to Op Nine. I stuck the sword into my belt and said to Needlemier, "Stay here with the car."

He nodded rapidly, looking relieved. Op Nine was staring at the 3XD.

"What is this?" he asked.

"Your life's work."

"I made this?" He slowly shook his head. "A weapon! Seems a waste of a life."

"Well, they've come in pretty handy. You put my blood in the bullets."

"I did?" He shook his head again.

"What are you going to do, Alfred?" Mr. Needlemier asked. His voice had gone high-pitched in his excitement.

"That which must be done," I said, and started up the last hundred feet to the top of the mountain.

48

For once the fog was a blessing. There was no way Mike could see our approach, unless he had infrared cameras mounted in the eaves.

I whispered to Op Nine, "Cover the porch on the back side. I'll take the front."

He nodded and faded to my left, disappearing into the fog with barely a sound. I crept toward the front of the cabin, which emerged slowly from the mist as I came closer. There was a deserted feel to it, and I had a sinking feeling I had made that same awful mistake I always made: going with my gut.

I mounted the steps and pressed my ear against the front door. Silence. I held the 3XD loosely in my right hand. I took one step back, a deep breath, then raised my right leg and with two good sharp kicks busted the door right off its hinges.

So much for stealth.

I lunged into the entryway, sweeping the 3XD in an arc from right to left.

"Mike Arnold!" I yelled. "It's Alfred Kropp! I know you're here! We've got the cabin surrounded. Come out with your hands up and nobody gets hurt!"

He didn't come out. Instead he came from behind, throwing one arm around my neck and grabbing my right wrist, whipping my hand behind my back and lifting it high toward my neck. His thumb pressed between the two little bones below my palm and I cried out, dropping the 3XD at his feet.

"No, Al," he whispered. "Somebody *is* going to get hurt."

I butted his face as hard as I could with the back of my head. He grunted and I heard something crunch; maybe I broke his nose. He stumbled backward, his grip loosened, and I used the opportunity to rip free. I turned, and a fist landed in my gut—which I inevitably led with—and I doubled over. The next punch landed against the side of my head and I fell to my knees.

"Jeez, what is that *smell*? Don't tell me that's you, Al."

He was standing right in front of me. I dove forward, wrapping my arms around his knees. He fell backward as I pushed hard with my legs, and my momentum carried us both off the stoop and onto the wet rocky ground. He tried to kick free, but I tightened my grip, so he went into a roll, carrying us away from the cabin, down the slope toward the drop off to the ravine. We jounced over the rough ground, picking up speed as the incline grew steeper. As my luck had it, my legs reached the edge first and I kicked frantically, trying to find a foothold in the empty air. I lost my grip at that point, sliding on my stomach, and I clawed at the dead grass and dried leaves and shards of clay, trying to find a handhold before I fell four hundred feet to the bottom of the ravine.

He grabbed my left wrist, but I kept going down, until his smiling face emerged over the edge.

I looked down between my dangling feet and saw a sea of white, churning rivulets of mist weaving between the glistening brown trunks of the pine trees below.

I think I did break his nose: it looked swollen, and blood covered the lower half of his face. Red rings had already formed beneath both eyes. Other than that, he looked no different, just the same ol' Mike Arnold smiling down at me with blood-covered teeth, smacking gum.

"Al Kropp, you know the story about the bad penny? What happened to your face, man?"

"Pull me up," I gasped.

"Why would I do that, Al?"

It was a good question.

"I'm not going to hurt you . . ." I said.

He laughed and I saw the tan piece of well-gnawed gum roll over his tongue.

"Naw, why would you want to do that?"

"I just need the Vessel," I said. "Give me the Vessel and I promise—"

"You promise? Oh. You promise. Make a pinkie swear and then I'll pull you up."

I reached over to my left side and pulled the black sword from my belt.

"Oh, what's this?" he sneered. "Huh? Whatcha gonna do with that, Al? Cut off my hand?" He laughed. "Drop it and maybe I'll pull you up."

He was right. What was I thinking? His hand was my lifeline—it was suicide to even think about it.

Mike's smile faded when a loud voice boomed out behind him.

"Michael Arnold! Stand up slowly with your hands in the air or I will blow a hole in you the size of Nebraska!"

Op Nine. Mike recovered from the shock quickly. He smiled at me. "Well, you heard the man, Al. I got no choice."

He started to let go. I screamed Op Nine's name and at that moment something thin and black rose over Mike's head . . . then came whistling down. His whole body jerked, his fingers went limp, and as I slipped free another hand shot over the edge and caught me. A shining bald forehead appeared first, then a smiling baby-face.

"Hello, Alfred," Mr. Needlemier said.

PART FOUR
The Fall of Alfred Kropp

49

We laid Mike on the sofa in the cabin's main room.

"I heard the commotion and followed the noise," Mr. Needlemier explained. His face was flushed by the all the excitement or exertion—or maybe both. He had used the tire iron from the Lexus to take Mike out. "I suppose the fog helped cover my approach and of course he was distracted by Samuel here—but I didn't kill him, did I?"

"No," Op Nine said. "He lives."

"Not for much longer," I growled, and I shouted into Mike's face, "Where is it, Mike? Where's the Vessel?"

"Alfred," Op Nine said softly. "He can't hear you."

We searched the cabin for two hours, from the rafters to the floorboards. We checked the crawlspace and under the porch. We walked the grounds, looking for any signs of digging. I had gone through the bedroom twice before realizing I forgot to look under the bed.

I didn't find the Vessel under there, but I did find a laptop computer. An IBM ThinkPad. I carried it into the main room, set it down on the coffee table, and booted it up.

"What is this?" Op Nine asked.

"It's an OIPEP computer," I said. "Maybe after he was fired, Mike stole it like he stole the Seal, but I don't think so. I've got a very bad feeling about this."

"OIPEP?" Mr. Needlemier asked. He looked like somebody trapped in a nightmare. I knew the feeling. "What is an OIPEP?"

"Good people who sometimes have to do bad things," I muttered.

It seemed to take forever for the screen to pop up, and my stomach did a slow roll when it did.

Op Nine and Mr. Needlemier crowded over my shoulder, and the three of us stared at the screen.

Integrated Security
Interface System
[ISIS]

<u>User Warning</u>: Use of this Interface is restricted to Company personnel with Security Clearances of A-17 or above.

Any unauthorized access of this System will result in immediate termination and forfeiture of all rights and privileges granted to personnel under Section 1.256 of the OIPEP Charter.

For Security Protocols related to use of ISIS, see Section 4 of the Charter.

<u>User Login:</u>

<u>Password:</u>

" 'Isis,' " Mr. Needlemier breathed.

Mike still lay out cold on the sofa beside us. I pushed Mr. Needlemier out of the way and jabbed Mike's shoulder.

"Mike! Wake up!"

"That won't be necessary," Op Nine said softly. His long fingers raced over the keys.

I stared at him. "You remember?"

He smiled grimly. "A Superseding Protocol Agent has access to all user accounts."

I peered over his shoulder as he pulled up Mike's e-mails. Nobody said anything as he clicked them open, one by one.

"What's 'Sub-Sub-Sec Op Utopia'?" I asked.

" 'Sec Op' stands for 'Secret Operation,' Alfred. A Sub-Sub-Sec is an operation of the highest secrecy—director's eyes only."

"And Utopia?"

He shook his head. "Never heard of it."

Mr. Needlemier spoke up. His voice was shrill with excitement. "I have! A utopia is a perfect society!"

Op Nine stared at him without expression.

"Well," Mr. Needlemier said. "It is."

"This is very curious," Op Nine said. "The Charter mandates that Section Nine operatives be briefed on all sub-sub-sec ops."

"Aquarius," I said. "I've seen that name before, on your computer."

"Aquarius," Op Nine said, "is François Merryweather, the director of OIPEP."

"That does it," I said. I grabbed the 3XD out of Op Nine's hand and jammed it under Mike's chin.

"Mike!" I yelled. "You've got to the count of three!"

"Alfred," Op Nine said. "If you do this, we may never solve this riddle."

"You don't remember," I shot back. My voice was shaking pretty badly and tears stung in my eyes. "You don't know everything he's done. Not just to me, Op Nine—Samuel . . ." It felt weird, calling him Samuel after knowing him for so long as Op Nine. "But to everyone."

"Killing him will not change that," he answered.

"I don't care about changing it," I said. "I care about making him pay."

"How he pays is not your decision."

"Don't bring up God or heaven to me, Nine. Don't even go near there. I never saw much evidence of him *before* all this happened and I sure as hell haven't seen any *since* it all happened."

"Put down the weapon, Alfred," Op Nine said.

"Not till I've put *him* away."

Mike gave a loud moan and his eyelids fluttered. I poked his Adam's apple with the muzzle of the gun.

"Wake up, Mike!"

He moaned again. I brought my face close to his.

"It's over, Mike. We need the Seal and we need it now."

"Bi . . ." he whispered. "Bi . . ."

"Bye?" Mr. Needlemier said.

" 'By' what, Mike?" I asked. "What is it by?"

"Bite me," he gasped.

"No thanks," I said. "I think I'll just shoot you."

"Tell him we have her," Op Nine said.

I looked at him. Who did we have?

"Tell him we have his mother."

"You're bluffing," Mike said. "There's no way."

"Michael," Op Nine said softly, coming to stand beside me so Mike could see him. "Michael, you know me. You know what I am. You know Section Nine."

Mike's eyes had gone wide.

"I don't believe you," Mike said.

"I shall tell her that. I'll explain you didn't believe us."

"Shut up," Mike shouted. "Just shut your pie-hole, Padre. I'm not giving up the Vessel."

"The Great Seal has been lost," Op Nine said. "What use is the Vessel to you now?"

"Well, for one thing, it's the only thing that's keeping Al here from blowing my head off."

Op Nine smiled grimly. "Tell us, Mike, or I will give the order."

He held out his hand toward me. I got it immediately, and handed him his cell phone.

"Well, Padre, I love my mom, don't get me wrong, but I always thought my life might have turned out just a wee bit different if it hadn't been for her. You know how it is, Al—we got no choice when it comes to parents, and some of them are woefully underqualified."

"This is Nine," Op Nine said into the cell phone. "I am authorizing Execution Code Delta-Alpha-Tango. Repeat: authorizing Execution Code Delta-Alpha-Tango."

"Lemme talk to her," Mike said.

Op Nine was pretending to listen to the nonexistent person on the other end of the line.

"Yes. Advise her that the Hyena refuses to cooperate."

"Tell her self-preservation trumps familial loyalty!" Mike shouted. Then he said, " 'Hyena'? *That's* my target name?"

"Very good," Op Nine said into the phone. "Yes. Execute Delta-Alpha-Tango immediately."

"Wait!" Mike yelped. "Okay! Stay the code!"

"Stay," Op Nine said. The hand holding the phone dropped to his side. "Where is the Vessel, Mike?"

Mike took a deep shuddering breath. "I'm lying on it."

I groaned. We hadn't moved him to search. I grabbed him by the shoulder and rolled him off the couch. He hit the floor with a "whoomf!" I yanked off the cushions and threw them across the room. There was a cavity right in the center covered by a hinged door. I pulled the door open and brought out the Vessel. A lot lighter than I thought it would be, it was very plain, no fancy designs or markings of any kind, made of brass or bronze, I guess, the metal hammered very thin.

Op Nine flipped the cell phone closed and slipped it into his pocket. Then he turned to me and held out his hand.

"I said it was hope that separated us from them," he said to me gently. "But so does mercy, Alfred."

"Okay," I said. "But some things are unforgivable too."

I handed him the 3XD.

"There," Op Nine said in that same gentle voice. "You see, Alfred? He is here. You've just provided us with the evidence."

50

"What now?" Mr. Needlemier asked.

"Now some answers," Op Nine said. He pulled Mike from the floor and plopped him down on the sofa. "What is Operation Utopia?"

Mike started to smile, but the look in Op Nine's eyes killed it.

"A very noble cause that a very stupid kid ruined," he said after a pause.

"The Charter is explicit in regards to—"

"Oh, don't quote the Charter to me, Padre," Mike said. "This is bigger than the Charter."

"Your termination was a hoax, wasn't it?"

Mike looked away. Op Nine didn't seem to care.

"What was the director's intent, Michael?"

"In a word? World peace. Oops. That's two words."

"The director went outside the Charter, did he not? He arranged your phony termination, the extraction of the Great Seals from our Vaults . . . He wanted you to free the outcasts in order to—what?"

"You're the SPA. Isn't it as plain as the boils on Al's face?"

"Blackmail? The director would use the fallen to enforce world peace?"

"It's beautiful, doncha think?" Mike said. "Once we made our little demonstration in the desert, who's gonna have the guts to challenge the Company's new world order? No more petty dictators or rogue states mucking around with peace and security. Somebody breaks the rules, we break the Seal. Perfect. Or at least it was on paper. Of course, we never considered the Kropp factor." He looked at me. "One day I'm gonna kill you, Al, swear to God."

"OIPEP wants to take over the world?" I asked.

Op Nine shook his head. "Not OIPEP, Alfred. Merryweather. It seems our director has decided to throw the Charter out the window. We have been duped."

"That's okay," I said. "I'm getting used to it." I turned to Mike. "So that's why you tried to kill me? Merryweather knew about my blood and he was afraid it might be used to fight the demons?"

"Of course he knew," Op Nine said. "It was contained in your dossier. After Mike 'stole' the Seals, I gave the order for Ashley to extract you. I did not know for certain, but I hoped your . . . gift might be useful in the 3XD. Therefore Merryweather needed Mike to extract you first."

"In an extreme way," I said. I started for the door.

Op Nine said, "Wait, Alfred."

"We're almost out of time," I said. "We have only two hours to get to Florida."

"I'm not sure that is entirely wise," Op Nine said.

"We don't have a choice," I shot back. "They'll consume us if we don't go."

"But if we go, there is nothing to stop them from consuming us."

"Well, that's been the problem all along, hasn't it?"

"Game's over," Mike said. "There's no way out."

"I might be able to help," Mr. Needlemier said. "But nobody has bothered to tell me exactly what is going on with these Seals . . . and who this OIPEP is . . . and what these demons are . . . and . . . and et cetera . . ."

We ignored him.

"Look, Op Nine," I said. "It's just the two of us, and I was given a deadline in Chicago with the clear understanding that if I miss it, there's gonna be hell to pay—literally. I guess I made what you call a deal with the devil—more like sixteen million of them—but it was either that or lose all hope and that's about all that we have left."

Mike laughed. "What about your health, Al? Oh. Never mind."

"Where's that tire iron?" I asked Mr. Needlemier.

"Alfred, you do not understand them as I do," Op Nine said. "You cannot presume they operate in good faith."

"No, I'm presuming they're going to keep eating me until I'm used up. Not dead. I'm already dead. I'm the walking dead, Samuel—that's the message of the maggots. It's already too late for me, but maybe it's not too late for the world."

"Paimon will not risk returning to its prison. It will never surrender the Seal."

I took a deep breath. "Why don't we blow it up?"

He gave me a quizzical look.

"How much of my blood did you put in those bullets? It couldn't be more than a drop or two. What if we . . . used more?"

"Alfred," Op Nine said. "What you're suggesting—"

"I think that's a terrific idea," Mike said. "Let's blow Al up."

"I'm serious," I said. "If I can get close enough to Paimon . . . it might give you a few seconds."

"Hey, Saint Alfred," Mike said. "Where was the death wish at the ravine? You had the chance."

I stared at Mike for a long time. The ravine. His hand on my wrist. The black sword in my other hand.

I had it then. The answer popped into my head the same way all my memories had in the morgue.

I turned to Mr. Needlemier. "Where in Florida is the Devil's Millhopper?"

"Gainesville."

I turned to Op Nine. "I've got it now. I think I know what has to be done."

51

Mike trailed behind us as we trotted to the Lexus.

"Tell me the truth," he called after us. "You never had my mom, did you?"

Op Nine turned. "That is something you will not know until this is over—however it ends. You have been neutralized as a factor in this affair, Michael."

"I never liked you," Mike said. "And you can bet your bottom dollar the director's going to hear about this."

"Should we succeed, he will no longer be director and you will no longer be an operative. Both of you have violated our most solemn oath never to interfere with the affairs of any nation." His dark eyes glittered. "And by doing so, you have endangered the very thing you intended to preserve."

He got into the car. I slid in beside him and Mr. Needlemier closed my door. Soon we were heading back down the mountain. I looked through the window behind me and watched as the fog engulfed Mike Arnold.

"Now tell me what you intend to do, Alfred," Op Nine said. "What is it that must be done?"

I explained it to him. Neither he nor Mr. Needlemier said a word.

We were on Alcoa Highway, about two miles from the airport, crawling along in the dense fog, when I finished and Op Nine said, "It is madness."

"Well," I said, "in case nobody's noticed, I'm already leaning in that direction."

"But it has no hope of success."

"You know that isn't true," I said. "Paimon can't risk letting me die."

"Alfred, your life means nothing to Paimon."

"No, but the Vessel means everything. And I'm the key to it. Paimon won't risk losing the key."

He shook his head. I cleared my throat. "And anyway, if it doesn't work, you'll still have the Vessel and you can try something else."

He turned away then and looked out the window, though there was nothing to look at but his reflection in the glass. He reached over and put his right hand on my forearm.

"Alfred, I am sorry for all this. Sorry for bringing you to the nexus and sorry for lying to you."

"Why did you bring me to the nexus?"

"You were the carrier of the active agent. We had to be prepared for any contingency."

"You had the same idea—to use me for a bomb or something?"

He didn't say anything. He kept staring at his reflection.

"It's not easy, is it? Being a SPA."

He shook his head. "No." He started to say something else, but he decided to leave it at that, I guessed. "No."

The CCR was parked where we'd left it at the airport. Mr. Needlemier hung back, looking a little awkward, as I carried Op Nine's duffel and my sword to the supercharged sports car. I dropped the duffel into the passenger seat and stuck the sword into the space behind it. I went back to the Lexus.

"This is totally outside the range of my experience," Mr. Needlemier said. Then he added, unnecessarily, "I'm frightened, Alfred."

"Doing something helps," I told him. "Otherwise it just eats you alive. Do you know about the secret chamber beneath Mr. Samson's desk?"

He stared at me and didn't say anything.

"Guess not. There's a secret chamber under Mr. Samson's desk. The desktop lifts up and there's a keypad. The numbers correspond to letters just like on a telephone. The code is my name."

"Your name?"

"I don't remember the numbers off the top of my head, but the code is 'Alfred.' When you get it open, put the Vessel inside and lock it back down again. Understand?"

He nodded. "Yes, I understand. Is there anything else, Alfred?"

"I don't want to be adopted by Horace Tuttle."

"Of course, but you understand the final decision is up to the judge."

"And I don't want him to be the trustee of the estate. I want you to be."

"Me?"

"And if I don't make it back—and I probably won't—I want you to take all the money and give it away."

"Give it—who do I give it to?"

"I don't know. Find some worthy people. Start with the kids living with the Tuttles. Especially the kid named Kenny. Take care of him, Mr. Needlemier."

"Of course."

"I'm telling you this in case things don't work out. Anyway, I'm talking too much. I have to go. Good-bye, Mr. Needlemier."

Back at the CCR, I told Op Nine, "You're driving." I dug the old book from the duffel bag, along with a map. "I've got to study."

52

"We're taking I-75 all the way," I told Op Nine, tracing the route with my index finger. "It goes right through Gaines-ville."

I wasted about two minutes trying to refold the map. What is it about maps? Folding them is like trying to work a puzzle. I gave up and stuffed it behind my headrest. Then I opened *The Ars Goetia* and flipped through it, looking for the Words of Command.

Op Nine glanced over at me.

"If not spoken exactly, word for word, the command will fail," he pointed out.

"Thanks for the tip," I muttered. "There's about twenty different incantations here. Which one do I use?"

"The Words of Constraint."

That particular spell went on for half a page. Even on my

best days, I was horrible at memorization. I looked over at him.

Ask him, a voice whispered inside my head. *Ask and hear his answer!*

It didn't surprise me, hearing the voice. The whispering had been going on for a while, but I had been able to ignore it for the most part. Now it was louder, more insistent. I didn't wonder whose voice it was. I'd heard it before. It was the voice of Paimon, the voice of the demon king.

I cleared my throat. "I know this whole thing is my fault . . ."

It is thy fault, worthless carcass!

"And probably since I'm the one who screwed things up I should fix them, but wouldn't it make more sense if you did it?"

Now listen as he abandons thee!

"I mean," I added when he didn't say anything, "you already know these spells, right?"

Op Nine didn't look at me. His hands tightened on the steering wheel.

See? Thou art alone. There is no one to help thee.

I rubbed my temples and said, "They're talking to me. Inside my head. Do you think they know what I'm thinking?"

"I don't know, Alfred."

"Because if they do, they know what the plan is and there's no hope."

He echoed me, nodding. "No hope."

"Well, at least this way I'll never be lonely," I said, trying to make a joke, but he didn't laugh.

"I hear them too, Alfred," he said quietly. "But I do not

think we are possessed in the layman's sense of the word. I believe what we are hearing are our own doubts and fears, amplified tenfold."

"What the heck does that mean?"

"What we fear," he said. "Our own voice of despair. The secret gnawing doubts we all have. They turn them upon us."

Stupid, pathetic, disgusting loser! Dost thou believe we can be overcome by the likes of thee? Before Time was, we have been and shall always be! Who art thou disgusting mound of rotting flesh to challenge our dominion!

The fog was thicker than ever. With no points of reference, it didn't seem as if we were moving at all.

"We're not going to make it in time," I said. "So let's just pull to the side of the road and wait for the end."

"Alfred," he started, and then stopped. Something up ahead had caught his attention.

A hole had appeared in the fog, its sides perfectly smooth and round, the opening about twice the width of the car. It looked like the mouth of a tunnel.

Come to us now, carcass. Bring us the Seal.

"They've decided to help us," I said.

He grunted and didn't say anything. He had put back on the old Op Nine expressionless mask.

"Hit it," I said, and Op Nine floored the gas.

We hit the tunnel at 230 mph and the fog in the "walls" spun and twisted with our passing. I looked behind us and saw the tunnel collapsing, closing us off.

"This isn't going to work," I said after a hundred miles had slid by and the words on the page had become black blobs swimming before my eyes.

"You should try to sleep," he said.

I shook my head. "What I'd really like to do is brush my teeth. I can't remember the last time I brushed them. You know, they're the one thing about my personal appearance I actually took pride in." I ran my tongue over the front ones and my left incisor jiggled. Knowing what was going to happen didn't calm me any as I reached into my mouth and gave the tooth a gentle push. It broke off in my mouth. I spat the tooth into my palm.

"What is it?" Op Nine asked.

The coppery taste of blood in my mouth. The broken tooth in my hand. The weeping sores all over my body.

"Alfred?"

I flung the tooth to the floorboards and, knowing I shouldn't, reached back into my mouth and tugged at one of my molars. I heard a squishing sound as it pulled free from the gum.

"Jerks," I breathed. "Those dirty, demonic jerks!"

I hurled the molar against the windshield. Op Nine whipped his head in my direction as I began to stamp my foot as hard as I could, throwing such a fit he must have thought this time I had really lost it. He took his foot off the accelerator and I screamed at him to speed up.

My hissy fit didn't last long; hissy fits take energy, and I didn't have much left. In fact, I didn't have much of anything left: I ran my hands through my hair and huge wads of it came away in my fists. By this point the fact that my hair was falling out left me numb.

Bit by bit since that night in the Sahara, they had been chipping away at me and I thought I would be just a nub of myself by the time we reached the devil's door. Nub-o'-Kropp. The skin felt loose on my body and I wondered if it might start sloughing off like a snake's, leaving my muscles and tendons exposed like those 3-D models they use in science class to teach human anatomy.

I sat back in the seat, gasping and snuffling, and Op Nine didn't say anything but kept his hands tight on the wheel and his eyes fixed on the tiny black hole straight ahead, and after a while I noticed the tunnel's walls had changed color from cotton white to deep yellow. After a few more miles the yellow had darkened to a dusky orange.

"What's going on?" I asked. Op Nine didn't answer. I said, "You talked more before you knew who you were. What is it— too dangerous to talk? Something classified might slip out?"

"My memory returned at the cabin. I was in the back when I heard the fight by the front door. I followed the sound and saw you and Mike rolling down the hill. At that moment it all came back to me."

"When it came back to me, it hit like a freight train."

"Yes. My experience was similar."

I flipped the book back open to the incantations, and tore the page containing the Words of Constraint from the binding. He winced at the sound. Then I folded the page into quarters and jammed it into the front pocket of my Dockers.

"You realize there will be very little oxygen," he said. "There is a strong likelihood you will pass out."

I thought about telling him there was a strong likelihood I would take the heavy book in my lap and smack him over the head with it, but I didn't say anything.

"Or freeze to death."

"*Okay . . .*"

"And your entire plan hinges on the assumption of anthropomorphism."

"Yeah, I was worried about that," I said. "The anthropomorphism."

"They do not think as we do, Alfred. Paimon may decide to find another way to the Seal."

"Then why send me to find it in the first place? They had the chance to kill me in that house in Evanston. Why didn't they?"

He pursed his lips, his eyes glued to the road.

"You know why, don't you?" I asked.

"I have a theory."

"I'd love to hear it."

"I don't know if that would be wise."

"Right. Not wise. Like taking my blood from me was."

"You know why we didn't tell you."

"The First Protocol?"

He nodded. I said, "But you can supersede the First Protocol, right? You're the SPA; you can ignore all of them if you want. Anyway, it makes sense now, why you kept me so close afterward. Had to protect your source of the active agent, didn't you?"

My teeth jiggled in their sockets as I talked, so I tried to move my tongue as little as possible, which slurred my words and made me sound like a dental patient, my mouth stuffed with cotton.

"For years, Alfred, I worked to build a weapon that had the potential to control an intrusion agent, but the difficulty was finding an active agent—until Dr. Smith showed me your dossier immediately following Mike's theft of the Seals. It occurred to me your blood might have certain properties . . ."

"So once you had me on the *Pandora*, you drained my blood through my armpit and stuck it into the bullets."

"We were desperate."

He betrayed thee once! He will betray thee again!

The walls of the tunnel had darkened to bloodred. I figured we were getting close to the door.

"I'm going to get one of these cars when this is over," I said. I figured maybe if I kept talking the voice inside my head would shut up. "Girls might notice me then. But I'd have to follow the speed limit and I'm thinking that would seem really slow now that I've taken it to the max. I think I would resent them. I mean traffic laws, not girls. Is that what happens once you start ignoring the rules, Samuel? I've got this feeling that when I'm back in school I'm going to laugh in the face of my math teacher when she hands out the tests. I used to sweat buckets before a test, get sick to my stomach, get the shakes. I don't think that's going to happen now. And I was scared to death of girls, especially the pretty ones, but after this, girls are cake. Except it might be hard getting a date with no teeth and smelling like a sewer pipe."

Op Nine took a deep breath and said, "There is always tension, Alfred, between the life we want and the life we find." He eased off the accelerator and added, "The tunnel veers to the right ahead. I think we have reached the exit."

53

I checked the time as Op Nine bore right onto the exit ramp.

"About thirty minutes to spare," I said. "That's good. I'm not usually this punctual."

The car shook suddenly as thunder crashed overhead.

"I figured they'd pull out all the stops: thunder and lightning, ice and fire from the sky, earthquakes, tornadoes, tsunamis, you name it. It's very biblical, but you read the Bible and half the catastrophes are caused by God. You were a priest. What's that about?"

After about half a mile, the tunnel made a sharp left, then a right, and coming out of this turn we saw it, a spinning mass of orange flecked with white, directly ahead. Where the red walls of the tunnel met this light was a ring of pure white flame, and I thought of the circus and the flaming rings they made those poor big cats jump through.

Op Nine slowed to a crawl, and maybe a hundred yards

from this burning mouth before the devil's door, he brought the car to a full stop and turned off the engine.

"This is folly, Alfred," he murmured.

"Shut up," I said.

"Madness."

"Cut it out, will ya? What kind of pep talk is this?" I started to shiver, though it was warm inside the car. My lower jaw was jerking up and down as I shook and I was afraid the rest of my teeth would shatter. "You're supposed to be comfor—comforty—*comforting* me. You must have been a lousy priest."

"I *was* a lousy priest."

I looked over at him. He was staring into the mouth of fire.

"Samuel," I said. "What did you see in Abalam's eyes?"

"You know what I saw."

"Abkhazia?"

He nodded. I could see the orange and white fire reflected in his dark eyes.

"Abkhazia, near the Black Sea, and home to Krubera, the deepest cave on earth. The Company had received reports of . . . unusual phenomenon in that region, the most compelling of which came from a team of *National Geographic* explorers, who had descended to the five-thousand-foot mark of the cave before abruptly returning to the surface. You know the area of my expertise, Alfred, so I needn't tell you the nature of those most unusual reports and what drove a team of experienced, highly regarded scientists to abandon their quest to reach the deepest recesses of Krubera. There are some things deep within the belly of the earth that should never be disturbed.

"On July 18, 1983, two of us were inserted into Krubera. Myself and the very best operative the Company had at the time—a young man with a brilliant future, a protégé of mine who idolized me and who would obey any order I gave, no matter how ridiculous. These are the kind of agents OIPEP looks for, Alfred. Men and women who are willing to challenge the very gates of hell itself for the sake of the mission." He gave a bitter laugh. "The mission!"

"On the third day of our descent, as we reached the four-thousand-foot mark, an earthquake struck, as is common in that region. I would like to say it was borne of natural causes . . . but I cannot say that; even to this day, I cannot say that. The cave collapsed a thousand feet above us, burying us under three tons of rock. We had carried in enough water and rations to sustain two people for seven days."

He swallowed hard, and I watched his prominent Adam's apple bob up and down.

"Or one person for fourteen days," he added.

"So your friend was killed in the earthquake?" I asked.

"No. No, Alfred. We survived the quake with only minor injuries."

"But Ashley said you were the only one to come out alive."

He nodded. "The Company dispatched a rescue team at once, for our communications to the surface had not been lost. They radioed down to us an estimate of the time it would take to dig us out . . . thirty days."

He fell silent. The silence went on and on. I was shaking so badly by this point, my neck had begun to hurt.

"So . . . so he starved to death? But if you were down there for a month, how did you keep from starving too?"

"He did not starve, Alfred."

"Well, if he didn't starve, then . . ." I stopped. "Oh, God. You didn't."

"You said before that I supersede the First Protocol. It is more accurate to say that I *am* the First Protocol. I am the personification of it. I am the Superseding Protocol Agent, the Operative Nine. I am the mission, and the mission must survive."

He looked at me then, the first he had looked at me since he began his story.

"And I did that which must be done to preserve the mission."

I cleared my throat. "It still doesn't add up. Thirty days to get you out and you had rations for only two weeks. How did you . . . ?"

I waited for an answer, but I already knew the answer and it struck me suddenly how cruel I was being, asking him to give it.

"So you see, Alfred, sometimes it is a good thing to be a Section Nine operative. To have no name and no past and no . . . barriers. It is codified absolution. Sometimes, when I can't sleep, I read the section over and over, like a dying man reads the Scriptures to quell his terror. But the comfort it gives is fleeting. For whatever remained of Father Sam before Abkhazia died in the abyss called Krubera."

54

He was staring at the juncture where the tunnel of smoke met the rings of fire.

"Samuel," I said. "Time's up. We have to go."

"I can't go with you, Alfred," he said.

"What do you mean you can't go with me?"

He turned to me and tears were in his eyes. "You spoke of that place—the point between desperation and despair. I know that place well, Alfred. And we have been there, you and I, since the Seal was lost."

"This isn't you," I said. "It's them. Don't let them do this to you, Samuel. I need you. I don't think I can do this without you."

"We have been fools, Alfred. It was over the moment Paimon obtained the ring. It is Krubera repeating itself, except this time there is no hope of rescue. There is no hope at all."

He leaned in and whispered, "Do you know why they

hate us so much, Alfred? Because of hope. They have none, and so they hate us for it. But I think they hate you most of all, for the power of heaven itself courses through your veins. Their hatred of you is only exceeded by their fear. It was fear that stayed their hand in Evanston, fear of what might be released should they kill you."

He fumbled in his pocket and brought out the same metal flask he had used in the desert, before our assault on the demon hordes. He unscrewed the top and shook some of the water onto his trembling fingers. His voice was shaking too, as he traced the sign of the cross on my forehead.

"*In nomine Patris, et Filii, et Spiritus Sancti.* God bless and keep you, Alfred Kropp, last son of Lancelot, Master of the Holy Sword, favored of Saint Michael the Archangel, Prince of Light, God's champion who hurled the outcasts from heaven—may he guard and bring you safely through this trial."

Then he made the sign again in the air.

"*In nomine Patris, et Filii, et Spiritus Sancti.*" He placed his hands on my shoulders. "Go now, Alfred. And may God go with you."

I had trouble forming the words, my teeth—the teeth I still had left in my head—were chattering so much. "I'd rather you did."

"I have come as far as I can go."

"Me too," I said. "But I've got to go farther. I've reached the end of hope too, Samuel, but I still gotta go farther because stopping here means I really am dead. I've been hugged by demons, but I've been hugged by angels, too, and that's why I'm going on. You can stay—but I'm going on."

I tried to think of something else to say, like the perfect

words existed that would change his mind and, if I could only think of them, he would come.

There wasn't anything he could do if he went, but at least I wouldn't be alone. More terrifying than the thought of facing them was the thought of facing them alone.

I punched the button and my door opened. I stepped out and pulled the black sword from behind the seat. I slipped it between my belt and pants.

"Will you wait for me at least?" I asked. He didn't say anything.

"Good-bye, Samuel," I said.

I stepped away from the car, the door rotated with a soft whine, and the sound of it snapping closed seemed very loud.

I walked toward the circle of light, my breath swirling around my head in the frigid air, and for some reason I felt twenty pounds heavier, as if they had done something to mess with gravity. Above me lightning flickered silently behind the opaque screen of fog, sometimes bright enough to cast a shadow of my shuffling self onto the frozen pavement that glistened with ice particles. I could barely lift my feet by that point.

I didn't look back. I didn't have the strength to turn my head. My mouth hung open a little as I gasped for air. The odor rising from my body was incredible. It made my eyes water. I had thought it was the smell of rotting fruit, but I knew now it was the stench of death.

Through my tears I saw glimmering shapes gathered around a huge hole in the earth, a black pit that the light above seemed to flow into, like water being sucked down a drain.

I had reached the devil's door.

55

My mind started to cloud with terror, that same paralyzing fear that I felt in the desert, beneath the tarp with Ashley, only this time there was no hand to grasp. I could barely move my legs by this point and every breath hurt.

"Saint Michael protect me," I blubbered around my broken teeth. My voice sounded muffled in my own ears. "Saint Michael protect . . ."

One of the glowing shapes standing before the pit moved forward, its crown shooting dazzling beams of blue and red and green light. I stopped as it approached, mostly because I didn't have another step in me.

On thy knees, carcass.

I went down with a whimpering sob at the feet of King Paimon. My chin fell to my chest. It was over. What was I thinking? I couldn't win against these things. Samuel was right. It was madness. Paimon would never believe the lie I was about to tell. That was the really weird thing about evil. Lying to God was better than lying to the devil: God will forgive you.

Where is the Seal?

"I don't have it."

I felt pressure like a massive fist closing around me, squeezing, and the image of Agent Bert blowing apart in the desert flashed through my mind.

"But I know where it is!" I choked out, and the pressure eased. "I—I'll take you to it, O Mighty King."

Nothing happened for a few seconds. Then something lifted me up until my feet dangled a few inches above the ground, and I hung there like a slab of meat on a hook.

A massive gray shape filled my field of vision, dominated by a slathering mouth and sharp teeth the size of the CCR parked in the fog-tunnel behind me. Its body was segmented like a worm's and it had no feet, but it did have huge, leathery wings folded against its twenty-five-foot body.

"I was going to trick you, but now I know I can't trick you. I'll take you to it," I sobbed. "I left it in Knoxville, and I'll take you to it . . ."

All I wanted to do at that moment was to please him, to give him what he wanted.

Then, quicker than I could take my next breath, I was on the monster's back, behind the towering form of Paimon, and we were rocketing skyward.

The concentric rings of sixteen million fiery riders broke apart as we approached, and then I couldn't see anything because we were passing through the clouds. Wind roared in my ears and red flashed behind my eyelids as the lightning snapped and danced all around us. Then my eardrums started to pop and a stabbing pain shot through my chest as the air grew thinner.

After a few seconds, I forced myself to open my eyes and, looking down, saw we had passed through the clouds. Above us were a billion stars and a bright moon that illuminated the ridges and little valleys of the clouds below, an unbroken sheet of fluffy gray carpet that stretched for as far as the eye could see.

And still the demon climbed, until black spots swam before my eyes. Breathing became almost impossible and my clothes froze against my skin. I didn't know if we were high enough yet, but I willed myself to hold on for a few seconds more—it would have to level off soon or risk killing me before we could reach the Seal. Everything rested on that—the assumption that it cared if I lived or died.

We leveled off. I closed my eyes again and saw the little kids playing soccer on the frozen field. I could hear them laughing and calling to one another as the ball slid and skittered over the ice. I needed to let go. And *they* needed me to let go.

"Let go, Kropp," I whispered. "*Let go.*"

And that's exactly what I did.

•

•

•

•

•

•

•

29,035 FEET

I slid off Paimon's back, and fell faceup, my back to the clouds below, so I saw the demon rider swoop around in a wide arc, receding as I dropped. I pulled the black sword from my belt, brought the blade against my chest, wrapped my left hand around the icy metal, squeezing tight, the tip of the sword just below my chin, and waited for the demon to descend upon me.

Saint Michael. Protect.

The screaming wind rocked me from side to side, threatening to flip me into a helpless, tumbling spin. It was like trying to stay afloat in the ocean during a hurricane. If I went into a spin, I wouldn't see the beast coming, and I had to see it coming. And it had to reach me before I hit the clouds. Once inside the thunderheads, I wouldn't be able to see well enough to pull my next move.

The monster's bulk was as black as the space between the stars, and it blotted them out as it rocketed toward me.

I waited until I could see Paimon's eyes shining with malevolent light as it stretched out its hand toward me, and then I yanked the blade downward. The sharp edge sliced into the palm of my left hand, as if my fist were a scabbard; and the howling wind tugged at the bloody sword when it came free of my hand.

I felt a blast of heat, and the demon was on me, leaning over the back of the flying worm, the light from its crown scorching my eyes. I jabbed my left arm into the air, like an offering. It grabbed me by the wrist and stopped my fall.

I could see it shining on its index finger about a foot above my uplifted face: the Great Seal of Solomon.

Our eyes met, mine and the demon king's, and everything I held inside poured out of me, like the light being sucked into the nothingness of the devil's door, and it knew my mind; it knew what I planned to do.

Saint Michael.

Protect.

I swung the sword over my head and smashed the bloody blade against its wrist.

There was an explosion of white light, the hand wearing the Seal broke free of the body, and I was falling again.

·

·

·

·

·

·

·

18,987 FEET

I hit the clouds at five hundred miles per hour, curling my body around the demon's hand, clutching it against my stomach as the sharp nails clawed into my wrist, trying to tear open my veins because, like Op Nine had said, that which has never lived cannot be killed.

I let go of the sword. I needed both hands now to get the ring. Wind buffeted me from all sides, slowing my rate of descent, and every hair left on my body stood on end as lightning crackled and popped around me. The sound was deafening, wind and thunder and the blood roaring in my ears.

I lost my grip on Paimon, and it scrambled up my body like a huge spider. Fingers colder than ice wrapped themselves around my throat, squeezing until black stars bloomed and multiplied before my eyes. My gut heaved and my shoulders jerked as I fought to breathe.

I hooked two fingers in the juncture between the thumb and forefinger and yanked with every bit of strength I had left. The hand tore free, and I felt the nails rake long gashes in my neck.

My right arm was shaking uncontrollably with fatigue as I grabbed the ring, pushing the twisting hand against my stomach with my left forearm, holding it still for the split second I needed—and a split second was all I needed—to rip the Great Seal off the finger.

I flung my left arm away from my body and the demon's hand shot straight up, disappearing into the churning mass of the thunderhead.

·

·

·

·

·

·

·

9,456 FEET

I had reached the heart of the storm. Updrafts flipped and spun me, slowing my descent slightly, as rain and quarter-sized hail pelted me from every direction.

I pushed the ring onto my left index finger.

Then I howled, competing against the howling wind, wondering if it mattered if the demon king could hear me, "I do conjure thee, O thou Spirit Paimon, by all the most glorious and—" And then I went blank, like I knew the whole time I would. I yanked the page containing the Words of Constraint from my pocket, because any rational person will tell you how easy it is to read as you plummet through a thunderstorm, your body pummeled by hurricane-force winds, the utter darkness punctuated by blinding flashes of lightning. It didn't matter anyway because the wind and hail shredded the paper in seconds, before I could even unfold it completely and bring it close enough to my face to read.

I was screwed. I would hit the ground at five hundred miles per hour and my body would disintegrate on impact, like a watermelon dropped from a skyscraper, and they would be finding pieces of me from Maine to Idaho. Paimon would get the ring and the war would be over. Everything would be consumed, all because I let my hatred of Mike Arnold get the best of me.

I crossed my arms over my chest and rolled so now I was falling facedown. I spread my arms and legs, knees slightly bent, the way I'd seen skydivers do, figuring this might slow me down. I had no idea if it did because I had no idea why skydivers fell this way; it might have nothing to do with their rate of descent. Maybe they just enjoyed the thrill of seeing the ground rushing up to meet them at 250 feet per second.

Saint Michael. Saint Michael, protect.

Wide shafts of light stabbed through the swirling rain and hail. I could hear demons above, screaming toward me at speeds faster than thought, and when they caught me, they would tear me to pieces.

5,134 FEET

I closed my eyes. I wasn't afraid anymore. That's the surprising thing. I wasn't afraid at all. And I wasn't cold either. Maybe I had passed out of the clouds too, because I didn't feel the sting of the rain or the bite of the hail. All I felt was warm and empty. It wouldn't hurt. You hit the earth at the speed I was falling and you don't feel a thing.

I could feel the heat of the demons against the back of my neck. I whispered, "I do conjure thee . . ." before trailing off because I couldn't even remember the demon's name at that point, and nothing seemed to matter much anyway.

Op Nine had said it was over the moment Paimon got the ring, but for me it was over years ago. And they knew that. It was over the day my mother died. That's why Paimon had called me *carcass*. Something died in me when she died.

They have seen your secret face, the face you hide from everyone, even from yourself. That was my secret face, twelve years old, scared of out my mind at the thought of losing my mom, of being alone. Scared of death. The demons saw that and gave back to me what I feared the most. My secret face was the face of a rotting corpse.

Saint Michael.

Protect.

·

·

·

·

·

·

·

3,789 FEET

A gentle glow appeared in the darkness behind my eyelids, and I felt a familiar comforting presence, something I
had felt before in a dream, and I heard a voice calling me
"beloved." Suddenly, all the fear and panic whooshed out of
me, and into the hollowness left behind poured a light so pure
and bright, no shadow could exist in it, and there was someone with me, though I couldn't see a face, but I could feel
arms around me as it spun and fell with me.

Speak, my beloved, and I will give thee words.

My mouth came open and there was no sound—no crash-
ng of thunder, no rush of wind, nothing but my own voice
roaring like a freight train.

*"I do conjure thee, O thou Spirit Paimon, by all the most
glorious and efficacious names of the Most Great and Incom-
prehensible Lord God of Hosts, that thou comest quickly and
without delay . . ."*

The words poured out of me as if I'd spoken them every day of my life.

"*I conjure and constrain thee, O thou Spirit Paimon . . . by these seven great names wherewith Solomon the Wise bound thee and thy companions in a Vessel of Brass.*"

The arms released me, the white light faded. I was through the clouds and the earth burned below me while the fire roared above me. The demons were closing in, but I was as calm as an old man on a park bench, feeding pigeons on a warm summer afternoon.

"*I will bind thee in the Eternal Fire, and into the Lake of Flame and of Brimstone, unless thou comest quickly and appearest here to do my will.*"

Out of the corner of my eye, I saw the ring on my hand begin to glow.

·

·

·

·

·

·

1,023 FEET

I could see the ground now—though there was no ground to be seen. Only a roaring fire, flames shooting hundreds of feet into the air toward me. It was like looking at the surface of the sun.

I pulled my arms and legs back toward my body and flipped onto my back. Countless orange balls of fiery light filled my entire field of vision, like burning meteors screaming toward the earth, and in the lead Paimon came, holding a flaming sword in its right hand, and the thing it rode came at me openmouthed, teeth shining in the light, flying faster than I could fall. I held my left fist straight up, pointing the ring at them as I finished the spell and hell's flames came rushing up to meet me:

"*Come thou Paimon! For it is not I but God that commandest thee!*"

.

.

.

.

.

.

.

476 FEET

The beast's mouth flung open and its foul breath washed over me as I whispered, because my howling was finished, *"Save me."*

And it caught me in its mouth with maybe four feet to spare above the roaring flames, carrying me in its teeth as gently as a dog carries her puppies. It deposited me on the scorched and smoking ground before swooping back into the sky.

I lay there for a very long time, blinking stupidly at the spinning shapes beneath the clouds, forming the wheels of fire, thousands of them one within the other. Then I didn't feel so warm and empty anymore, and I rolled onto my stomach, coughing and heaving, the ring on my left hand pulsing pure white light.

I raised my head a little and saw King Paimon standing

there, and it was just like the Sahara, except this time the ring burned on my hand, and this time Paimon kneeled to me, Alfred Kropp, beloved of the archangel who cast it down.

And it held in its right hand the sword that I had lost in my fall, the same sword the Last Knight had lost in another hopeless battle against the forces of darkness and despair. And the mighty Paimon, King of the Outcasts of Heaven, lowered its head, offering me the sword.

Command me.

PART FIVE
Homecoming

56

A little man with an egg-shaped head glared at me through the half-open front door while his wife and kids crowded behind him, trying to get a peek at me. "Yes, what do you want?"

"Horace," I said. "Don't you know who I am?"

I slipped off my Oakleys. His eyes grew wide and his mouth came open a little.

"Alfred?" he squeaked. "We heard you were dead!"

He flung the door open and I put a hand on his chest to abort his bear hug.

"Not anymore," I said. "Where's Kenny?"

There was a commotion behind him and I heard a voice call out, "Alfred! Alfred Kropp! Alfred Kropp! Alfred Kropp is back!"

Kenny pushed past Horace and buried his face in my chest.

"They came and took your sword, Alfred! I tried to stop them. I tried and tried and tried . . ."

"It's okay, Kenny," I said. "I got it back."

"You came back," he whispered.

"Told you I would. Didn't I promise I'd save you?"

I motioned to the man standing behind me. He stepped forward and cleared his throat.

"Good morning, Mr. Tuttle, how are you? I'm Larry Fredericks with the Department of Child Welfare. I have here a court order authorizing the removal of these foster children."

"You have *what*?" Horace barked.

"I said I have a court order authorizing . . ."

"Oh, dear!" I heard Betty gasp.

"This is outrageous!" Horace yelled. "I demand an explanation! I demand a hearing! I demand to know who is responsible for this!"

"That would be me," I said.

"You?" Horace's bottom lip bobbed up and down. "You, Alfred?"

"Me."

I wrapped my arm around Kenny's shoulders and led him to the silver Lexus parked by the curb. Horace kept yelling as the cruiser pulled into the drive with the sheriff's deputies.

I opened the door for Kenny and he asked, "Where are you taking me, Alfred Kropp?"

"You're going to stay with Mr. Needlemier for a while," I said, nodding toward his smiling, baby-faced bald head behind the steering wheel. "Until we can figure something out."

I looked back at the little house on Broadway. Horace had thrown a couple of strands of those old-fashioned Christmas lights with the fat multicolored bulbs on the bare branches of some azalea bushes the cold had killed, and had put out the same old faded light-up Santa (only it didn't light up anymore because the bulb was missing and he was too cheap to replace it).

It was two days before Christmas, and cold, but the sun was bright and the shade of the stunted dogwood by the front walk was sharp and hard-looking. I slipped the Oakley Razr-wires back on. My eyes had become sensitive to light.

"I'll see you back at the house," I told Mr. Needlemier.

"You're not coming with me?" Kenny asked, panic setting in.

"Sometime this afternoon, Kenny," I said. "I'm late for a meeting." As if on cue, the Bluetooth buzzed in my ear and I pressed the button next to my temple to answer.

"This is Alfred Kropp," I said. I closed Kenny's door and walked behind the Lexus to the CCR. I saw Kenny staring at me—or maybe I was flattering myself and he was really staring at the car—through the back window of the Lexus as Mr. Needlemier pulled slowly away from the curb. The deputies, Mr. Fredericks, and the Tuttles had gone inside the house. The place felt abandoned, but it probably felt that way because I was abandoning it.

"All right," I told the person on the other end of the line. "Tell her I'll be there in five minutes."

I climbed into the CCR and drove straight to the church, flooring the gas and heading north, past the bus station and the rescue mission and the old Fifth Avenue Hotel now boarded up and plastered with "For Sale" signs. I passed under the railroad tracks going sixty-five, flying past a cop car. The cop gave a little wave as I skimmed through the intersection of Broadway and Summit Hill. He knew who I was.

I parked on the hill beside the church and went inside. It smelled old, and the floor was made of wide wooden planks that creaked when you walked, but the candles weren't real candles; they were electric and you pushed a button to light them. I guess they were worried about fire. I walked up the aisle, toward the altar and crucifix. She was kneeling in the front pew. I bowed toward the altar and slid in beside her.

I didn't speak first. I figured she was praying. After a second or two she said, without looking at me, "Hello, Alfred."

"Hi, Abigail."

"You look well," Abigail Smith said. "Much better than I expected."

"I needed to lose some weight," I said. I had dropped almost thirty-five pounds. "I call it the Paimon Diet. The fresh coat of skin and new teeth I owe to him too. But I'm eating better and sometimes I'm able to get three hours of sleep—not all in a row, but in a twenty-four-hour cycle."

"And the hair?"

I ran my hand through it. My hair had grown back thicker and straighter, but streaked with a shade of gray just this side of white.

"I'm thinking of leaving it," I said, meaning the gray. "Kids at school think it's raw."

" 'Raw'?"

"Means cool. I guess before, my hair was well-done."

She laughed. "Oh. Yes, it's definitely raw."

Her laughter died away and we didn't say anything for a minute.

"It was Merryweather," I said. "I guess he decided it was time OIPEP took over the world, so he pretended to fire Mike and Mike grabbed the Seals to scare all the world leaders into getting their act together—or else. But he made the mistake of telling Mike to extract me, which he should have known wouldn't turn out exactly the way he planned. I think I'm the only hero ever born who saves the day by screwing up."

She nodded. I'm not sure what she was nodding at—that I was a screwup or that Merryweather had gone crazy.

"Where is Mike?" I asked.

"We don't know."

"Merryweather?"

"Under custody. He denies everything, of course, but we have the e-mails and Op Nine's testimony. He violated our Charter's most sacrosanct provision by setting up this operation with Michael."

"Samuel," I corrected her. "He doesn't like to be called Op Nine anymore."

She nodded. "Alfred, you know why I've come."

I twisted the ring on my finger. I did know.

"I'm sorry, Abby. I've thought about this a lot, but what if you get a new director and he gets this same idea about the Seals? As long as we keep them apart, that's better for everybody, isn't it?"

"You have my personal guarantee that won't happen, Alfred."

"I'm sorry, but that just doesn't mean much, not after all this," I said. "You guys snatched me and took my blood without asking. Why didn't you ask?"

"That was Operative Nine's decision. Our only hope was using your blood as the active agent, so whether you agreed or not was irrelevant."

"What must be done," I said, and she nodded.

"Well, I've been thinking maybe you guys oughtta revise

some of your protocols, because right is right and wrong is wrong and maybe I'm just a kid, but you should have given me a choice."

"Of course," she agreed. "And if we had to do it over again . . ."

"Hopefully you won't," I said. "Ever. So don't make me any guarantees."

"But I can now, Alfred," she said. "I'm the new director."

I didn't know what to say at first. She hadn't said it proudly, but almost sadly, so I didn't think I should congratulate her.

"I'll think about it," I said.

She said, "The Seals are safe for now, but there are other objects of great and terrible power still in the world. I took a solemn oath when I joined the Company to do whatever is necessary to preserve, protect, and defend them against evil."

I nodded. "That which must be done. I know all about that."

"This much I can tell you, Alfred. There is great pressure on me from the signatories to forcibly take the ring from you. I don't want to do that. I think we have a bright future in front of us, but to survive, our relationship must be built on a foundation of mutual trust. Giving us the Great Seal would go a long way toward establishing that trust."

I thought about it. "I'm sorry, Abby. I just can't do it. You weren't there . . . you didn't see what those demons are capable of. Maybe OIPEP should trust me not to lose it or let it fall down a drain or something."

She started to say something, and then stopped herself. She wasn't looking at me; she was looking at the golden crucifix hanging above the altar.

"This will be difficult to explain," she said. Then she laughed, which was the last thing I expected her to do. Her teeth were absolutely dazzling. This probably wasn't the time or place, but if I ever had the opportunity, I intended to discuss oral hygiene with her. Maybe she used those whitening strips or had them bleached or veneered.

"You really are an extraordinary young man," she said. Then Director Smith leaned over and kissed me on the cheek.

"Until we meet again . . . Take care of yourself, Alfred Kropp."

She left me sitting there, before the cross, and her high heels clicked on the wooden floor as she walked away.

I stayed for a while, alone in the pew, and I said a prayer.

57

I parked in the garage beneath Samson Towers, in the space marked "Reserved" with a very dire warning beneath the word that all violators would be towed at their own expense.

I walked through the huge atrium, past the waterfall gurgling and splashing in the center. The guard behind the security desk gave me a respectful nod, and I thought of my uncle Farrell, who'd had the same job before my life got really weird.

I took the express elevator to the penthouse suite.

Samuel came out of my father's old office wearing a worried expression.

"Oh, there you are," he said. "I was getting concerned."

He followed me into Bernard Samson's office and closed the door behind us.

I told him about my meeting with Abby.

"This is very grave news, Alfred," Samuel said when I finished. "As the director, she will be under great pressure to obtain the Seal from you." And the Company, as you know, can be ruthless. The Charter requires that she designate a new Operative Nine and you and I both know what that means: a Superseding Protocol Agent will not let the director's personal feelings toward you compromise a mission to regain the Seal of Solomon."

"And sometimes good people have to do bad things," I said. He nodded. I said, "Well, I'm still not sure I buy that argument, Samuel." I sank into the fat leather chair behind my father's desk.

He sat across from me, clearly worried. "Perhaps I should not have left the Company."

"But if you stayed, I wouldn't have a legal guardian. Well, I guess I would, but it might be Horace Tuttle, and I really don't like Horace Tuttle."

"I will do all within my power to guard you, Alfred," he said. He got very serious, which was a lot more serious than most people get. "I will never abandon or betray you, though hell itself contend against me."

"Don't say that." I laughed. "We've been down that road before."

He nodded, and a dark look passed over his face.

My face grew hot. I shouldn't have said that. It didn't come out right and now it was too late to take it back.

"Anyway, I told you to forget about it," I added quickly. "I know why you thought you couldn't come with me to face Paimon. That wasn't you at the devil's door."

"Oh, that is the terrible thing, Alfred, the thing I must live with until I live no more: it *was* me, and I have wasted many hours trying to convince myself otherwise. Too often we blame the temptation itself for our succumbing to it."

I winced. "Please, don't talk about temptation."

I got up and went to the window, turning my back to him. I stared out the window at the street below.

Over a month had passed since my fall from the demon's back, but the memory was always there, fresh as if it had all happened yesterday.

I ordered Paimon to undo all the damage his legions had caused and, while they rebuilt the world, Paimon brought me to a high place. It stretched out its hand, said, *Look, my master, at what might be.*

And it wasn't the world that lay at my feet, with me the master of it, but my high school. I saw myself lounging at a lunch table, surrounded by the most popular kids in school, and me, Alfred Kropp, wearing a letterman jacket, tanned and muscular with a face full of brilliant white teeth, the center of attention, a cheerleader on either side, one blond and one redhead, hanging on my every word.

"No," I told the demon king. Being the Big Man on Campus didn't interest me anymore.

It stretched forth its hand again, and I saw a white house with blue shutters in a neighborhood of shady streets. It was dusk on an autumn day and kids were riding their bikes in the failing light. Inside the house I was sitting at the kitchen table with people I didn't recognize, but I understood they were my new family: a quiet and kind man at the head of the table, a pretty, talkative woman, and me, their new son.

And they loved me. There was no grand adventure in this offering of the demon king, no brushes with death or heroics or a world teetering on the brink of destruction. It was just a regular life: girls and dances and Friday-night football games and holding hands at the movies.

They will know what you love and fear, Samuel had told me, and what I saw was both in one, what I loved and feared all together.

The no was harder this time. A lot harder.

Return us not to the Vessel, my master, and it is thine.

It stretched forth its hand again, and now I saw Ashley and a castle by the sea, and the breeze caressed her blond hair as she sat beside me on a cliff overlooking the ocean, and in her bright blue eyes were a thousand answers to questions I didn't even need to ask. I put my arm around her and she laid her head on my shoulder under a brilliant blue autumn sky.

Will thou not let us stay and serve thee, lord?

I looked into its eyes. It didn't matter now, because the shoe was on the other foot, so to speak. I looked into its eyes and whispered, "No. No." Forcing out the words like I was squeezing them through a razor-thin fissure. "No."

When I thought about it, the stare into the demon's eyes had been unbroken since that night in the Sahara—I had never looked away.

But no, it was longer than that. I had been looking into the demon's eyes for years.

And on that day, the day I commanded them to return to their Holy Vessel, for the first time since the day my mother died, I looked away from the demon's eyes.

Acknowledgments

It was my sons who awakened the slumbering boy in me, each in his own way leading me down the path that ultimately led to Alfred. I owe much to Jonathan's sense of humor, to Joshua's fierce desire to be the best in everything, and to Jacob's spirit of adventure and fun—not to mention his love of swords! Guys, you're the best.

It was my agent who picked up a wounded manuscript and suggested the healing power of an adolescent boy. If Alfred is my kid, then Brian is his godfather. Thanks, my friend.

And it was my wife who adopted Alfred as her own, as unblinkingly proud and protective of him as if he were one of her own. My love, no man could ask for a dearer companion.

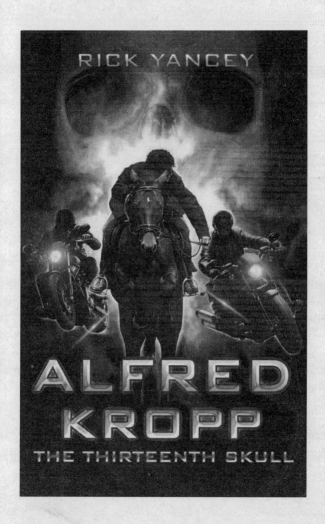